Stories by Enrique Ande

Woven on the Loom of Time

Selected and Translated by Carleton Vail
and Pamela Edwards-Mondragón

Introduction by Ester de Izaguirre

University of Texas Press, Austin

First Edition, 1990

Requests for permission to reproduce material from this work
should be sent to Permissions, University of Texas Press, Box
7819, Austin, Texas 78713-7819.

These short stories were originally published at various times by
Ediciones Corregidor.

ⓧ The paper used in this publication meets the minimum
requirements of American National Standard for Information
Sciences—Permanence of Paper for Printed Library Materials,
ANSI Z39.48-1984.

The Texas Pan American Series is published with the assistance
of a revolving publication fund established by the Pan American
Sulphur Company.

Library of Congress Cataloging-in-Publication Data
Anderson Imbert, Enrique, 1910–
    Woven on the loom of time : stories / by Enrique Anderson-
Imbert ; selected and translated by Carleton Vail and Pamela
Edwards-Mondragón ; introduction by Ester de Izaguirre. —
1st ed.
        p.   cm. — (The Texas Pan American series)
    ISBN 0-292-79054-6 (alk. paper). — ISBN 0-292-79060-0 (pbk. :
alk. paper)
    1. Anderson Imbert, Enrique, 1910–   —Translations,
English.   I. Vail, Carleton, 1912–   .   II. Edwards-
Mondragón, Pamela, 1944–   III. Title.   IV. Series.
PQ7797.A594W6   1990
863—dc20   90-35737
                                                   CIP

Contents

Introduction

I know that Professor Enrique Anderson-Imbert would not recommend that a study of his short stories begin with information about his life. He belongs to that family of formalistic critics who defend the autonomy of literary works against the indiscretions of historians, sociologists, and psychologists. His major concession to the biographical method was rather terse: "The biography of the author, although useful, is not indispensable," he said in *La crítica literaria*. Agreed, but I believe that certain facts would not be out of place in an anthology such as this one, which presents to the North American public the creative activity of an author little known to the reader. Donald A. Yates, professor at Michigan State University, observed that "Anderson-Imbert's stature as a teacher, critic, and literary historian is widely acknowledged, but only in recent years has his importance as a writer been appreciated" (*Cuentos de la Metrópoli: Quince narraciones porteñas* [Englewood Cliffs, N.J.: Prentice-Hall, 1975]). Julio Cortázar, referring to the precursors of the story of the fantastic in Río de la Plata and speaking to readers in the United States, said that "an apology should be extended principally to Enrique Anderson-Imbert who has lived among you as a professor at Harvard for so many years and whose works have not attained the recognition they deserve" (*Books Abroad*, Summer 1976). In Argentina, on the other hand, he was recognized very early on. Fernando Rosemberg, professor at the Universidad Nacional de Buenos Aires, declared that "due to the magnitude and hierarchy of his work, Anderson-Imbert can be included among the primary Argentinian and Hispanic writers of the short story" (*Homenaje a Enrique Anderson-Imbert* [Madrid: Anaya-Las Américas, 1973]).

What place does Anderson-Imbert occupy in the history of the Argentinian short story? This question deserves three very careful responses, one concerning periods of time, the second the genre, and the third aesthetic values. María Rosa Lojo, in her preliminary study in the anthology *El milagro* (Buenos Aires: Kapelusz, 1985), places him in "the generation of the thirties": or, let us say, in the same group with Manuel Mujica Lainez, Julio Cortázar, Adolfo Bioy Casares, et al.; among "the generation of the twenties": Jorge Luís Borges, Silvina Ocampo, Roberto Arlt, et al.; and "the generation of the forties": Marco Denevi, María Esther de Miguel, Adolfo Pérez Zelaschi, et al. Fernando Ainsa, in "Revuelta y rutina en lo fantástico," *Río de la Plata* (Paris, 1985), says that "the first ones to enter into the genre of the fantastic in the Americas were Jorge Luís Borges, Adolfo Bioy Casares, Enrique Anderson-Imbert, and Julio Cortázar." For Silvia Zimmermann del Castillo, "Enrique Anderson-Imbert is one of the most notable figures in contemporary Argentinian literature, and certainly one of the great story-tellers in the Spanish language" ("Una estética del tiempo," *La Nueva Provincia,* 1988).

Curriculum Vitae

Enrique Anderson-Imbert was born on the twelfth of February in 1910 in Córdoba. His parents were Argentinian, but among his grandparents were a Scotsman and an Irishwoman and a Frenchman and an Argentinian lady (this last being a descendant of old Spanish families who arrived in South America in colonial times). He spent his first four years in Córdoba and the following four years in Buenos Aires. The city where his literary vocation awoke was La Plata, where he lived between 1918 and 1928. There he studied with eminent professors. Some among these—the humanist Pedro Henríquez Ureña, the poet Ezequiel Martínez Estrada, the philosopher Alejandro Korn—exercised a decisive influence on his intellectual formation. His adolescent short stories and essays appeared in the La Plata newspapers; and with adolescent naïveté he already considered himself a literary professional when, having moved to Buenos Aires in 1928, he started publishing them in important periodicals, such as *La Nación, Nosotros,* and *Sur,* and to earn his living writing editorials and managing the literary page of the socialist daily *La Vanguardia* (1931–1939). In 1931 he entered the School of Philosophy and Letters and from that point on his life divided between activities not necessarily unrelated among themselves, but still mutually distracting.

One needs only to glance at the first thirty titles in his bibliography in order to realize how his creative narration alternated with his works of research. In 1940 he changed his profession from journalist to educator: he was professor at the National Universities of Mendoza (1940) and Tucumán (1941–1946); with a Guggenheim Fellowship in 1943 he went to the United States and, after teaching in Smith College, Northhampton, Massachusetts, he returned to Tucumán in 1945, but not for long, since the fascist political violence that successive military dictatorships had unleashed obliged him to expatriate himself with his wife and children. From 1947 to 1965 he was a professor in the Department of Romance Languages of the University of Michigan, in Ann Arbor. When the autocratic regime of General Perón was defeated in the revolution of 1955, Anderson-Imbert returned to Argentina and obtained professorships at the National Universities of Buenos Aires and La Plata. But the political tumult did not permit him to remain. So he decided that from then on he would live half of the year in his own country and the other half in the United States. In 1965 Harvard University named him the Victor S. Thomas Professor of Hispanic Literatures. In spite of the fact that since 1980 he has been Professor Emeritus, Anderson-Imbert continues to be active, giving courses and delivering lectures at various universities, attending international conferences, and, above all, publishing books of his creative writings and criticism.

It would be appropriate to add to this biographical résumé a list of the academic associations to which he belongs (including the Academia Argentina de Letras and the American Academy of Arts and Sciences), of the awards that he has received, of the honors that have been accorded him, of the journeys that he has undertaken, but now is the time to pass on to a more important matter, which is not the biography of the author but the quality of his work.

Theory of Literature

I will paraphrase, without putting into quotes, the opinions of Anderson-Imbert that help in understanding his writings. His philosophical position is radically sceptic. We know nothing, he says, about the chaos from which we have emerged by pure chance. All that we know are the phenomena presented to us from within our own consciousness, and those phenomena are already conditioned by our individual nervous organization. We human beings, by virtue of being members of the same biological species, can understand each other, more or less, thanks to language articulated in words. In this language of symbols at times we express our most subjective feelings and thoughts, and at times we communicate what we pretend to know in a factual, objective manner. Expression, on the one hand, communication, on the other. Clearly, the functions of the mind are inseparable and the modes in which the mind acts tend to blend together, but, even so, it is plausible to distinguish at least two attitudes in facing any experience: we express it or we communicate it. That is, we express intuitive knowledge or we communicate conceptual knowledge. The first is aesthetic; the second, logical. Anderson-Imbert, in order to differentiate between the aesthetic expression of intuitions and the logical communication of concepts, presents the case of an experience that may be complete, deep, rich, concrete, lived with all the potentialities of our personality, in a momentary circumstance that will never be repeated. Such a unique experience, in its totality, in its plenitude, will remain ineffable. Nevertheless, if our attitude is aesthetic, it is possible that with imaginative language we may manage to express valuable intuitions of that experience. On the contrary, if the attitude is logical, what we will do is to abstract from our experience concepts common to similar experiences we have had before, and also common to experiences of other persons; and with a conceptual, discursive language we will communicate verifiable knowledge. For greater clarity I turn to an example from Anderson-Imbert himself:

> I have seen a hummingbird. Shall I say: "I saw a bird"? If I say it like that I am communicating an enunciative sentence and nothing more. The word "bird" does not give the totality of my experience, but rather points out a concept that is the common denominator of innumerable birds in the experience of many people. But in my experience it was not just any bird. I was a little boy, and one spring morning I saw for the first time in the garden of my home, in La Plata, a hummingbird: it left a flower, trembling, and went away brushing with one wing the silk of the air. I felt intuitively not only the hummingbird, but also the modesty of the flower, the surprise of the sky, my envy of the freedom and audacity of that unique hummingbird. If I were able to objectify in words this personal experience, then I would be creating literature.

(Teoría y técnica del cuento)

To sum up: we give expression to intuitions, which give form to concrete and singular perceptions (and thus, from image to image, we approach a poetic creation); or we communicate logical forms, very abstract and general (in which case we approach, from concept to concept, a scientific explanation). In this introduction we do not concern ourselves with the intellectual knowledge of Anderson-Imbert, communicated in some twenty books of history, criticism, and essays, for which reason we will pass directly to examining his artistic expression as it appears in this anthology, *Woven on the Loom of Time*, a selection of short stories taken from Anderson-Imbert's latest six books, dating from 1965 to 1985, a series originally published under the title of *En el telar del tiempo*. It is a good title because the ingenious plots of his narratives are cleverly woven, and the loom on which he weaves them is the psychic time in his characters. They reveal the complete personality of Anderson-Imbert: exalted lyricism, lucid intelligence, penetrating knowledge of the human soul, humanistic culture, concern for politics, and the free will to play with the incongruencies of life and with forms of art.

The Short Stories

In *Teoría y técnica del cuento*, Anderson-Imbert has denounced the fallacy of any kind of story classification that follows a logical and therefore antipoetic criterion. For example, the fallacy of measuring the distance between an event that exists only within a fiction and an extraliterary event proven by science. Nevertheless, Anderson-Imbert himself, for reasons that are more pedagogical than aesthetic, has resigned himself to classifying his own stories in four categories that extend from the real to the unreal.

1. *The Realistic Story.* The narrator with aspirations toward realism, says Anderson-Imbert, stands in the midst of daily life and observes it with normal eyes from the perspective of a man in the crowd. His aesthetic formula consists in reproducing reality exactly as he believes it to be. Beginning more or less from *El estafador se jubila* (E),* 1969, the stories become each time more realistic.

*The books to which the stories belong will be indicated by the following initials:

Ch   *The Cheshire Cat/El gato de Cheshire*
E   *The Swindler Retires/El estafador se jubila*
J   *Two Women and One Julián/Dos mujeres y un Julián*
K   *Klein's Bottle/La botella de Klein*
L   *Madness Plays at Chess/La locura juega al ajedrez*
T   *The Size of the Witches/El tamaño de las brujas*

Nevertheless, they never reach the point of reproducing things exactly as they are. The restless temperament of Anderson-Imbert prohibits him from behaving like a common witness. Even the picture of common customs is converted by him into a caricature: see "Murder" (L). What begins as real ends by being grotesque, "William Faulkner Saw a Ghost, and Then . . ." (K); or sick, "The Pruning" (E); or tremendous, "I'll Teach Her a Lesson" (E). The whirlwind of forms and dreams blurs the cruel reality in "Anonymous Manuscript concerning a Sad Waltz" (L). The verisimilitude of an anecdote ends in a flash of irridescence in "Anchored in Brazil" (K), "Ovid Told It Differently" (L), "The Eyes of the Dragon" (K), "The Size of the Witches" (T). A historic event, like that of the fall of the famous balancing stone of Tandil, is a pretext for the analysis of the psychology of resentment, "The Stone" (E). With the brush strokes of a realist Anderson-Imbert lends credibility to his fictions so that immediately, in one blow, he can destroy it.

2. *The Ludic Story.* Ludic (from the Latin *ludere,* to play) are those stories in which the narrator enjoys himself and entertains us with happenings that are surprising, improbable, and extraordinary. Paraphrasing the definitions from Anderson-Imbert himself in his *Teoría y técnica del cuento,* I will say that in this kind of story he does not reach the extreme of violating the laws of either nature or logic but you can sense in him the wish to violate them. In any case he specializes in exceptions. He exaggerates. He accumulates coincidences. He permits chance to direct man. With subterfuges he makes us believe that we are facing a prodigy; a prodigy which then turns out to be the effect of a cause that is not at all prodigious. He searches and searches again. He looks for exotic climates, eccentric characters, unheard-of situations. And he searches deeper again for explanations of that which at first sight appears inexplicable. Esoteric is the explanation for "Frankly, no" (E): just when a theater director convinces himself that he has perceived in an extrasensory manner a case of a physical "double" of a body, the actress in the case confesses that everything has been a joke. The explanation in "Esteco: Submerged City" (K) is also esoteric: the extraordinary vision of the poet, Duffy, turns out to be a mirage produced by the atmospheric changes after a rainstorm in northern Argentina. In "Bats" (K) he plays with the feelings of the principal character and probably also with those of the reader.

3. *The Mystery Story.* The events, no matter how real they may appear, produce the illusion of unreality when Anderson-Imbert envelops them in a mysterious, hallucinatory light that suggests magic even where there is none. We may say that it is a "magic realism"

because instead of presenting the magic as if it were real he presents the real as if it were magic. Magicians do not take part, but rather neurotics who distort reality. Everything that occurs in the story could be logically explained, but it is so ambiguous, so problematic, that it disturbs us with its feeling of strangeness. Although possible, it seems to us strange and doubtful that the protagonist of "The Wisteria" (T) should see in the falling of petals the form of a loving and invisible woman, or that the protagonist in "Forever Sweetheart" (J) may see an old woman as eternally young.

4. *The Fantastic and Miraculous Story.* The events of these stories are absurd and impossible, because in them supernatural factors intervene. The intervention of the supernatural may be partial or total. It is partial when an ordinary, daily, familiar situation is suddenly altered by the eruption of agents that do not exist in nature. Anderson-Imbert classifies this kind of story as *fantastic.* For example, in "The Innocent Child" (T) the situation of a Jewish family in an anti-Semitic political atmosphere leaps from an Argentine reality to an absurd level when, suddenly, a mythical figure enters the scene. In "The Moon" (Ch) the dinner of an ordinary married couple is interrupted by the intrusion of a child who, transgressing the universal law of gravity, slides up and down a moonbeam. The intervention of the supernatural is total when the events happen in a world completely foreign to our own, whether it be in the kingdom of the fairies, in an Olympus of pagan gods, in the paradises or the hells of whatever religion, in extraterrestrial dimensions, and so on. Anderson-Imbert classifies this kind of story as *miraculous.* There is not a particle of reality in the events of "Theologies and Demonologies" (Ch), some of which take place before the creation of the universe. Nor is there in the reelaboration of myths in "Heroes," "Orpheus and Eurydice," "Narcissus," or other mythic plot lines (Ch). Some stories are difficult to classify. For example, is it legitimate to consider as fantastic a story that narrates the supernatural events of dreams or nightmares, the hallucinations of the insane or drugged, the beliefs of the superstitious or parapsychologists? In "The Fallen Hippogriff" (J) and "Madness Plays at Chess" (L), the apparent subversion of the world happens only within two demented minds.

Themes, Forms, and Style

Themes. The themes of Anderson-Imbert are varied but one is so frequent that it acquires the force of a leitmotiv: that of Time. Not the physical time that we measure with clocks and calendars adjusted to the movement of the stars, but rather the psychic time that each person lives in a concrete manner. We are conscious of the temporality of our existence. This preoccupation with time becomes the metaphorical madness in "Instantaneous" (Ch). Another of the dominant themes in the stories of Anderson-Imbert is that of Freedom, derived from the above. Since time is a movement of life toward goals, we have to choose among those goals, and one of the goals that we choose is that of freeing ourselves from the coercion of nature and society. We fight for freedom and we achieve it more in the imagination than in action. Anderson-Imbert imagines freedom to be an aspiration toward higher values; therefore, in his stories there is a proliferation of flights, levitations, and things that ascend and point upward, like a tree, smoke, a mountain, a tower. Anderson-Imbert is an aerial spirit, like Ariel, and he conceives art to be an exercise in freedom.

It is well known that what is interesting in a story is not the subject but rather the humor with which the writer covers it. The humor of Anderson-Imbert is sometimes melancholic. In "El hijo pródigo" the mystic vision of chaos (it was published, significantly, in *Las pruebas del caos*) moves us by its tone of anguish. In other stories one notes, if not melancholy, then at least a sadness for the human condition. Anderson-Imbert knows loneliness and the difficult relation of man with his neighbor. The compassion for Ines, protagonist in "Ovid Told It Differently" (L), is evident in spite of the mythological pedantry. When it is not clearly shown it is divined, as in "Baby Bear" and "Would to God" (T) and in "Juancito Chingolo" (J). In some of his stories an ingenious construction hides the serious depth. In "The Stone" (E), the narrator, like a prestidigitator, hides until the very last sentence the historic name of that balancing stone, but the psychological analysis that he makes of the social resentment is moralistic. "Anonymous Manuscript concerning a Sad Waltz" (L) sets against each other, as in a showy wax museum, dolls of different color, but there are also words that comment with severity on the conflict between barbarism and civilization. As a matter of fact, concerning these two stories I should clarify that Anderson-Imbert is an intellectual of European formation, but he feels inextricably tied to his country. For him Spanish American barbarism is not so barbarous and European civilization is not so civilized. After all, the gauchos of "Anonymous Manuscript concerning a Sad Waltz" (L) were provoked by the Europeanized great landowners. And in "Anchored in Brazil" (K) a full professor from Harvard boasts before his colleagues of having behaved like a barbarian brawling in a brothel with drunken sailors.

I said that at times the humor of Anderson-Imbert is melancholic, but in the majority of his stories it is ironic. He plays and he laughs, not through frivolity, but because the world seems so amorphous that he would gain nothing by explaining it seriously, and language seems so conventional that it is not worth the trouble to write if not in some degree to shock with personal fantasies. Since for him the supernatural is a dimension of literature and not of reality, he teases with myths, with superstitions, with esoteric cults, with parapsychological phenomena without trying to offend believers. Some stories are frankly humoristic, "Patterns of the Possible" (Ch), for example. The reader expects something worthwhile and that expectation is turned into a joke when the supposed value is suddenly devalued and collapses. With laughter we punish the men who, through rigidity, destroy the free and creative energy of life. Not only the reader laughs. Various stories terminate with the characters loudly laughing: "Frankly, no" (E), "The Alleluia of the Dying" (J), "Esteco: Submerged City" (K). Even the angry man of "The Stone" (E) finishes in laughter. More subtle is the irony of stories where one thing is said and another is thought. So subtle, in truth, that sometimes the reader is not sure of the intention of the writer. For example, in "The Fallen Hippogriff" (J) does Perceval see a hippogriff on the rooftop or does he only imagine it? Does he thrust himself into the void trusting that he is riding on a winged hippogriff or is the hippogriff the one who falls to earth? In general, Anderson-Imbert, jealous of his authority as author, is very clear in his intentions and does not give any margin to the reader to interpret the meaning of the stories according to his or her own taste or wishes. When the stories are ambiguous it is because the ambiguity is deliberate, as in "One X and Two Unknowns" (J).

The ironic tone of the stories of Anderson-Imbert comes from his intellectual attitude. So dense is the erudite atmosphere of many of his stories that they might be read as essays. It amuses him to make literature with literature. In his stories fictional and cultural events are combined; he has recurrence to "scholarship" in order to find the key that resolves an enigma; he encloses a completely fantastic adventure in a historic framework; with a conjecture he fills a void in science; he attributes to an illustrious writer pages that he never wrote; he makes a parody of a literary genre in "Imposture" (T); through his pages real writers walk: "A Heart Outlined" (K) and "Nalé Roxlo and the Suicide of Judas" (K); there are characters who,

like the author, are teachers: "Intelligence" (Ch); literary traditions
are reelaborated: "The Rival" (Ch); literary problems are discussed:
"Two Women and One Julián" (J). In "The Kingdom Bewitched"
(E), we hear the echo of a limerick. "A Famous Conversion in the
XIVth Century" (K) is inspired by a story of Boccaccio. It is not
that Anderson-Imbert encrusts his stories with literary material
from mere pedantry, but rather that he is a man of culture, a professor of literature with his curiosity open to history of religion, the
arts, ideologies, and science. Culture excites his vitality with the
same intensity that nature does. An idea delights him as much as a
landscape. A book impassions him as much as a woman.

Forms. And now let us take note of the length of the stories of
Anderson-Imbert. They áre miniature engravings, not murals,
painted al fresco. Behind that thin surface is a theory: Anderson-
Imbert believes that the brevity of the story has the virtue of captur-
ing the short impulses of life. In many of his books is a section called
"Casos," containing "ministories." *El gato de Cheshire* (1965) is
made up of hundreds of these "ministories." Even in these minia-
tures, plots may be discovered, but only when the action extends
into the space of several pages do the threads of the plot weave together in more elegant embroideries.

The dominant form in these stories is linear: a beginning, a middle,
and an end. And the end is always a surprise. Examples: "Murder"
(L), "The Tomb" (T), "Lycanthropy" (T), "Eyes (Mine, Peering Up
from the Cellar)" (K), "The Palm Tree" (J), "The Last Glances" (J).
On one occasion I asked him why he preferred this technique of the
surprise ending, and he answered me with the following letter:

> Suddenly I feel excited by a poetic intuition, by an interesting event or by a conflict,
> which may be that of the will which cannot make up its mind to take a certain course of
> action or, if it has already made up its mind, runs into obstacles. At times I feel the desire
> to turn a place upside-down, to give a new feeling to something which I read; or I feel
> simply the desire to get something off my chest. However it may be, with my imagination
> excited I'm transported in one leap from the problem to its solution, and immediately I
> return again in one leap to the original setting of the problem. Now I repeat the journey,
> from the point of departure to the point of arrival, except that now I do not leap again over
> the void but rather, with pencil in hand and leaning over my paper, I make my way
> among words, I interpose between the problem and the solution characters, dialogs, scenes,
> epochs, acts. Thus the story writes itself. The sentences in the beginning prepare those in
> the end; and I develop the middle with the necessary strategy so that the reader's attention
> will be maintained. The ending of the plot has to be aesthetically satisfactory: a profound
> observation, a mysterious suggestion, a dilemma, and, above all, a surprise. I never begin
> to write a story if I am not sure that the beginning and the end will fit together perfectly,

with a click! The middle is the least of it. This is so true that, in the process of writing, the people, the place, the atmosphere can all change. What does not change is the intrigue and the outcome.

Anderson-Imbert prepares surprises also in more complicated structures: shifting points of view, leaps forward or backward in the chronological sequence, parallel constructions, counterpoint and cycle, confrontations with mirrors, frames and fragmenting of frames. In his *Teoría y técnica del cuento* he has diagrammed the stories having a more complex structure. Those stories do not figure in the present anthology, but even in the simpler stories, which do figure here, one may see the desire to experiment with forms. These examples will suffice. In "The Gold Doubloon" (K) each time that the child cries "Mommy! Daddy!" the story backs up and begins again. A favorite procedure of Anderson-Imbert is to have a character in his story begin to tell another story, giving us two stories in one: "Glacier" (L), "The Alleluia of the Dying" (J), "The Eyes of the Dragon" (K). Another form is that of the "metastory," which narrates one story already narrated, and the "story-object," which is, precisely, that story that was already told: "North Wind" (L) is a metastory that is focused on the story-object "August Heat" by W. F. Harvey. (Semiotics calls this "intertextuality.") There are stories that have the form of a jack-in-the-box, which, when it opens, releases a doll. It is what occurs in stories that in the last lines reveal the true personality of the narrator, until then hidden, and for that reason all that has been read turns out to have been a subjective and untrustworthy testimony: thus it is in "William Faulkner Saw a Ghost, and Then . . ." (K) and in "Anonymous Manuscript concerning a Sad Waltz" (K). I should have pointed out before the form of the "double," so insistent throughout all the work of Anderson-Imbert that it lends itself to a special study: "Spiral" (Ch), "Madness Plays at Chess" (L), "One X and Two Unknowns" (J). I must leave to one side, since they are untranslatable, other verbal forms, such as alliterations, antithesis, symmetries, repetitions, puns, acrostics, and rhetorical games.

The Style. The style of Anderson-Imbert is masterly. The words, exact. The syntax, flexible. The rhythm, harmonious. Because he searches for the exact word for each one of the innumerable objects that come into his mind, his vocabulary is probably the richest among today's Argentinian writers. His syntax is so flexible that it unfolds from the shortest and most elliptical sentences to sentences that surpass even the longest of Proust. Whenever possible he avoids cacophony, and thanks to a good ear he achieves harmonious rhythm.

He has that which the philologists call "drive for style." His prose is articulated logically with his thought and often reads like poetry. His metaphors flow incessantly. They do not compare images, they create new ones. His metaphors are the richest element of his style. Since in this introduction I already lack space for a thorough study of the stylistic features of his prose, which is so frequently poetic, I will limit myself to pointing out a single one, that of the richness of his impressionistic and expressionistic images.

He, like every writer, transforms his impressions into expressions. His prose is impressionistic when in it the immediate reaction of the senses prevails over the stimuli received from the exterior world. When the consciousness of Anderson-Imbert uses impressions in order to convey ideas, his prose acquires expressionistic features. The impressionistic style analyzes the sensorial experiences of the writer. He does it in two ways. In one, the physical world appears through the sensations of the narrator or of his characters. In the other, the feelings of the narrator or of his characters appear translated into sensations of the physical world. In "The Pruning" (E) both types of impressionist style complement each other. A man gravely ill looks through the window at how the trees in the street appear now after a brutal pruning. The trees impress him as suffering human creatures, and he, in his turn, feels as wounded as the trees themselves:

> I saw them with skin and flesh. The wood became my flesh, the bark of the entire slashed grove became my skin. I suffered for the plantains, and for myself in seeing myself like them, with one foot in the grave. . . . I felt, rather, that those truncated bodies were recalling their amputations, as I myself, ill, was recalling my lost health.

The expressionistic style lifts the impressions to a new plane. It prolongs them, it enriches them with new ideas, it integrates them in an artistic conception in which all the facets of the writer's personality combine. Anderson-Imbert is expressionist above all in his stories of intellectual content but he never reaches the extreme case of allegory, where images symbolize concepts.

Ester de Izaguirre

Woven on the Loom of Time

SELECTIONS FROM

The Cheshire Cat (1965)

Prologue

I have always preferred brief forms: they better encompass a rela-
tivistic theory of the world and an imaginative method in literature.
In the short stories of *El grimorio* (1961), even in the novels *Vigilia*
and *Fuga* (1963), the smallest rhetorical unit is the metaphor, the
prose poem, the magical situation, the play of fancy. If it were possible, I would relate pure intuitions, but technique requires substance. I describe that substance in two different inks, one delible,
the other indelible, so that when the substance fades out there remains a trace of the intuition, like a smile in the air. The smile of
the Cheshire Cat. Lewis Carroll, mathematician and poet, tells us
how Alice, in Wonderland, saw a cat that was grinning at her from
the branch of a tree and then would vanish only to appear and disappear over and over again:

> "I wish you wouldn't keep appearing and vanishing so suddenly: you make one quite
> giddy!" "All right," said the cat; and this time it vanished quite slowly, beginning with
> the tip of the tail, and ending with the grin, which remained some time after the rest of it
> had gone.
> "Well! I've often seen a cat without a grin," thought Alice; "but a grin without a cat!
> It's the most curious thing I ever saw in all my life!"
> (Alice's Adventures in Wonderland, Chapter VI)

Here you have my grins without the cat. They grinned this way
from the branches in the woods of La Plata, when in 1926 I started to
describe them (do you remember, don Ezequiel Martínez Estrada? do
you remember the fourth-year classroom of the Colegio Nacional?).

Those attempts became less and less awkward, thanks to the library. Because storytelling, which began in mythology and folklore, later developed into the most familiar form of literature. The narrator of classical taste—for whom "originality," differing from the narrator of romantic taste, is more stylistic than thematic—combines without dissimulation what he has invented with what he has created from the inventions of others. In the act of making use of ancient fictions he feels the pleasure of twisting traditional sources and achieves, in a new surge of spirit, a surprising effect.

The books from which I learned how to tell stories do not communicate among themselves—they are like monads, as Leibniz, another mathematician and poet, would say—but they communicate within me, the reader and writer, and the origin of the preestablished harmony in my private library. My little stories, too, are monads, psychic atoms reflecting from different perspectives the totality of a vision of life. To encode it, the key word would be: liberty.

Enrique Anderson-Imbert

Twelve Notes

"What times they were!" said the Hydra to its charming visitor. "Not a month passed without some hero coming to kill me. Very proud, they used to arrive on this shore, lean out over the water, challenge me with shouts; I would emerge (slowly, to make the show more dignified) and they, whirling their swords, would lop off my heads. One would fall, and instantly, before a single drop of blood spurted out, another head would be born. I let my heads taunt those vehement swords; to make them easier to reach I used to stretch them out toward the heroes, whistling and dancing, my twelve heads, always twelve, however many they cut off. Finally the heroes, exhausted, no longer had the strength to lift an arm. (Then I would relieve them of the humiliation of returning to their homelands defeated.) And thus, month after month, I would amuse myself with those harmless decapitations. Now they don't come any more. The fame of my immortality has discouraged them. I regret it. Those games of swords and heads were a party. More or less tense, I would wait for the blow, which was sometimes delayed and sometimes hurried; and immediately I would feel that the new head that blossomed out was a change in my life, or that it would continue the expression of the former, or repeat it exactly. Thanks to this expectation of mine, in which the return of each head was inevitable, but, nevertheless, surprising, I enjoyed myself as if I were listening to music.

Tempo. Pure tempo. Now I am bored; and these twelve heads that you see now no longer sing like notes in a melody, but like yawns in empty space."

"You have spoken," said the visitor, "of your expectation of change, of continuity, and of repetition. You will see that you needed to learn to wait for the best part of the melody, which is the ending. Would you like to play it one more time?"

And, getting to his feet, Hercules waved his sword.

The Pomegranate

Nathaniel, who has failed as a writer, decides to commit suicide. He loads his revolver, places it at his side on his desk, and starts to write his letter of farewell. The letter lengthens, brightens, breathes, lives. It is the Masterpiece, the yearned-for Masterpiece! In order to publish it, Nathaniel does not commit suicide.

&

Robert told a secret and Basil, upon hearing it, promised, "I will be silent as a tomb." Thus was born a great friendship. From that point on, they were always together, Robert speaking, Basil listening. In time Basil became more and more silent and hollow. One day Robert noted with disgust that Basil was in fact a tomb, and, with his eyes—open like the REST IN PEACE on a tombstone—was inviting him to jump on down.

&

The children gather in the square, each one with his stick, as they had all agreed. They gather hanging from crutches, perched on stilts, mounted on broomsticks. The air is stiff with javelins, canes, lances, flags. Martin arrives with a toothpick in his mouth.

&

"Rejoice! Your wish has been granted! You will write the best stories in the world. However, no one will read them."

&

He made himself wings of ostrich feathers, climbed up the bell-tower and threw himself out into the air. When they picked him up, with his legs broken, he explained that he had fallen because the feathers were too heavy.

"Next time," he said, "I'll fly without wings."

8⊷

The man empties his revolver into his terrible enemy. Five shots. Yet he squeezes the trigger one time more. On hearing the click of the empty weapon, he feels helpless. Now, alone with the corpse, he is afraid.

8⊷

He received a grant to travel. Where? America? Europe? Asia? Africa? Oceania? The morning suddenly became dark, and when he looked up, expecting to see a cloud, he glimpsed an enormous hand that drew back quickly behind the sky. If that hand was the one that was going to move him around on the chessboard of the world, what would he be: a pawn, a king, a rook, a knight, or a bishop?

8⊷

A tiny island, round and green, lost in the blue sea: in the middle, just a single tree with gray branches.

From far away an angel, coming down head first, thought that the tiny island was the round, green foliage of a tree flying through the blue sky, and that the branches of the tree were gray roots that it was trailing.

8⊷

They were unable to explain either the chemistry or the theology of his halo. Meanwhile that human beast went strolling about the jail yard, displaying the beautiful halo on his head.

8⊷

I bathed, shaved, and dressed; I looked at myself in the mirror. "Let's go!" I said to my agoraphobia, and together we went out to take a walk in the park.

8⊷

In a dividing wall between two old houses in Babylon, there was a hole. During the last few weeks, the hole had taken on the shape of a mouth, the shape of an ear; after that certain night it started to take on the shape of an eye. Now the hole looks out from side to side: "Aren't they going to come? Won't they come tonight either?" it asks. And it listens for the slightest sounds, with the hope of hearing the silent steps of the lovers. A useless wait. Time passes and the hole, which will never learn about Pyramus and Thisbe, slowly fills with cobwebs.

ह≥

Someone passed along the street whistling "Salome." The man began to accompany the melody, closed his eyes, saw his old neighborhood by the railroad tracks, to which he had not returned since childhood, and felt cold in his legs: the cold in his bare legs at a time when he was wearing short pants and was whistling "Salome." He got down from his bed and dragged himself to the door. Seated on his little platform with rollers, pushing himself along with his arms, a legless beggar, he rolled along the streets like a happy child.

The Sun

The demiurge created them in order to play with them for a little while, but made his first mistake in giving them consciousness. With this consciousness the homunculi, in turn, devised their own society. When the demiurge, tired of his game, wanted to cancel them out, they were already living and holding firmly to their way of life. He thought, "If only I could surprise them all at the same time! If they were all asleep it would be easy to snip off their little remaining thread of life."

Ah, but it was too late! The demiurge had committed a second error; to live on, he had given them a round planet that rotated under the lanterns of heaven. One of the lanterns saved the homunculi. On the side toward the sun there were always brothers mounting guard in rigorous shifts: if some of them, becoming sleepy, relaxed their watch, others, now alert, would intensify it. By force of thought they converted the demiurge himself into the servant of the homunculi.

ह≥

Spiral

I returned to my home in the early morning, heavy with sleep. As I entered, all was in darkness. In order not to wake anyone I went on tiptoe and came to the spiral staircase that led to my room. Scarcely had I put my foot on the first step than I wondered whether this was my home or another, identical to it. And as I went up I feared that another boy, just like me, might be sleeping in my room and perhaps dreaming me in the very same act of climbing the spiral staircase. I made the last turn, opened the door, and there he was, or I was, all lit up by the moon, sitting up in bed, with eyes wide open. We remained an instant, staring at each other. We smiled. I felt that his smile was the same as the one on my own lips: as in a mirror, one of the two was false. "Who is dreaming whom?" one of us exclaimed, or perhaps both of us together. At that moment we heard footsteps coming up the spiral staircase: in one motion we merged together and thus started to dream the one coming up the stairs, once again ME.

Heroes

A hand touched him from behind. He was afraid to turn around for fear that, in looking over his shoulder, he would see at his back, vengeful, a Past that was calling him. Oedipus departed, deep in thought, and continued on the road to Thebes.

ا&

Some of the sailors that were returning from their long voyages were accustomed to visiting Sinbad, the paralytic. Sinbad would close his eyes and tell them adventures from his own inner voyages. In order to make them more believable, he would attribute them to Odysseus. "I'll wager," thought Sinbad when he was alone, "that he never left his house either."

Theologies and Demonologies

In Paradise, from time to time, they avail themselves of the services of Hell in order to sharpen the joys of the Blessed. From time to time they experience shrieks, sulphurous flames, lashings of shadows, parades of ugliness and despair, all for the sake of contrast. In its turn, Paradise lends something of its felicity to Hell in order that the Damned, also by contrast, not forget that they are suffering.

ا&

A boy climbed up a mountain in Armenia and saw Noah's Ark. "Ah, so it is true that Noah's Ark existed!" he said to himself. "The flood, in receding, left it grounded among these peaks. Unless Noah built it right here, so high above sea level, confident that the waters, after forty days and nights of rain, would rise up to it and set it afloat. But there never was such a flood. In this case the fish were right in not believing a word of it when they were told that Noah had saved all the creatures of the animal kingdom from the water."

&

Elohim, pleased, looks down on the wars. He believes them to be part of a mysterious sacrifice that man is rendering to him. The affair began with Cain and Abel. Little by little, killing each other had become a ritual. Wars are now massive sacrifices that convert the entire world into a vast temple. Elohim, honored, looks down on the ceremony and smiles.

&

In heaven. An angel—the most devilish of them all—said to another: "Do you know what is annoying in this place? It looks like a waiting room. Look at that: all those seraphim and cherubim look as though they are waiting for something. I'm getting bored. Or could it be that they are waiting for me to do something awful?"

&

The danger was not that anyone might be preparing to climb up to heaven through the tower of Babel, but that, once it was constructed, someone might want to climb through it down to earth. This had already happened once. It could not be permitted to happen again. So the tower was destroyed.

&

I told him that I did not believe in guardian angels.
"That must be because you don't have one," he answered. "I do."
He turned his head, gave an order to some invisible person:
"Your finger, Raziel!"
And taking off his hat, he left it hanging in the air.

&

"Any good stories from down there?" God asked.
And the angel who had just returned from a long sojourn on earth, without saying a word, held out an open book—it was by Descartes—and indicated a passage: "God, who is omnipotent, could deceive me. But how can that be? Is not God pure goodness, is he not total truth? Well, might there not be some power or malign spirit, no less clever and mischievous than powerful, who deceives us?"
And God blushed.

&

He hesitated a moment, but then made up his mind and took hold of the weapon: "Bah!" he thought. "After all, I can't damn myself. If man is free, I have the right to kill myself. If he is not free, then it is God who consents to my suicide."

ટે

Abel, the shepherd, offered Jahveh a lamb. Cain, a farmer, offered him some fruit.

Jahveh preferred Abel's bloody sacrifice to Cain's offer of fruit.

With the passing of centuries, religions have imitated Cain and not Abel. Nowadays we consider it more civilized to place flowers on an altar than to cut the throat of an animal. Cain, then, was right. If he made a mistake, it was later on when he killed his brother. But why did he kill him? They say it was for envy. That is possible. But nevertheless . . .

"So you are pleased to see blood?" he must have said to Jahveh. "So here is the most precious blood that I can give you; not that of a lamb, but that of my brother."

Did Cain misunderstand the wishes of Jahveh and carry his obedience to an extreme? Or did he kill in a violent spasm of irony?

ટે

The Prisoner

When they shoved Luis Augusto Bianqui into a cell it took him a few days to discover that he was able to dissolve into air, escape like a breath through the transom, reassume his bodily form on the other side, go about in the streets, and live his life as usual. There was one inconvenience: each time that a guard came along to inspect his cell, Bianqui, wherever he was, had to drop everything, return in a flash, and resume his image as a prisoner. A matter of conscience! If the jailors were forgetful, Bianqui's freedom became real. He studied the timetable of the guards' rounds in order to walk around the city only during hours more or less safe, without fear of interruption. He would spend a whole night out. Even so, in the jail they were accustomed to making unexpected inspections. More than once he had felt the pull from his cell and had had to dissolve while in the arms of a woman. Very unsatisfactory. Little by little, he began to renounce his power to evaporate; finally, in the end, he stayed in jail.

Antonius

Back in the third century an Egyptian youth lost his mind in such a way that he was no longer able to distinguish the difference between what he perceived and what he imagined. Antonius was a Christian and, although neither a hermit nor a cenobite, he purified himself as best he could. At night he would pray and dream in the desert and during the day he would meditate and struggle in the villages of the valley of the Nile.

He would pray in the desert until his eyes closed and, with the presentiment that his prayers were useless to free him from his sinful dream, he would fall asleep.

In the villages he meditated so as to be strong in virtue and, thanks to the example of Jesus Christ, he struggled in the full light of day and with his eyes wide open against the temptations of the flesh, the world, and the devil.

In the desert, all nights merged into one long night. All nights were the same, profound, immense, into which Antonius, asleep, entered like a slave, totally deprived of any ability to reason or choose.

The days, on the other hand, multiplied in the villages under a carousing sun. The days were disconcertingly different, with things, people, and places that Antonius imagined were placed there in order to test his chaste spirit.

The night was real, when Antonius, stupified and inert, was delivered into the empire of his dream; the days were unreal, when his consciousness conjured up phantasmagoric thoughts and resolutions.

In the desert he would dream of the same woman and always would succumb to her witchery. That woman took possession of him but never revealed herself completely. Antonius, passively, docilely, learned her, night after night, in a series of discoveries and possessions. Now she was the sudden image of a mouth created by the mischievous look in her eyes, or a chart of blue veins surrounding a nipple, or now a mole newly revealed on her stomach, or a new shadow hiding in her thighs, or the lips of her vulva, half open like a rose. And although he perceived her only a little at a time, and vaguely, there was no doubt that she was a complete woman. Her features were harmonious and comprised a woman so real that she even had a name: Ophelia. And Ophelia, in her turn, was connected with that shadowy background of reality from which implacably she would emerge. Antonius' emotions—desire, anguish—were real; the reactions of his body—sweat, orgasms—were real. So real that Antonius was more afraid of falling asleep in the desert than of wandering around in the villages: he knew that transported into sleep he would succumb, awake he would not. Ophelia was irresistible. Perhaps some day she might disappear forever from his nightmare, but if she did, it would not be because he had dismissed her, but rather because the king of hell was calling her from down below. It would be a desertion, not an expulsion. Meanwhile, the persistence of that dream, coherent as reality itself, tied him to that woman: she, he, were conjugal, bowed down under the weight of a common yoke. And Antonius went on sinning remorselessly throughout an extraordinary, persistent, and imperious night.

When on the following day he would mix with the people of some village, women would cross his path trying to insinuate themselves, trying to offer themselves. Antonius would reject them: each different from the other, they seemed to him unstable, illusory, mere images floating around in his imagination. They were images within images within his consciousness; and Antonius, faced with them, would take a position: he declared them nonexistent. He conceived them, he repudiated them. Freely. Those heterogenous women were what they were, mental images, complete as ideas but, like ideas, deceiving, fluttering, and evanescent. They were not linked among themselves, nor with anything exterior.

Thus Antonius enjoyed a single woman in his dream and abstained from many women while awake. Real was his prolonged sin in the desert night when, asleep, he could imagine nothing. Unreal was his intermittent chastity when, awake, he repelled the temptations of his imagination. And because for him the real was the essential element of the erotic nightmare and the unreal the contingency of his ascetic will power, Antonius considered himself the most lecherous sinner in the world and suffered from his repeated offenses against Jesus Christ.

He was a saint without realizing it. A saint insane. His madness consisted of his feeling responsible in his dreams and irresponsible in his actions; in sum, unable to appreciate the value of freedom.

The Knife

Today, while rummaging around in the trunk in the attic, my hands once again encountered the knife. It's old. I have seen it an infinity of times since my childhood. According to what they told me, it came from Japan, among other things that my grandfather left when he committed suicide. Now it serves for nothing, and I ask myself if at some time it had served for something; rather it seems a knife of mere adornment or for some futile ceremony. For me it wouldn't serve even as a paper knife, since the blade is too long and curved. Why do I keep it? The truth is that it is not I who keep it. It keeps itself. It is simply here and stays here. And today, after stumbling on it, I thought I would throw it out. But what resistance! I can't throw it out. Forcefully it clings to me. Now I see that it will cling to me until the end of my life. Wherever I go it goes too, among the pieces of furniture. Apparently it has no other place to go, and it stays at my side. We don't say anything to each other. All we have in common is the time we spend together. Useless: useless my desire to throw the knife out with the trash. What can it want? I'm starting to worry about it. When I pick it up it pulls at my hand and its blade touches me in the belly.

Nature

"Listen to the song of the wind in the casuarina trees: it sounds like the song of the sea."

"Yes. I hear that song. But I would rather hear the other song, the one that the casuarina trees sing to each other, the one we cannot hear."

ह

Mario was strolling through the garden. Something (a movement?) caught his attention. He turned his head and looked around. They were flowers. Nameless flowers, unknown flowers that had just opened there, newly arrived from the future or from some paradise. Their forms and colors still held the movement of their coming. Those new flowers, did they decide in that instant to stop being light or, the reverse, were they trying themselves to be light? Be light! Be light! Throughout the planet, Mario thought, the flowers go on opening their corollas, in succession, and make the sun follow their path, flattered by their bows.

ह

I stop in the middle of the garden when I hear the sound of the bell. The bell is not difficult to locate. It is there: round, celestial, crystalline in the spring morning, suspended from the sun. But, the clapper? What is the clapper that has drawn that sweet sound from the bell. This tulip? Perhaps my head? All things appear to understand the message of the bell and remain immobile, silent. I myself do not dare take a single step. And suddenly I see a butterfly, fluttering at the level of my eyes; I look higher up. Nothing. But the air is full of feeling. And although I see nothing, I sense that a great descent is happening, as from an invisible ship. It must be something very light if it wishes to hold on to our world by letting down a butterfly as an anchor.

Intelligence

Ramón, an atheist, decides to invent a utopia. When the moment arrives to write it, he will do it in a single verbal tense: the future. Meanwhile, he goes on completing it in his mind, detail by detail. He suppresses what does not serve his purpose and founds institutions that suit him. At first he establishes a population of millions and millions of men, identical with himself; then he has the courage to introduce slight changes in human nature. And in that ideal framework one begins to enjoy peace, order, justice, liberty, happiness, abundance, progress, and culture. This is a long and complicated thought. At the end, the Utopia is rounded out, perfect.

Perfect? To be perfect it lacks nothing more than to be real. Through what routes, with what journeys can one arrive at Utopia? Ramón imagines a miracle to make functional that admirable enterprise: he imagines that one fine day a fine God . . .

Ah! No sooner has he thought of God, than Ramón loses interest in his Utopia. If God exists, who cares about an earthly paradise?

҉

The first day of class. The professor rested his text on the lectern, faced his students, lifted a hand, was about to speak but suddenly stopped with his mouth half open; on tiptoe, a little nun had entered, who, with a slight and gracious little bow, excused herself for arriving centuries late. The professor started to lecture and, from time to time, stole a glance at the little nun, unreal as Time itself, always quiet, modest, with lowered eyes.

> *Lovely eyes has the heron,*
> *and never lifts them.*

Weeks pass. Now the medieval little nun looks up from her notebook and the professor receives her long gaze. If the professor pronounces a brilliant sentence, the little nun drops the bright hint of a possible smile. To bring out the smile, the professor multiplies the brilliant sentences.

The blessed habit, with its ample and deceiving folds, was planned, cut, and sewn with the specific intention of removing from man any desire to imagine the woman enclosed within. But that nudity was what the professor, hours later, alone in his room, entertained.

> *I was in my room*
> *alone and studying*
> *and I remembered my love.*
> *No—no longer could I study.*

His imagination penetrates back through the dense history, the sulky night, the unknowable distance, the opaque walls of the convent, the black mantle of the little nun, and he sings to himself the song Francisco Sánchez collected from the time of Charles V:

> *Don't show me them again*
> *or I will die!*
>
> *The nun was in the convent,*
> *her little white breasts*
> *were beneath the black veil.*
>
> *Oh,*
> *let me die!*

જીજ

Khon, the new professor, rented a small apartment near the library. He was one of those absentminded professors who wander along the street without seeing anybody, as if living on a cloud, or in a dream, or in oblivion, and the Dean, meeting him, had to repeat his greeting. Khon saw him appear from nothingness and apologized with the same humility that he would have used before an angel.

"Are you comfortably settled?" the Dean asked him.

"Oh yes. Thank you. The apartment is lovely, with windows looking out onto a garden. All that it lacks is the floor. It is disconcerting to walk around the room without being able to touch the floor, but in general I am very comfortable. Thank you."

જીજ

With computers the technicians established an Academy of Philosophy. First they chose the most important works in the history of thought. Then, through very rigorous analysis, they stripped it of its nonessentials—language, libraries, era, landscape, polemics, anecdotes—until they reduced it to the essential views of the world. Finally, with these fundamental nuclear ideas they prepared electronic brains. So that the philosopher-machines would be able to talk to each other, they gave them the same language. A few—those with mechanistic philosophies—functioned satisfactorily, although nothing they said surprised the technicians. On the other hand, those that corresponded to philosophers who did not believe in machines, emitted extravagant combinations of symbols. The philosopher-machines for whom reality was a behavioral characteristic of consciousness, produced only verbs. Others suppressed the verbs but on the other hand linked nouns together or threw them around followed by hordes of adjectives. There were philosopher-machines that, with desperate neologisms, strained themselves to reestablish the interior structure of the national language from which original thought had arisen. To the point where there were black dialects whose words—if they were words—no one could identify. The technicians, confused by so much gibberish, searched for a third code that—as in the argument of the "tritos anthropos" of Aristotle— would permit them to go from the cybernetic code to the personal code. They found it. In translating it, metaphors emerged. For example, to the questions "What is the Universe?" one code would answer "An eye"; another, "A yawn"; another, "A soup." This was not serious. They were forced to dissolve the Academy and return all the machines to the Ministry of War.

The Future

Truly it was alarming. Mankind was covering the surface of the earth with hard substances: pavements of stone or asphalt, cities of high buildings squeezed one against the other, machines spreading out into the country squashing everything, forests demolished, rivers forced into pipelines, nets of subways, tubes of iron and cement, rubbish and waste of tin and earthenware buried in the subsoil, machine gun shells and artillery dug down deep . . .

"Let's have a little more patience," one blade of grass said to another, from the edge of a humble tile patio. "Man won't be around very long. Then we'll return, with our captains, the forests."

ৈ≫

It was total war. With the latest weapons. Everything was destroyed. One poem turned out to be indestructible; but then there was no one left to read it.

Orpheus and Eurydice

Orpheus recalled how the Kings of Death had warned him, saying, "You will be able to take Eurydice back with you, fully restored to life; go and she will follow you; but when you leave this subterranean kingdom of shadows you must not look behind you; if you do so, you will lose Eurydice forever."

Then Orpheus, realizing that she could mean nothing to him because he, by nature, was unable to love any woman, turned his head and looked at her over his shoulder.

From the depths of Hell he heard, like a distant echo, the voice of the twice-dead Eurydice, and the woman's "Goodbye" carried all the contempt of a terrible accusation.

The Moon

Jacob, the half-witted child, was accustomed to going up on the roof to spy on the activities of the neighbors.

That summer night the pharmacist and his wife were on the patio drinking soda and eating cake when they heard the child walking around on the roof.

"Shush!" whispered the pharmacist to his wife. "That half-wit is out there again. Don't look. He must be spying on us. I'm going to teach him a lesson. Follow my lead and act as if we were just talking . . ."

Then, raising his voice, he said, "This cake is delicious. You must hide it when we go in, so no one will steal it."

"How could anyone steal it? The door to the street is locked. The windows are shut off by the blinds."

"But . . . someone might come down from the roof."

"Impossible. There are no stairs; the walls of the patio are smooth . . ."

"All right, I'll tell you a secret. On nights like this it would be enough for a person to pronounce the word 'tarasa' three times for him to be able to throw himself headlong down a moonbeam and arrive safe and sound down here, grab the cake, climb back up the beam and return very happy. But let's go in. It is late now and we must sleep."

They went in, leaving the cake on the table, and peeked out through the blind on the bedroom window to watch what the half-wit would do.

What they saw was that the child, after repeating "tarasa" three times, threw himself head first toward the patio, slid down as if on a smooth, golden toboggan, seized the cake and like a joyful salmon leaped up into the air and disappeared among the chimneys of the rooftop.

Instantaneous

At that time I was a normal man. Let no one come to me with mysteries: matter is matter and that's all there is to it, and if man-kind were to disappear from the universe, things would remain just as they are. Imagine then what must have been my surprise when, as I was strolling one night along a deserted beach, there appeared out of the sea spray a totally naked maiden who approached me and, after learning that I was a materialist (the discussion started because I looked at my watch!), told me that time had nothing whatever to do with a watch, and lectured me as follows:

"You, I, all of us, open our eyes wide in order to get out of our-selves and consider the world outside. But as soon as we open them, not the world, but an image of the world sneaks into our mind and we spend our lives trying to understand it. Observe more closely the long look that you think you are casting on the reality outside you. You carry it always attached inside you: it is like one of these waves that appear to free themselves to skip along the beaches and bluffs but that are never separate from the sea; and in that gazing wave there is a shoal of gazing wavelets moving out in all directions. Some are moving from the present toward a possible something new. Others take off from what is approaching to become the present which is about to happen. Others take off from a past which is push-ing back an earlier past. Still others reopen a past that was obliter-ated, reopen it to install themselves into that instant in which such a past had not yet happened but still held the touch of the future. Others, after waiting, again recall how something kept surviving and, after remembering, stop to wait for something suddenly to break into the present. Little gazing waves so diaphanous that they can see all through each other into the broad expanse of one large gazing wave, pure time, continuous and indivisible, unique and di-verse, irreversible in spite of being a fluctuating turbulence. You break your watch and nothing happens because we continue reading time in the movement of the stars; on the other hand, you withdraw your consciousness from the world and there remains neither move-ment nor stars. Without consciousness the entire world would be blacked out in one immutable and simultaneous mass. Without the metaphoric madness of man, the moon, ignorant of its own existence, would not distort its golden body in the deforming mirror of the night. Without that madness, trees would not constitute assemblies of magicians who, in the spring, draw out green garlands from their fingertips or, in the autumn, release their dry leaves at the bidding of the wind. Without that madness, no one would be able to say of the elephant that his trunk is a pseudopod remaining from the time when he was an amoeba. Without the metaphoric madness of man, the moon, the tree, the elephant, would all be one and the same thing, black, unmoving. Our consciousness invents these things and orders them into files, makes them wait and pass slowly, one behind the other. All this would happen, once and for all, in a single instant, if it were not that you and I and everyone else make the instant move slowly or quickly."

As she said all this, the maiden (who since she was naked thought herself a Greek) started, with a round motion of her arms, to outline the entire world, as if wishing to sketch the sphere of Parmenides in the air. It must have been a proscribed magical gesture since her body disappeared; her consciousness was suspended for a second like a soap bubble which then broke in the night, leaving not a trace behind. With a certain apprehension, I looked around to see whether something was missing. After what I had just heard, it seemed to me possible that the maiden, in fading away, had taken with her at least a tiny piece of the universe. But I relaxed. Everything—the waves, the wind, the grove of trees, the light of the moon—all continued as before. Everything except my materialism, since I realized that if things continued as before it was because I, who was still present there, in a certain fashion substituting for the maiden, was also carrying within my body the bubble of consciousness. So I undressed and joyously began to swim out into the sea.

Narcissus

One day, leaning out over the fountain, Narcissus could no longer see his face. It was as if his face had fallen to the bottom of the fountain and had dissolved there. Disgusted by the sensation of a face faded away, he stretched out on the ledge. "What is happening to me?" he thought. "What is happening to me that I see the water and don't see myself?" He glanced at the things that surrounded him and for the first time found them beautiful. Suddenly he discovered another beauty: the girl who was approaching him. The maiden leaned over him, Narcissus, and silently started to make faces as if over water: she smiled, threw her head back or turned sideways to see the lines of her cheeks, rehearsed the expression of her eyes, arranged the waves of her hair, and even, with a rapid movement of her lips, kissed herself.

Narcissus, meanwhile, hidden behind himself, now a pure mirror, remained trembling, trembling like water when it is touched.

&

The nymph Echo listened amorously to the beautiful Narcissus and then repeated his last words, and Narcissus, hearing himself in the voice of Echo, was as enchanted as when he looked at himself in the pool.

After some time, Echo noticed that in reality Narcissus was ignoring her and that she was for him scarcely more than a sounding mirror. She realized this only when Narcissus said "Goodbye." "Goodbye," Echo answered, believing that he was saying goodbye to her; but then she understood that he was saying goodbye to himself because he was going to die.

The Rival

King Arthur had known Guinevere since she was a child. He saw her as she grew up. He saw, on an April noon, how as she passed under the branch of a rosebush, a rose petal fell and left her stained with red. Then he decided to marry the maiden.

A maiden, without doubt. Nevertheless, after a few days of marriage King Arthur heard Guinevere talking in her sleep about a former spouse, more handsome than he, stronger than he, more loving than he. Jealous, King Arthur searched for him in order to make sure. He let his horse wander at will, dismounted on the bank of a river, boarded a barge without a sail, without oars, without a tiller, disembarked on a beach of golden sand, crossed through a tangled wood, passed over a bridge to an island, climbed up a mountain and at the top saw a castle of crystal turning in the wind like a mill wheel while four griffins, perched on four marble pillars, beat their wings. King Arthur made a great leap, caught hold of the drawbridge, and managed to enter the castle where he met his rival—whose head had the shape of an omega, with the face erased—and from him he learned that on certain nights Guinevere had been his wife.

Understanding that all this was from another world, and that therefore nothing that had happened there affected his honor, King Arthur returned to the arms of his wakened bride, and was happy ever after.

Danse Macabre

On the first of November Armand went to the cemetery, expressly in order to place some flowers on the tomb of Laura, who had died in July. But the bus on which he was traveling crashed into another. One of those accidents that occur every day. Getting off the bus, he saw Laura in the crowd of people attracted by the blood. Armand approached to speak to her, but she gestured to him that he should not do this, and disappeared.

"How can this be! I have just seen my dead sweetheart alive!" he thought. And that was when, suddenly, Armand realized . . .

Bestiary

The horse lashed itself with its tail, as if to frighten off horseflies. But there were no horseflies. Then I understood that the horse lashing itself was a form of flagellation. In order to help it in its ascetic self-punishment I attached a piece of barbed wire to its tail. The animal continued lashing itself to the point of drawing blood. From time to time it looked at me gratefully. I don't know if it had found its God.

All men, you, I, everybody, are under the constant watch of animals that follow from afar our slightest movements and at times surround us, feigning indifference. Can this be because they find us too dangerous and are preparing to wage war with us? I don't know, but it is certain that, positioned on all the rungs of the zoological ladder, they watch and wait. Some pretend to flee. Others hide. There are some that permit themselves to be hunted and, from the cages of the zoological garden, peer at us on the sly. There are those that draw near, apparently distracted or indifferent, but they are like those detectives that disguise themselves as vagrants and move along the streets with an air of boredom. One time a squirrel—young, naive—started to play with me, and I noticed immediately that what she wanted was to tame me. When I refused to go along with her she went away. Believe me, they are plotting something against us. Our only hope is that, sooner or later, a dog will end up revealing to us the secret animal plan. He is the only animal capable, as a favor to us, of being a traitor to the others: have you never observed how a dog sometimes seems to want to tell us something?

Patterns of the Possible

After the last birds died, the cage took off from the patio and began to fly toward heaven. "It is coming to us to ask for forgiveness," thought the angels, unaware.

è❧

The cat Aknatun still conserved the memory of having been a man and, thanks to this, was able to get along with Cleopatra, who, in turn, recalled, also vaguely, her preexistence as a cat.

è❧

Applause. Feet tapping. Song. Laughter. If only he could see something of the party! But he could not. A prisoner in the darkness of the guitar, he lifted his gaze, looked up through the large hole, and saw only the enormous fingers that came down on the strings . . . and plucked them.

è❧

He found a postcard in his pocket. He had never seen it before. It was not addressed to him. Someone passing by had confused him with a mailbox. Or was he really a mailbox?

è❧

They were talking in the room, very animatedly.
"I don't believe it," interrupted Estela, who, until that time had remained quiet because she had not yet been born.

è❧

"I," said one ghost to another, upon meeting in the attic of a very old big house, "am different from you: I have never died. I started by pretending to be a ghost, and look what happened."

è❧

Other amnesiacs forget their name, their profession, their family. Samuel forgot that, being a man, he was unable to fly. He leaped up to pluck a fig, continued rising up through the air, and was lost in a cloud.

è❧

Nobody knew how the statues passed the word through the parks, museums, temples, and palaces of the most remote cities, but the strike was general. All of them, at the same time, dropped whatever they were carrying: mantles, weapons, even children—and un-dressed. Those who had always been in the nude were shocked at this sudden immodesty.

Fame

The poet saw her pass, hurriedly, and hurriedly he ran after her and complained, "Still nothing for me? You have already honored so many poets less worthy than I. When will you get to me?"

Fame, without stopping, looked at the poet over her shoulder and answered, smiling as she hurried even more, "In two years exactly, at five o'clock in the afternoon, in the library of the School of Philos-ophy and Letters, a young journalist will open the first book you published and start to take notes for his special study. I promise you that I will be there."

"Ah, I shall thank you so much!"

"Thank me now, for in two years you will have no voice."

The Doorman

Gustave has to enter the palace about an urgent matter, but the doorman holds him back and tells him to wait. Gustave sits down in front of the doorman and waits. Meanwhile, other people are enter-ing and leaving. Entering and leaving, they greet the doorman with smiles. Gustave, timidly, "And I?"

"Not yet."

Gustave waits. For weeks, months. One day the doorman asks him to do him the favor of replacing him for a moment. And a little later the doorman does, in fact, return.

On another day the doorman repeats his request, but this time he disappears and never returns. Gustave continues waiting. Weeks, months. The people who enter and leave start to greet him, to smile at him with growing familiarity.

Gustave now realizes that he is the doorman, but he is not yet certain whether he ought to permit himself to enter the palace where he still needs to take care of an urgent matter.

For Eternity

The angel put his hand on his shoulder and with a silent gesture indicated to him that it was now time to leave.

Enrique, having trouble becoming accustomed to the idea that he was dead, started following the steps of the angel while for the last time caressing with his eyes the furniture in his room. And seeing through his window the jacaranda tree that was in bloom on the patio, he asked, "Up there where I am going, will there be any jacaranda?"

"No," answered the angel; but after glancing at the jacaranda he added, condescendingly, "Well, from up there you will be able to look down on this one here, while it lasts."

Time

Time felt remorseful in seeing what it had done to that poor man: covered with wrinkles, white hair, toothless, bent over, arthritic. It decided to help him in some way. It passed its hand over all that there was in the house: furniture, books, paintings, dishes. . . . From that time on, the old man could live (whatever remained to him of his life) by selling his belongings at a high price, belongings that now were rare antiques.

ৡ

Time was accustomed to entering homes (as it entered, every clock ironically greeted it by sounding the hour) and it was bathed in the awareness of man. When mankind disappeared, Time understood that since now there was no more awareness, it would have to flow forever like a dirty river, with all the weird memories that mankind had left it. Then it turned toward the river Lethe to merge into its waters and forget itself.

Gods

From the pews we saw only the head of the preacher, above the high pulpit; when he smiled, the slash of the smile circled around his head and cut it off. The head said:

"Man knows nothing of God and has nothing to gain by setting himself the insoluble problem of His existence; nor can he formulate a single theological proposition which in truth signifies anything. But God exists. He exists outside the awareness of man. The fact is that one of His perfect attributes is modesty: the admirable feature of modesty in having created man and yet not permitting him to perceive his Creator. I wish you could have seen the gentility, the humility with which He said 'I do not exist,' when I happened to bump into Him."

&

The madman did not harbor any sentiment of guilt before God. Rather he held a strong resentment against God.

"God," he said, "must have thought everything over very carefully before deciding to create the world. Creation was, after all, the result of slow rumination. He put an end to chaos, began the cosmos. If it was He who began everything, why, much later, did He accuse Adam and Eve of having committed the Original Sin? The sin of Adam and Eve was of secondary importance and nothing very terrible. Paradise must not have been a great affair: it took so little to destroy it! And why bother about the other little human sins that followed? If we men sin, it is because God is willing. We do not sin in spite of the Divine Will—nothing can occur against the Will of God—rather it is God who sins against Himself, man willing. Why does He punish Himself? Because God desires to punish Himself for His great Original Sin: Creation."

&

"God," said the old man, and as he said it his smile trembled within his beard like a bird in foliage, "is far above what all religions, present and to come, are capable of conceiving. He is so different and superior to the world that human experience will never even be able to guess how He is. At times God ceases being God. He expands, multiplies, changes form, recognizes Himself, comes down, observes His own children, speaks with a few of them, and even intervenes in their lives. Only when God has ceased to be God does man imagine Him and worship His Image. So God, annoyed at being worshipped only in His lesser forms, flies back up again and gathers Himself within His unfathomable absence. This absence of God causes even the most religious of men to appear to us as atheists."

The Frightened Priest

No one respected the priest. There was no weakness of flesh or spirit from which he did not suffer. All his congregation knew him to be sensual, obsequious, ignorant, inefficient, petty. The more pious prayed for him. One fine day an angel appeared before him. It came to infuse him with a sense of the mission of his priesthood. It reminded him, among other things, that however insignificant he might be as a man he was still a minister of God on earth.

"In the ceremony of the Holy Mass," it told him, "you can do more than all men put together. The Virgin Mary gave life to Jesus

Christ only once, but you conceive him every time you say at the altar, 'This is my body.' God has peopled the world, but you people heaven each time you say at confession, 'I absolve you.' The liturgy unites you with the absolute, and since the absolute contains nothing relative, there are no priests more priestly than others, just as there are no souls more soulful than others. You . . ."

The angel suddenly became silent. It was astonished to realize that the only thing it had infused into the priest was a dreadful fear.

A Puzzle of Possibilities

I'm with Rodríguez (I think that is his name) on the corner of Florida and Viamonte. A few minutes ago, along the sidewalk opposite us, the ugliest woman in the world hurried by. Her flesh was stuffed tightly into a green dress, her hair was dyed in multicolored streaks, her features were masked in cosmetics. She was a caricature of a figure from time-gone-by, who refuses to grow old. And she disappeared into the crowd.

"Did you see? Did you see?" I exclaimed, laughing. "Did you see that old parrot?"

Rodríguez turned toward me, gazing calmly, and said, "Yes. She is my wife."

Confusion. While during an embarrassed silence we acted as if we were watching a parade of women along Florida Street, I cogitated:

"Rodríguez pretended that the grotesque woman was his wife in order to punish me for my lack of gentility. If, in fact, that rag doll was his wife he would have sounded offended. But he didn't. He said 'She is my wife' with such calm that it was equivalent to proving to me that she wasn't. And so, at the same time that he was giving me a lesson in manners, he was saving his vanity as the handsome man who would never marry such an ugly woman. Except that Rodríguez must have foreseen that I would think this and, in order not to let me escape from my awkward situation (not to relieve me from the shame of having committed such a blunder), he exaggerated his calmness; knowingly he exaggerated it to the point where the calm itself was incredible, as if Rodríguez wanted to pretend that he was pretending, so that I, discovering his game, would not let myself be deceived and would understand that, in fact, that caricature of a woman was indeed his wife, at which point, after all, I would have to be ashamed of my faux pas. Or let us say that the tricky Rodríguez pretended that he was pretending to pretend only in order that I should be ashamed of having been ashamed of my shame. I suspect that Rodríguez has calculated that I am going to get out of the mess of pretendings proliferating within pretendings with some doubt as to whether that hideous creature is or is not his wife. Unless Rodríguez is imagining in me the same mental mess that I am imagining in him, so that when he heard me exclaim 'Did you see that old parrot,' he thought that I was trying to make him fall into a trap, because that grotesque, ridiculous, hideous caricature of a parrot was in fact my very own wife."

Dreams

Guillermo is in mortal danger: they have tied him hand and foot to a tree and a rattlesnake is going to sink its fangs into him. Suddenly Benito appears and prepares to save him, but in order to save him he must die.

Nobly, Guillermo says, "I cannot consent to such a sacrifice."

"As you wish," says Benito, backing away. "It's all the same to me. After all, it's your dream."

The Evil Eye

When I met him (they had instructed me to go and pay him a visit), Eugenio Gaudio was very healthy, rich, and happy.

"How have you managed to have such good luck in life?" I asked him, not without a certain professional curiosity.

He explained to me that he had not always been so lucky but that for about ten years he had been dedicated to pursuing a lady, a certain Mrs. Jinx, and that this had brought him all kinds of good luck.

"Oh, yes? And how is that?"

Foolishly, he continued explaining:

"You must understand, my dear friend, that the total number of misfortunes is limited, and no two are alike. When a misfortune falls on a man, it uses itself up and cannot be repeated. Or let us say that each time a misfortune touches someone, there is always some other person who automatically is freed from it. For that reason, although we don't admit it, the misfortunes of others give us pleasure. Well then, I have learned to avoid them. I decided to follow, as I told you, that Mrs. Jinx, that fatal shadow who goes along dealing out misfortunes among all she meets. And as I follow her at a discreet distance, always behind her, never exposing myself to her evil eye, she never includes me in her distribution."

"Aha," I said, smiling perversely, "I fear you exaggerate the importance of Mrs. Jinx. She is no more than a modest assistant."

Eugenio Gaudio looked at me, first without understanding, but when he did understand, he hid his face in order to avoid my eyes, and crossed himself.

"From now on," I advised him, "we will be seeing each other frequently."

I don't know whether he managed to hear me because at that very moment a cornice fell on him.

The Big Head

We were flying. The pilot who during a long interval had remained silent, looked at me as if he wished to say something but did not dare, lowered his eyes, turned toward me again and then spoke. Evidently he was preparing me for some bad news.

"The universe, sir, is an animal with a soul. Since outside itself there is nothing to be heard or seen, it lacks ears and eyes. Since it contains within itself all the air there is, it does not breathe. Since there are no enemies that threaten it, there is no need for it to move, nor does it have hands or feet. But it is an animal that thinks, and for this reason its form is the most perfect of all forms, that of the sphere. The sphere of the universe is a head, and the human head, also filled with thoughts, resembles in its turn the sphere of the universe. One head understands the other . . ."

"Well, go on. Stop the metaphysics and tell me what you need to say to me," I interrupted him, "I'm not a child. What is the matter?"

"We have to go back. We cannot continue."

"Why not?" I asked him, alarmed.

"Don't you see? Over there. Beyond those clouds. It's the inside wall of a big head. We have to go back. Something is telling me that the big head has started thinking about a disaster."

"You're crazy."

"Crazy? Ha! I'm telling you that inside my little head I am feeling that the big head has started thinking about a disaster. We must land."

The man was crazy.

"Yes," I told him, so as not to contradict him, "we should land. The sooner the better."

SELECTIONS FROM

❦

The Swindler Retires (1969)

Prologue

In my early books of fiction fantastic situations predominated. In
order to remind my friends that frequent playing with ghosts had
not entirely turned me into a ghost, I therefore included a few realistic situations. Now, in *El estafador se jubila (The Swindler Retires)*, reality appears with greater frequency, but I include unre-
alities so that those same friends should not believe that I have
changed my game and am moving away from fantasy. Images of a
normal life or testimonials of a magic life, all is invention. The important thing is that the reader not escape the trap that has been set
for him. That trap is a plot: finally, a surprise. The surprise, at times,
is that the story has no ending. Too mechanical a procedure? It
would be if within the artifice there were not beating a conception of
the world: ironic, perhaps poetic.

Enrique Anderson-Imbert

Frankly, No

What I am going to relate happened to me during a frustrating vacation in Córdoba. Although young, I enjoyed a certain degree of
fame as a theater director. My secret vocation, nevertheless, was to
write: poetry, stories, and, at just that moment, a play. If my reper-
tory playwrights were benefiting from the scenic tricks with which I
was enhancing their dialogue, why shouldn't I benefit by directing
my own play during the next season? Ever since I had seen *The Tail
of the Mermaid* by Nalé Roxlo, I yearned to present an even more

brilliant spectacle, with a mermaid so deep in the sea that she really left the spectators breathless. In those days I must have let my tongue run away with me—probably from having one glass too many at some party. I confided in someone I believed to be an actor and it turned out that he was a journalist—because I remember that *Crítica* devoted several lines to me, picture and all. After praising, with a wealth of details, my activities as a director, he pointed out how vain it is to risk a well-deserved reputation for a doubtful literary adventure. These, he declared, are not the days of Lope de Rueda, Shakespeare, and Moliere, when it was possible to be author, actor, director, and producer all at the same time, but of specialists; and the specialty of the director, "ever since 1874, when the Duke of Saxe-Meiningen organized his company in Berlin," is to dominate the author, the work, the actors, the make-up, the costumes, the lights, and the music to give to the spectacle a unity of interpretation. At the end he gave the news that I was going to retire to a chalet in Santa Catalina to attempt one more dramatization on the theme of the mermaid and he wished me success, not without indulging in the irony that, with so aquatic a theme, instead of spending my vacation on the island of Capri "where Odysseus saw the first mermaids," I would bury myself in the countryside of Córdoba, notorious for its dry rivers.

The learned journalist didn't even suspect that the true reason for my trip to Santa Catalina—where indeed I owned a chalet—was that I needed to rest my nerves, shattered by a year of excesses and frictions.

I took a train, got off at Jesús María, rented a sulky and an hour later entered the little town, which smelled of mint and history. The church was a story in stone, impoverished by having been visited so much by traveling monks. They came there from Peru in the XVIIth century and started to rebuild the church, forgotten by the XVIIIth century. Poor little church, resting there with its timid facade and a crazy bell tower. We went around the breakwater, crossed through a ranch and, after three kilometers, we stopped.

I dismissed the coachman and smiled at the chalet. The white of the walls and the red of the tile shone down from the height of the hill, gilded by the sun. With a garnish of gray clouds at the side, the sky rose up, blue. Little dandelion stars shone yellow at my feet. I walked up among the greens—greens of the cocoa trees, green of the carob tree foliage, green of the clover, green of the chanar's trunk—and, finally on the patio, I pondered my wide solitude. For only a moment—just enough time to fill my lungs with the pure air—because I had to get the keys at Antonio's hamlet on the other side of the river.

I trotted to the fence, crossed the drainage ditch on a few planks, straightened up, and, from the bank of the ravine, I saw, at the bottom of the sharp slope, a few threads of water separated by pebbles. That was all that was left of the river! The journalist was right: a dry river. What mermaid was I going to see there? Unless it was that fish, that, stranded in a pool when the water evaporated, had drowned in the air of man. I went down a rough and stony slope, grabbed the fish and returned it, dead, to the dead river. I had never seen the canyon full, but it was so deep and broad that formerly it must have been carved out by a true river. Now I was able to cross through that rocky gallery as if it were a sculpture museum. Jumping from rock to rock (to show off; not because I had to), I came to a field of long grass on the other bank and climbed up toward Antonio's hamlet.

The old man had rented a neighboring farm and was charging me a few pesos for taking care of my chalet. He had already seen me and was coming down, silhouetted against a large cloud.

"How are you, Don Antonio? I'm glad to see you. Still handsome as ever, eh?"

When he was a child a cow had kicked him in the mouth and he was left with a twisted jaw. Although his mustache covered his lips, one could see his tongue licking a single tooth. I asked him for the keys. He went to the hamlet and brought them.

"And my mare, Don Antonio?"

"She's over there. She's getting fat. A little galloping would do her good. Shall I saddle her for you?"

"Yes, please."

I petted the mare—chestnut, lustrous, beautiful. I mounted and went off for a ride. The wind was becoming more and more lively. On the side of the Pinto Canyon black clouds were piling up. It must already have been raining on the north hills. Perhaps for a few days. I noticed the restlessness of the thrushes. By about five o'clock in the afternoon the sky was a single huge cloud vibrating with lightning and thunder. A flash of lightning and a crash of thunder that lasted longer than the others, warned me to return. I returned. I unsaddled the mare, gave her an affectionate pat on the withers and released her. I went through the rooms and lay down. I wanted to read but the kerosene lamp irritated my eyes and I went to sleep. I woke at nine o'clock in the morning. I hadn't slept like that for a long time! Through the open window I heard a strange clamor, like the harsh clearing of a dry throat. I looked out. No, it was not raining. What was it then? Ah, the river! And in order to see what was happening, I repeated my little walk to the fence and the ditch. When I reached the ravine, what a change!

Over the river bed, yesterday empty, a flood had come with the dawn. Without doubt it had been traveling all night, from the far distant and for me unknown waterfalls where the rains came together. The torrent had ripped out thickets of bramble and, muddy with branches, clamorous as a cataract, dreadful as a destroying witch, had rolled over the land. Only the tips of the highest rocks were left in the air. Now no one could wade across that river. I was fascinated by the destructiveness of the flood and, in spite of feeling that the storm could begin again at any moment, I sat down on one of the rocks, unnoticed the day before along the ridge of the ravine, but now, with the rising flood, taking on the dignity of a vast shoreline.

Suddenly I saw a bulk swept along, twisting and rolling in the tumbling waves. It was a girl, nearly drowned. She was waving her arms helplessly. The current dragged her under and pushed her up. I sprang to my feet but did not dare to plunge in. What floated highest—inflated like blisters—was her blue dress; and blue was the shipwrecked glance that she threw at me when for the last time she managed to lift her head. After that I could make out only her hair, long and blond. At a bend in the river a willow tree hid her from me.

It was all so rapid that for a moment I imagined that I had just lifted my eyes from a novel where a girl was described as being carried away in a river similar to this one; and that, with the shift of my eyes from the work of fiction to the real landscape, I had confused a fictional river with the real river. But the mistake did not paralyze me. I began to run through the ups and downs of the ravine to reach the dyke before the girl, and to rescue her. A desperate race. I stumbled. I fell. Up again! A leap! Another leap! The river was outracing me, but nevertheless it stayed always at my side, mocking. I ran, I ran. I cursed. The sky descended on me. It wasn't a squall, it was a deluge. The world dissolved, sped by me, faded away. And the drops battered my eyes. I thought, "One slip and I tumble forward down the ravine. But keep going!" With the energy of a man who does all he can to do his duty and so feels free of guilt; because the truth is that I had no hope of saving that girl.

I heard a voice from the other bank. It was Antonio, on horseback, somewhat blurred through the crystal shards of the downpour.

"Is something wrong, sir?"

"Ah, Don Antonio! There goes a girl, drowning!"

Antonio started up the cowpath. I could no longer be of any help. I had dislocated my ankle. I lay stretched out in the mud, under the whip of the storm, nearly unconscious.

When I recovered my strength I returned to the house, limping, done in, miserable.

Hours later, Antonio appeared. "It's useless," he said. "My boys have gone as far as the dyke. They have found nothing. Who was the girl that fell in?"

"I don't know. Just a girl."

"Who could it be? At first I thought that it could be one of my own. Thank God, it's not. It could be a tourist."

"Are they still looking for her?"

"Yes, sir. But it seems strange to me that she hasn't appeared yet. Unless she is caught between two rocks under the water. But at the moment there's nothing we can do. When the flood goes down . . ."

The flood did not go down. The rain, which lasted a few days, fed it even more. As my ankle got worse, I stayed in bed, but every day they brought me news. Farmers, neighbors, and civil guards with poles were dredging the river from the banks; and umbrellas sprouted up like mushrooms among the curious crowd coming from far away, unwilling to miss the drama of a search for a drowned person. A local newspaper reproduced the article from *Crítica*, with the same photograph of me: my past successes in the theater, my proposed drama on the theme of the mermaid . . .

That afternoon, a police lieutenant about my age appeared. I noticed immediately that he was less interested in the girl than in talking with me. He admitted that he was an amateur in literature. He had started his career—"for professional reasons"—by reading detective novels, and from there he had moved on to murder mysteries. Now he was intrigued by my project of bringing a mermaid onto the stage. Was I going to make the stage into an aquarium or into a bubble?

I interrupted him by requesting that he please get to the point, since I was in pain, had no desire to talk and needed rest.

"Very well," he said to me arrogantly, "you understand that I have to investigate. If a corpse appears: was it an accident? a suicide? Or was it a crime? Personally I don't believe that the corpse will appear, for the simple reason that it doesn't exist. Two hypotheses. Let us look at the first: that you invented the story of the girl who drowned. You're preparing a drama with a mermaid as the protagonist, right? It's only natural, then, that to assure yourself of free publicity in the newspapers you invent a vacationing mermaid who drowns in a flood. But I discard this hypothesis. Mythical mermaids can't drown, and if on your opening night you drown your mermaid, that will be a confession that all this present upheaval has been a publicity stunt in very poor taste; in which case you would have to answer before justice for disturbing the peace. Your mermaid will have been a false alarm. So there remains the second hypothesis: that the story was invented, not by you, but by the girl. You said you saw her go by, dragged by the current, and you lost sight of her behind a willow tree, didn't you? All right. It could be that the girl, right there, touched bottom, walked out of the river, shook herself off and beat a retreat, safe and sound. If she has remained in hiding since then, it's because the mermaid was a red herring: she didn't fall into the water. Rather, she dove in head first. Why? Elementary, my dear sir, elementary! Since you have announced that you will direct your play about a mermaid in a Buenos Aires theater, an actress, hearing of this, wants, at any price, to be cast in the role. That actress follows the author-director from Buenos Aires to Santa Catalina. Surprising him, drenched in the pouring rain, splash! She leaps into the flood. Being an excellent swimmer, she can pretend to be swept along by the current. Her plan is that you save her and that you become good friends and so . . ."

I couldn't stand any more and interrupted him again, "You're a humorist."

"Me? No, sir. The girl, perhaps."

"Stop reading so many novels, lieutenant. If you want to take my statement do it once and for all and let's be done with it. I'm falling asleep."

As soon as I was able to walk I had them take me to the station and I waited for the train. To my beloved Buenos Aires! I leaned my head against the window and closed my eyes. When I opened them who did I see? The girl! She was seated in front of me, looking at me out of her large blue eyes, but now they were bright and teasing. I jumped. "What! You? So you didn't drown. . ."

"Who? Me?"

"But the whole town has been looking for you. Didn't you hear about the commotion? Didn't you read the newspapers?"

"No. These days I've been busy studying. Let's see; tell me about it. It interests me."

I described the scene.

"Ah! Now I understand," she exclaimed, smiling. "Don't worry about it. That girl really did drown, but they'll never find her because she had no body."

"But I saw her!"

"I saw her too, but she was bodiless, like a ghost. It's just as well that you didn't throw yourself in to save her: you would have grasped a form made out of water, nothing more. Let me explain. Are you familiar with *An Occurrence at Owl Creek Bridge* by Ambrose Bierce? They hang a man on a bridge. The hanging man feels the noose tug at his neck; he also feels the noose break, and he falls into the stream; they pursue him shooting; he swims underwater, comes out on the bank, enters a wood, arrives at his home, and his wife runs into his arms. But all this while the man is still hanging by his neck from the bridge. At the instant of dying, in a last burst of fantasy, he imagined that flight. In Montevideo we were thinking of dramatizing that story, but we abandoned it as too difficult. I was going to play the part of the wife (the wife who is only a hallucination in the hanging man's agony). Something like that, but different, happened to me. There, the same day. I was standing at the edge of the ravine, looking at the flood. I didn't see you. Suddenly the earth gave way under my feet. Nothing much—some clumps of mud. But I was frightened, as if it had been a landslide. In a kind of vertigo I became two people, me seeing myself before my own eyes. You understand? My fantasy produced the image of me, but instead of thinking about it, I forced the image away from me. My fantasy overflowed like the river and what flowed out from me was the image of myself, independent of me. Now do you understand? And the other Paulina—my name is Paulina—that other Paulina that I had projected into space stumbled, clawed the air, and sank. I not only saw myself, I also felt the rain whipping my body, and afterwards the force of the current that was pushing me. It lasted only a second. Immediately the illusion vanished and I, laughing at my fright, returned to the hotel. From what you have told me, you must have seen my double, drowning. You saw, as concretely as I did, the image that I had caused to materialize."

While I was listening to her, memories came, very vague, of my reading during adolescence. Nothing supernatural had ever happened to me; I never even knew anyone to whom it had happened. But it called up an arcane other world, inexplicable to science: extrasensory perception, eidetic trances, spiritualistic embodiments, metaphysical and parapsychological phenomena, psychokinetic and schizophrenic manifestations, exorcisms and demiurges. I remembered Nefele, Golem, the Ambulant Souls of the Great Chaco. Well, I was listening to Paulina ("Paulina"—what a name for an actress!) with a certain uneasiness. But suddenly I noticed a detail that did not fit in:

"Let's suppose that it is as you say (and please note that I am saying 'Let's suppose'). If you hadn't seen me, how is it that in an almost empty railroad car you sat down precisely in front of me? Don't tell me that by chance . . ."

"No, not by chance. I was walking down the aisle, looking for a seat, and when I saw you I stopped, astonished. What is this! I recognize that gentleman without having met him before! It was not a

sensation of false recognition, of déjà vu, so frequent with the absentminded who see an image accompanied by a shadow and believe
it is a matter of two perceptions, one before the other, and that as a
result they are remembering something past, since everything, the
image and its shadow, occurred at the same time. No, it was not a
double perception. It was a double personality. So I sat down in front
of you so that when you woke up we could clarify this matter. Now
it's clear. Would you like me to explain how I recognized you without having seen you? Because not I but my other self lifted her head
from the water, and that was when the two of you saw each other.
The eyes of my other self looked at you. And here is what is difficult
to understand: in some mysterious fashion, what that astral body
saw—a body that was like a feeling extension of my own body—
slipped into my own memory. Was smuggled in, as it were."

Perplexed and, I must confess, overwhelmed by a superstitious
feeling, I could only murmur, "Is it possible?"

Paulina looked at me, very serious. Then, unable to stand it any
longer, she burst into laughter and answered, "Frankly, no."

The Stone

Pedro had the soul of a stone. Like a stone, he fell into discourage-
ments and calamities. And while he was falling he would glance at
those above him and wish that they too would fall. The looks of the
basilisk—lethal missiles—at any bird that was flying above him.
Except that, unlike the basilisk, his glance damaged no one; weak
and impotent Pedro did not attack, for fear of counterattack. Perhaps
he might have defended himself against light offenses, but his real
enemy was no less than the vertical hierarchical order; with what
forces was he supposed to defeat something so indefinite, so permanent? He folded his arms and held in his rancor. His mouth, from
which all laughter had fled, spoke bitter words. Oh, if only there
were no superiors who were able to make him feel inferior! Oh,
if only society suddenly became level, like the vast plain where he
was born!

He had been born in a village lost in a nameless territory. Only
pampas. He grew up among women: his grandmother, his aunts. Of
his mother—he had seen her no more than once or twice—little was
said, and that in a low mutter. His father, they told him, was dead,
and then it turned out that he wasn't; he was alive but his name had

been dropped. Nevertheless, all things considered, Pedro realized that he was owed favors, those that his father, as he advanced further and further in his political career, did for him indirectly. Thanks to those favors from a remote authority which, however, like the sun, mysteriously shifted the shadows of the family, Pedro grew up in a home with possibilities. Others in his place would have profited from them; he could not. The over-sensitive child became an irascible adolescent and later on an explosive man. The least frustration wounded him to the quick. When he was not wounded he imagined that he should be. He was convinced that his destiny was to suffer insults. And in the face of that fate, he was passive. Feelings of revenge, envy, hatred, jealousy, and rancor, repressed and retained too long, had fermented into a black intoxicating brew. They were no longer sentiments but resentments, without a determined object. Through recommendations which, he supposed, proceeded from his father, he found a job. He lost it. He found another. Again he lost it. Now, at thirty years of age, he swallowed his pride and asked an elderly aunt to arrange (with whom if not with his father?) to get him out of that damned village. They brought him out. His next job—working in a granite quarry—took him to a city in the east, in the middle of a valley.

On the first Sunday he went to visit The Rock. Bad luck! Just as he was starting for the country, a speck of dust entered his eye; the earth, impatient, was looking for his corpse and, without waiting for him to die, already had started to bury him. It took some time to remove it. Ah, it was a radiant summer morning; the blue of the sky resembled the ideal blue, the hills also were bluish, although with a gray cast, and the plain—which still recalled the flood of the ocean, when the mountains were islands—rose and fell in a tide of brown velvet, violet, golden, green, with passionate waves of pointed daisies.

Pedro had promised himself a long walk, alone and relaxed. With disgust he noticed that a crowd of people was invading the area. To find out who they were, he waited for the most distinguished group. They walked away from the parking area, their gestures signaling the importance of one certain gentleman, dressed like a man from London, who was lending his arm to a lady wearing a Parisian dress. The lady was beautiful; the gentleman was one of those who are born to command. Pedro compared himself to him. He began by putting him down. "The well-endowed," he thought, "have less merit than people, modestly endowed, who must struggle to survive." And he ended up by denigrating the values that the man embodied. He thought, "Behind his vitality, education, charm, initiative, talent, and finesse, other qualities can be seen, less worldly, that neither he nor I possess, and in that we are equal." He approached other groups— they were commenting on the electoral law that the congress had approved unanimously a few days before—and confirmed his suspicion: that group was made up of nationally known politicians, as eminent as the mountains that were breaking the uniformity of the pampas. Officials, property owners, industrialists, journalists, police, rich neighbors who make up the politicians' cortege. What to do? Go away? It wasn't fair, since he had arrived first. Stay on? Then he would have to mix with them. Avoid them? Difficult: all of them were converging on the same vantage point. He stepped forward, puffing himself up so that his slight body would occupy the maximum of space, ready to protest if anybody brushed against him. As if against his will, he stood alongside the gentleman and observed him. He was truly elegant, sharp, happy. What rage! Wasn't he already envying him? How good it would be right there to strip him of his cane, his limousine, his impressive height, his regal gaze, his language, his wife! But he would never even be able to rival him; however hard he tried, he would never succeed in being like him. What was unpardonable was his existence itself, his animal integrity, his unique class. Pedro, on the other hand, subsisted in an ambiguous situation. Amphibian, rather. Here he was the frog, not daring to leap from one environment to another because his gills had not finished their metamorphosis into lungs. And meanwhile, from his pool he heard those on the shore making fun of him: "You could, but you can't," "You can but we won't let you."

They had arrived at the hill. Pedro wanted to erase from his mind all that golden crowd—hadn't he come alone to enjoy his solitude?— and he stepped forward to climb up before anyone else when, from nowhere, a guard came out who roughly forced him back; with his left hand he held him like a prisoner, while at the same time with his right hand he opened the way for the gentleman and murmured "Your Honor" with those negroid lips just begging to be split with a punch. The minister smiled graciously, yielded the way for the beautiful lady with a gallant bow from the waist, and the two of them started the ascent. Pedro, at the end of the line, with his eyes fierce, his teeth and his fists clenched, with a need to relieve his tension in some way, humiliated, once more humiliated. But this time he distinguished, in full clarity, the nature of that humiliation which for many years he had heard flapping about in black circles, like a bat. Before, he had felt himself insulted by the vague authority of an indefinable paternal and political regime. Now that authority was defined by a monstrous name: oligarchy. It was represented there by these personages, elegant tourists, coming from the capital to admire a famous rock that had no equal.

The rock was within reach of his hand. He could touch it. He did touch it. It had the shape of an enormous Phrygian cap that ironically saluted the valley. Or rather, of a crown which ruled a kingdom from the heights of privilege. It spread its two hundred tons over almost two hundred meters, and it was moving! A stone with anxieties, with intentions. Its shadow in the midday sun undulated over the ground like the skirt of a lovely lady. It was sensitive, graceful, playful; in an angle at the base they would place a nut, and it would crack it without crushing it; they would place a bottle and crack! it would be shattered into bits. Laughter. Jokes. A few of them, joining arms to form a battering ram, began pushing the stone. Ha, ha! Don't be so stupid . . . If Rosas hadn't succeeded with teams of horses . . . ! No, the idea is not to push it over, but only to make it wobble . . . Ah, that's it . . . Exclamations. Ah, ah, ah! Oh, oh, oh! An apparition. An Italian acrobat! With his feet up and his head down, like an angel bringing a message to man, balancing on one hand over the rock; and the rock, in turn, dancing with one finger touching the hill, a hill that rises up over the planet; a planet floating in the air . . . That was the ultimate. Aerial forms, as if things had no weight! The acrobat resumed his normal posture and bowed to the applause. Pedro noticed that the oligarchy and the rock, the two excellencies, continued in equilibrium. Why hadn't that occurred to him! What the devil! Neither one nor the other was that permanent. The electoral law would bring down the oligarchy from its pedestal; why shouldn't he, Pedro, anticipating it with a symbolic act, bring down the Rock from its pedestal?

For three days he searched for a way to execute his plan. He found it in a notebook with an oilcloth cover which an engineer had left on his desk. The rock would never fall by itself, he read. It had been balancing for centuries and centuries and would continue that way for centuries more if the workers who in every workday were making the hill shake with a hundred blast holes would only take certain precautions which the engineer recommended in order to conserve "that marvel of Argentine nature." On Thursday Pedro went up the hill and, with the punctuality of a timekeeper, stamped the date in the granite: February twenty-ninth, 1912. Then, reversing the engineer's instructions, he carefully measured the distance and exploded a stick of dynamite. It was five o'clock in the afternoon. A tremendous clamor, and the Moving Rock of the Tandil fell onto the plain and mixed with the anonymous mass of rubbish. And then that other stick of dynamite that Pedro had guarded for years and years in the cellars of his soul, also exploded. The resentment, so long contained, was discharged in one act of violence and cleaned him of his venom. For an instant he believed himself free, like the victim who conquers an aggressor. To his mouth, before twisted with rage, laughter returned. But immediately he heard, like an echo, the shrill cackle of Satan, another fallen one, and he understood that all he had managed to do was to move into another part of hell.

The Confession

I knew that my maternal grandfather had been a painter, but beyond that I knew nothing. And even that I learned by chance, since in my home his name was never mentioned. More than forgotten, it was forbidden. One time when, at the instigation of an older cousin, I asked my mother "What did grandfather do that was so bad?", she looked at me, very upset, and told me that she did not want to hear me speak of that ever again; afterwards from my room I heard her crying. Years later I went to Italy and by chance in a museum I saw a few paintings by my grandfather, one of them—according to the catalog—a self-portrait. His eyes impressed me. They looked out with hatred. I suspected that, having done the self-portrait in front of a mirror, that look of hatred revealed that he hated himself. I had to return immediately to Buenos Aires because I had been informed by cable that my parents had just died in a fire. The lawyer also informed me that I inherited a house belonging to my grandfather. I expected to find there many of his paintings, but I didn't. I found only one in the attic, and I was disappointed. It was a dark canvas, dirty with flyspecks and mould, dust, and spider webs. One could just make out the shape of a woman asleep on the ground in the middle of the shadows of a forest. I took the painting down and washed it. While I was washing it, the face of the woman began to resemble that of my mother. She was not sleeping but was in the agony of a scream. I continued cleaning the canvas: the lady's dress, that before was gray, now became white—a dress belonging to my grandmother—and at her breast was a bright stain of blood. Who could have killed her? A corpse without a killer is somewhat illogical, something that runs counter to our mental habits, something that disturbs like a magic capable of killing with mere thought. With a sponge I scrubbed other parts of the painting; the air shone over the painting as if it was dawning. The lawn was golden with daisies, the foliage was vibrant and through a few openings it was possible to see a sky every moment more bright. And suddenly, when I moved the sponge to one side, there appeared between the trees of the background a figure that before was not visible, darkened from the soiling: it was a man running away but with his face turned toward the murdered lady, and in his hand he carried a dagger that now was starting to drip blood. The face of my grandfather! He was looking with those same eyes of hatred that I had already recognized, except that he was looking with hatred, not at his image in the mirror as I had supposed, but at the murdered woman. I understood that my grandfather had painted there his confession.

My Shadow

We don't say a word to each other, but I know that my shadow is as happy as I am when, by chance, we meet each other in the park. On those afternoons I see him always in front of me, dressed in black. If I walk he walks, if I stop he stops. I too imitate him. If it seems to me that he has clasped his hands behind his back, I do the same. I suppose that sometimes he turns his head, looks at me over his shoulder and smiles tenderly to see me so excessively large in all directions, so colorful and plethoric. While we are walking along through the park I take care of him, I spoil him. When I feel that he must be tired I take a few measured steps—here, there, wherever— until I take him where he wishes to go. Then I twist myself around in the glaring light and assume an uncomfortable posture so that my shadow, in comfort, can seat himself on a bench.

The Pruning

A terrible illness had prostrated me for months. From my bed I used to look through the windows into the shady street, always in shade no matter how much sun there might be, since in Tucuman the foliage meets overhead in high vaults. That morning I heard voices and strange noises. I gathered together what little strength I had left and, leaning on a chair, I was able to reach the window. Pruners had come to clean the plantain trees of their black insects. A boy, pole in hand, opened the ceremony. At the height of the pole, they marked the trees with slashes of a machete. Then they climbed up like monkeys and started to prune. They chopped off the branches, mutilated the trunk, bound up the limbs and, pushing and pulling, dragged them down to the ground.

I returned to my bed, exhausted. In the afternoon, once again I looked out of the window. The scene was desolate. The house of plantain trees had lost its roof. A crude light, the sky filtering down from far above, inundated my eyes. A burning blue sky with no longer a trace of leaf-green shade.

Although cut to the quick at the same level, the forks of the branches, twisting and turning, some larger than others, created their own figures. In a moment of distraction those figures seemed to me almost like ornamental images: a candelabra, antlers, a piece of coral. Before they could become beautiful I recognized them as figures of pain. I saw them with skin and flesh. The wood became my flesh, the bark of the entire slashed grove became my skin. I suffered for the plantains, and for myself in seeing myself like them, with one foot in the grave. It was not a museum, but a hospital of mutilation. A dead hand, frightfully open. Two little arms, emaciated, lifted up, begging for help. The throats of arteries open to the air. Bloody wounds waiting for gangrene.

I was looking with such pain that I stopped seeing. I felt, rather, that those truncated bodies were recalling their amputations, as I myself, ill, was recalling my lost health. A healthy tree must believe—as a healthy man does—that it is a unique being, pregnant with purposes. The wound, the scar, old age, and death all come, on the other hand, to prove that we are all homogeneous forms through which life has passed with complete indifference. I dragged myself back to the bed from which I was never to rise again.

June, July, August, September.

Today I asked about the plantain trees.

"They are turning green again," I was told.

I can imagine them on the other side of the window, still the same, still the same as I: their hands filled with scabs and suppurating sores, they, and I, covered with green leprosy. I no longer believe in springtime.

Jealousy

Elisa woke up, tortured by jealousy; she had just finished dreaming that her husband was flirting with another woman. And what tortured her like an evil thorn in her flesh was that if her husband had dared to behave like that while she was dreaming, what would the beast not dare to do when he was alone in his own dreams!

The Writer and His Inkwell

In a crystal inkwell, seven genies are imprisoned. The owner knows that, writing with that ink, he will be assured of glory. He also knows that if he opens the inkwell, the seven genies will escape.

Soledad

From New York, Osvaldo sent a cable to Soledad, his wife: "Am returning soon. Since the company has given me no date, you cannot pick me up at the airport, but wait for me at home. After next Monday, don't go out. Yours. Osvaldo."

He arrived finally in Buenos Aires, at night. Impossible to warn Soledad, who had no telephone. Should he telephone Soledad's sister, who lived nearby? No, he was not going to force his sister-in-law to go out in the streets at that hour with so many woman-chasers running loose out there. Better to find Soledad in bed and wake her up with caresses.

It was midnight when he opened the door and entered his home, trying to make no noise.

A voice, alarmed, "Who is it?"

Before the woman had time to turn on the light Osvaldo was holding her in his arms and kissing her.

The voice said in his ear, "Osvaldo, Osvaldo . . . Soledad is dead. I came to clean up the house and fell asleep exhausted. . ."

In the darkness Osvaldo lifted his head, looked at the face of his sister-in-law and kept on seeing Soledad.

"Osvaldo, don't you understand? Osvaldo, it's me! But Osvaldo . . . !"

I'll Teach Her a Lesson

Mariano was a police official in a town in the province of Buenos Aires. One afternoon a neighbor ran in, screaming, "My husband! He has committed suicide!"

"Calm yourself, Señora."

Mariano put on his hat, his sword, and, accompanied by a pa-trolman, went up to the woman's room, who continued whining ex-planations. "I'm guilty, yes, I'm guilty, I'm guilty. We were having an argument and finally he told me that he couldn't stand me any more and was going to shoot himself. He shut himself in his room and pulled the trigger. Oh, what a tragedy! And just now when I'm going to have another baby!"

Mariano knocked loudly. Since no one answered he kicked the door down with his foot. The man stretched out on the bed looked at him very calmly. On the night table, the pistol.

"What! You're not dead?"

"No, sir."

"And the gunshot?"

"I fired at the ceiling. I was arguing with my wife, I shut myself up here and fired at the ceiling, to teach her a lesson . . ."

Mariano wanted to beat the man up, but he changed his mind. He took the pistol from the night table and holding it out he said:

"Right now you are going to commit suicide, you bum, and this time it's for real."

The man took the pistol, fired a shot at Mariano, another at the patrolman, another at his wife, and the last one, once again, into the ceiling.

The Complaint

Once again the raven was out there waiting for me along the road. He dotted the i of the post. When I drew near he said to me, "Listen, stupid, can't you avoid misfortunes on your own account? I'm fed up with playing this role of a bird of evil omen."

The Girlfriend

Ramón was born in Tucumán, but at the age of ten his parents took him with them to Buenos Aires. He would always remember his mandrake-like cry when he was uprooted from his native soil; what pained him above all was to be separated from the little girl-friend who lived on the other side of the fence.

Twenty years later he returns to Tucumán for the first time, in-vited by his uncle. He asks about his former little neighbor.

"Contrary to the universal law of gravitation," his eloquent uncle relates, "heavy-minded men rise, and light-minded women fall.

They took that girl to Buenos Aires too, at almost the same time as you. She grew up beautiful but wrong-headed. She got mixed up with a good-for-nothing and finally returned to Tucumán and died along with the child that she had borne."

Thanks to other details, Ramón realizes that his little childhood friend is the same lover that he had in his years in college and who one day left him without saying where she was going or why.

The Kingdom Bewitched

From the four cardinal points of the world came the four magicians convoked by the king to put an end to the extraordinary events which were driving his subjects mad and altering the very stability of the kingdom. Beforehand, however, they had to prove their powers.

They were on the patio, in the center of which was a large fig tree. The first magician cut a few little branches, changed them into bones and built a skeleton. The second shaped it with figs which were converted into muscles. The third wrapped it all in a skin of leaves. The fourth pronounced, "Let it live!"

The animal thus created turned out to be a tiger who ate the four magicians.

They proved their powers, but far from resolving the evil, they only made it worse, since the tiger, which had fled into the forest, intended to return and eat up the first person it met. The hunters who went in search of it either didn't find it or succumbed to its claws.

The king had a daughter, famous for her smile. She would smile and disarm the whole world. Moved by the suffering of her father, the princess, without telling him, went to tame the tiger with her smile. The same afternoon the taming princess and the now tame tiger returned to the palace: the princess within, and the smile on the face of the tiger.

SELECTIONS FROM

❧

Madness Plays at Chess (1971)

Prologue

Leibniz said, "Whoever knows me only in my latest publication doesn't know me."

Any story-teller could say the same.

"Here you have my latest little book, but please, read my complete works."

Vanity?

Yes, but . . .

"Portions of my writings that are known separately are, in consequence, mere fragments of a long confession," Goethe said.

In my case, *Madness Plays at Chess* continues the series of *Grimorio* (1961), *Vigilia, Fuga* (1963), *The Cheshire Cat* (1965), and *The Swindler Retires* (1969).

"And you pretend that one must read the entire series?"

"Naturally! And with careful attention. And then read it again."

"You're joking."

"Each one of my stories is a closed entity, brief because it has caught a single spasm of life in a single leap of fantasy. Only a reading of all my stories will reveal my world view."

"And are you sure that it is worth the trouble?"

"No."

Enrique Anderson-Imbert

North Wind

Shortly after I arrived in London in 1936, I was invited to a party. One of the guests looked so pallid, so wasted, that I thought, "Has this poor man had the horrible idea of coming here to die?" He wasn't old, fifty years at most, but from my twenty-five I saw him as ancient. Nor had he a weak constitution; his body, short if you consider that he was English, permitted one to assume a musculature that in better times would have made him able to lift weights in a circus. Nevertheless, the poor fellow was in a condition to be carried on a stretcher out into the sun; more than pallid, he was cadaverous. Certainly some accident had ruined him, and now his eyes carried a serene and distant blue, as if they had had a vision of death.

It could be that people avoided him or that he withdrew from them. Certainly this spectre of a man, thin, withered, trembling, was in danger of passing out in some corner. Before he might fade away completely, the hostess approached me and whispered, "He's a famous writer," and introduced me to him. His name, William Fryer Harvey, told me nothing. Famous, yes—famous to the owner of the house who, let it be said in passing, after having nailed me to that Harvey, fled in relief to join up with friends on the noisiest side of the room.

Since I was getting tired even looking at how tired Harvey was— he could no longer stand up straight; anyone could have pushed him over with a finger—I suggested that we sit down. He agreed and, at a turtle's pace we went through a corridor and ended up in an empty study. With difficulty and perhaps with pain, he settled into a white easy chair which, until then, in contrast with the austere grays of the room, had appeared very gay, but which, suddenly on receiving the weight of the sick man—goodbye gaiety—was reduced to one of those sad seats in the waiting-rooms of hospitals. I drew up a chair and sat down in front of him. The classic position, tête-à-tête, which invites storytelling.

From my accent he must have noted immediately that I was a foreigner, but with typical British discretion did not ask me where I was from. Only when, in the course of the conversation I mentioned Buenos Aires, did he ask me if I was Argentinian. When I said yes, he apologized for the London climate as if he were responsible for it, as if he, dry, white-haired, shivering, were winter itself.

"How you'll suffer from the London cold!" he sympathized. "You, accustomed to the temperate climate of your country."

"Don't you believe it." I replied. "I prefer winter. Out there in Buenos Aires it is summer. One roasts. Sometimes the temperature passes 100 degrees. And when the north wind blows, I can't explain it. It is born in the heated regions of the equator, joins with the steam of the ocean, passes through forests and swamps of the tropics, drags along all the viruses that it encounters, comes to rest in the misnamed Buenos Aires until the atmosphere gives up and lets

go in an electric storm. On those days it is impossible to live. Your
nerves can't stand it. Nothing can stand it: the walls drip, the furniture comes unglued, the keys in your pocket are wet, books are
covered with mold, the stitches in your clothes rot from sweat. Huy!
Viscous, everything is viscous. The irritability of people is such that
along with the mercury in the thermometers, the index of crimi-
nality shoots up. I'm not exaggerating. The police know it: there are
days of arguments, madness, beatings, and murders. Believe me, Mr.
Harvey, from a summer in Buenos Aires, especially when the north
wind blows, a writer can get a lot of material for stories of violence."

"So you too are a writer?" he asked, with a feigned and comic look
of apprehension.

"Oh no," I answered, laughing. "A journalist, thank you. But I enjoy regaling my writer friends with anecdotes. Do you want me to
tell you one?"

Mr. Harvey lifted his mouth from wherever he had dropped it, and
forced it into a smile.

"Let's see how this story strikes you. It caused a sensation in the
intellectual circles in Buenos Aires. A little bit more and it would
have been folklore. I was told it many times and in different versions."

And I told it to him, more or less as I tell it here now.

৯৯

On the nineteenth of January in 1934, at two in the afternoon, the
thermometer indicated its absolute maximum of 110 degrees. Masaccio, an Italian illustrator employed by the publishing house of Es-
pasa, was melting away in a hotel room. He started to fan himself
with a piece of pasteboard when suddenly, obeying a force inexplicable because it had no connection with his habit of doodling with his
pencil, he started to scribble a sketch. The pencil did not follow any
particular outline, but capriciously drew lines at random over the
board. What were those streaky lines for? A bench? A door? And this
profile, moving upward, where was it going? Ah, perhaps it wants to
outline a neck, a chin, a cheek. It was as if a second Masaccio, without having told his plan to the first Masaccio, was doing the sketching for him. But no. It was not his double. A double, using the same
imagination, would be duplicating Masaccio's style in the details of
the design. These, on the contrary, were not his. No, not his double.
More likely another artist, totally unknown to him, who had entered Masaccio's body and, from within, was directing his hand.
Now the features were coming together. Five, ten, fifteen minutes
later and the sketch was making sense. It was moving, living. Masaccio looked at what he had done and could not believe it. Was it

he, himself, who was doing that drawing? For the moment the scene he was sketching resembled those in the series of *People of Justice* by Honoré Daumier, but without the sarcasm and intent to caricature. A prisoner, front view, with hands clutching the railing, was staring, not so much in despair at the sentence he had just received, but in surprise at what he saw on a pasteboard that the judge, seen from the back, was showing him.

Masaccio had never seen that man. Nor had he ever witnessed a scene like this. Never had he taken a step into a courtroom. Nevertheless the sketch seemed copied from real life. The lines, vigorous and eloquent, brought alive an instant in the history of a crime. More than an object sketched for the pleasure of art for art's sake it was an expression of a judgment. Not only a criminal judgment brought in court, but a moral judgment of man over his neighbor, over his brother. With deep compassion, the artist was depicting an image. Of a poor man? Yes, but more. Of *poor man* himself. Of a criminal? Yes, but more. Of a Cain, judged by an understanding Abel, a little before the Final Judgment.

Masaccio was an illustrator, ornamental, imaginative, but this time, without knowing how or why, he had created a masterpiece of realism. The details were impressive. The bony frame of the criminal, although not visible, was present in the shape of his powerful anatomy. The shaved head, a scar across the temple, the swollen nostrils, the open mouth lacking a tooth, the astonished eyes, all gave character to that head, tormented by dark thoughts.

Masaccio held the pasteboard above the table, appraised it as if it were not his own, and murmured, "It is not in my style. Could it be that I have died in one period of my life as an artist and that from now on I will live in another period?" Disturbed by the apprehension that he had taken leave forever from what he was before, he glanced about the sordid room, at the unmade bed, cursed the hour when he became an exile, thought of his beautiful Italy, and rushed out into the street.

It was an error. The city was a furnace. His feet felt the heat through the soles of the shoes that sank into the asphalt. His shirt, soaked with sweat, stuck to his flesh, like a repugnant glue. Fleeing from himself, he walked and walked without knowing where he was going. Avenues, houses, trees vibrated in an unreal light. He was like a fleeing dog that could find no shady spot in which to rest. Then, at the point of fainting, he perceived, from a gate, that the high walls he had approached were those of the cemetery of Chacarita. He crossed the street. Above a large portal was a stone in which was carved, in golden letters: MARBLE BY DONATELLO. PEDESTALS, BAL-

USTRADES, ALTARS, FOUNTAINS, DECORATION ON TOMBS, INSCRIPTIONS ON STONE, AND EVERY CLASS OF WORK IN MARBLE.

The name, Donatello, and his own, Masaccio, seemed like echoes of quarreling voices coming out of the depth of centuries, or from the memory of something long ago read and forgotten, something, perhaps, out of the *Lives of the Most Excellent Italian Architects, Painters, and Sculptors,* by Giorgio Vasari? He sensed that a divine intelligence, hidden behind a heaven that would appear gloomy only to those below, was preparing to place a hand on the gameboard and play with the destinies of two little men who had been engaged in some former struggle and now were returning for a replay of the past.

Masaccio entered the patio, and from his left, together with the beating of his own heart, he heard the noise of hammer and chisel. What could it be? Buried in Buenos Aires, in those moments of general lethargy, could there be another soul in pain who, like himself in his hotel, was persisting in work despite the scorching heat?

He looked into the studio.

A man, seen from behind, was squatting in front of a block of marble, performing, it seemed at first, an esoteric ritual. His scarlet shirt was like a flame, and from his head, or from a hidden cigarette, an ominous smoke was rising.

Masaccio clapped his hands. The man turned, and as if in a nightmare, Masaccio recognized him. It was the man of the pasteboard. The same shaved head, the same swollen nostrils straining for breath, the same scar across the temple, and in his smile the same missing tooth. Except for his expression, now indifferent, he was exactly the same man.

"I am not feeling well," Masaccio said from the doorway, "could you give me a glass of water, please?"

The man stood up and wiped the sweat from his forehead on the sleeve of his scarlet shirt.

Masaccio, dizzy, leaned against a marble angel. But he had to withdraw his hand. The angel was wrapped in air that reverberated in waves of fire as if it had just come up from hell.

"Water, no. Brandy is what you need. Come over here and sit down," said the man as he went to the cupboard and returned with a bottle, two little glasses, and a cup of water. "Say what you like," he said, "but there is nothing like brandy. It's good for the heart. Drink from the cup, and then drink up the brandy."

He treated Masaccio with familiarity. Anyone would have said they were old friends. He even smiled shyly as if knowing that Masaccio was aware that the treat was only an excuse so that he himself might have a drink.

Masaccio swallowed the water while the other drank the brandy. "I am sorry to interrupt you in your work."

"No. Actually when you entered I was just finishing the date, which is all that remained to do."

"A tombstone?"

"Yes, but it was not a commission. I confess I did it in one stroke, as if it had come to me as an order during sleep. You wake up and all that you remember is that you have to make a tombstone. Today I wasn't expecting to work. Imagine! In this heat! But in the corner I found a flawed piece of marble. I don't know how it got there. I have forgotten whether I ever saw it before. Well. No sooner did I discover this flawed piece than there I was, like a man possessed, with my hands busy with hammer and chisel. I still ask myself what it was that made me work in such a frenzy. Huh. Whatever it was, it occurred to me to create a tombstone that would be outstanding. I will exhibit it on the patio, so everyone who passes will notice it. I invented a dead man to lie beneath it. Ha, ha, ha! I baptized him with a strange name that, I don't know how, came to me either from heaven, purgatory, or hell. And I engraved today's date. Come and look!"

Masaccio rose up, turned and stood in front of the stone. It said: HERE LIES MASACCIO. BORN NOVEMBER 20, 1900. DIED, DESTROYED BY FATE, JANUARY 19, 1934.

Masaccio reeled as if struck by a portent of death.

"What's wrong with you? Drink! Drink more! It's the heat."

And the man poured himself another glass.

"That's not it. Do you know something? The name on that tombstone is mine."

"Really? Masaccio? And I was thinking that in Buenos Aires there couldn't be anybody with that name! How strange! Well, it's a pleasure to know you. I am Donatello."

"I already know that," he said, and sat down, exhausted from a long voyage through the half-forgotten pages of the *Lives* by Vasari. Telepathy? More than that. Behind him he heard the steps of destiny, at every moment drawing closer to its victims.

"Masaccio . . . Donatello . . ." he murmured. "What are we doing in Buenos Aires?"

"Why do you say that? Because we are Italians? Bah! Buenos Aires is a colony of Italian ghosts."

"Not only is my name on the stone, but also the date of my birth!"

"You don't say! That certainly is a coincidence!" Donatello exclaimed and bolted another drink. "But at least there is one thing that is not a coincidence, eh? The date of death. Ha, ha, ha!"

Masaccio did not want to name the other coincidence, even more disturbing: his own portrait of the convicted criminal, Donatello. Back in the clouds and crannies of his brain there was a gleam of light, the gleam of a enigma shimmering like a tiny star.

After a moment he was no longer able to hide the suspicion stirring in his mind. He said, "Pardon me something . . . strange . . . somehow . . . that I would like to clear up . . . You have never heard of me before, right?"

"Right."

"For my part, I don't remember ever having seen you before. But even so, I have reason to believe that I must have seen you before, if not in person, then in a photograph. Tell me, have you ever had anything to do with the courts. Something you did that made them call you up?"

"Never. Not even a fine. Why do you ask me that? Explain. Do I look like a criminal?"

"No, no. Forgive me," Masaccio said, at the same time stepping back to avoid Donatello's alcoholic breath, a useless movement since the latter moved forward and continued breathing in his face.

"Bah! You must have asked me for some reason. Tell me!"

"Nothing. It is nothing!"

"Ah, not so easy! You're not going to leave me with a thorn in my side. Who do you think you are? You intrude into my house. I treat you well, and you come out with insinuations."

The more Masaccio tried to avoid a conversation that was turning bitter, the more the other became angry.

Donatello (how like the picture!) ended by shouting, flushed with brandy, maddened by the north wind, "You have insulted me, you ungrateful wretch!"

"Forgive me," sighed Masaccio, in a sympathetic voice, sad and resigned. He had finally understood that the game was coming to an end.

Now in a frenzy, Donatello turned and grabbed a chisel.

"So is this the destiny that according to your tombstone would destroy me?" Masaccio asked, not expecting a reply. But in the middle of his pain and his own scream he was able to hear the words:

"Unfortunately, yes."

With that, I ended the story.

Mr. Harvey had listened to it attentively, but when I finished he lowered his head and remained silent. We were tête-à-tête—I have already explained—in the classic position that invites storytelling.

Except that classically it is the older man who is the storyteller and the youth is the one who listens. Here, the reverse. Perhaps Mr. Harvey had not understood the story (besides appearing ill, he seemed somewhat dim-witted), so I explained it to him, just in case.

"You understand, Mr. Harvey? The judge, yielding to a hidden impulse—how can one know whether from amusement or perplexity—showed to Donatello, at the moment of sentencing, Masaccio's drawing that the police had seized in the hotel during the investigation of the murder. Donatello, recognizing himself, widened his eyes. This is precisely the expression that Masaccio had caught. Do you understand? A mix-up in time. The present, although still in the past, was already in the future. A mysterious cosmic cataclysm. The lives of Masaccio and Donatello coincided, as if two trains that were running on parallel tracks suddenly derailed, jumped their tracks, collided in the air, and fell back in a tangle. What do you think? If you like it, I make you a gift of it. Mr. Harvey, why don't you write about the event? It's strange, isn't it?"

Imagine my surprise when Mr. Harvey, who had given me the impression of being at death's door, with no longer the strength to speak, answered me, in a hoarse voice, yes, interrupting himself with fits of coughing, yes, but with authority, vehemence, irony, logic, and amplitude:

"Strange? Much more than you believe. In your story there is an abominable destiny that, on the same day, operates in the form of a premonition for two people who meet by chance. Let us call them *A* and *B* if you don't mind."

"Not at all."

"*A* makes a picture of the one who is to be his killer, and *B* engraves the name of the one who is to be his victim. The event of the sentencing of *B* whom *A* has pictured is after the death of *A*, which *B* engraved."

I pricked up my ears. I had read nothing of Mr. Harvey, the "famous writer," according to the owner of the house, but what doubt could there be that whoever was capable of such rapidity in reducing a story to its elemental theme must also be capable of constructing stories based on similar themes. He continued:

"Something similar to that derailment of time of which you were speaking is happening to us both. You and I have met here also by chance and are in the inception of a crime; in this case the crime is plagiarism. As the saying goes, the best plagiarism is that in which the robbery is accompanied by a murder, or let us say, the complete obliteration of the name of the true author. You heard the story in Buenos Aires, at various times in different versions, and now, amiably, you want to make me a gift of it so that I may convert it into an English story. Many thanks. But that anecdote which anonymous Argentinians are transmitting from mouth to mouth before it becomes folklore, was, in fact, literature. I suppose a book entitled *The Beast with Five Fingers* must have arrived in Argentina in 1928 and fallen into the hands of a raconteur. In the book there is a story, not as clever as your version, but with a similar situation: *August Heat.* Read it. I wrote it myself."

I opened my eyes. Of course; that's it! Why be surprised that Mr. Harvey was capable of reducing my story to an elemental theme? After all, that watchmaker with deft fingers did no more than take apart the pieces of a watch that he himself had put together previously . . .

I don't know whether from amusement or shame, I exclaimed, "Pardon, Mr. Harvey, pardon! What nerve! I, with the air of an important person, hand you a story, and it turns out to be your own. What a gaffe!"

My face must have been a picture of shame rather than amusement since I felt that Mr. Harvey observed me sympathetically. Surprised that in the dark hollow of his skull there were still eyes that could pierce, I lowered my gaze and murmured, "Pardon me. If I plagiarized you, it was without intention."

"Don't let it bother you," he said, gripping my knee with the five fingers of his bony hand. "Without willing it, we are all plagiarists. One believes he is inventing a story, but there is always someone who invented it before. Take, for example, the theme of the picture that absorbs the vitality of living beings or that influences their destinies; hundreds of writers have developed it: Oscar Wilde, Henry James, Galdós, Poe, Gogol, Novalis, Hoffman, Calderón . . ."

While he was reciting the list of names—it was much longer, but I have forgotten—Mr. Harvey leaned more heavily on my knee and lifted himself from the chair as if, having conjured up his shades, he would propose to accompany them into time past and leave each one at its historic home. And thus I saw Mr. Harvey as the popular imagination has always pictured the storyteller, as an old man, full of memories, in touch with the first dreams of men.

"One story emerges from another," he said, bidding me farewell with a handshake, "and each follows from the one before it, and so on back to their origins in mythology. When I published *August Heat*, Montague Rhodes James asked me if I had been inspired by his story, *The Mezzotint*. I suspect that he did not believe me when I said no. I did not lie. In *August Heat* I combined *The Prophetic Pic-*

tures of Hawthorne with *L'Esquisse Mysterieuse* of Erckmann-Chatrian and *Die Weissagung* of Arthur Schnitzler to clothe a Greek myth. Are you familiar with it? An oracle has prophesied to Iphitus that someone—he doesn't know who—will be punished for committing a murder. At the same time another oracle, in another city, reveals to Hercules that someone—again he doesn't know who—has been murdered. Iphitus, who is on a voyage, by chance visits Hercules at his home. The host, by Fate, murders his guest."

"Fantastic! And I believed all the while that this had taken place in Buenos Aires!" I told him, assuming an air of innocence.

Anonymous Manuscript concerning a Sad Waltz

This is the chronicle of a waltz which, forty years ago, was lost in the night. More exactly, during a summer night of 1857.

The estate of Don Agustín Yáñez y Arganaras was the most opulent of the province. Nevertheless, it was modestly tucked away at one end of a valley one league from the city. To find it, visitors had to travel along mountainous roads at the end of which the house came into view in profile, set against woods and hills. Only those who approached it by trudging over the hill could surprise it from the front; the smooth slope became a patio and then the mansion revealed itself, broad and imposing, light blue and white, surrounded by gardens.

One might say, why build a home so ostentatious if you plan to hide it away? But Don Agustín had not hidden it; rather, he had reserved it only for the select. He had built it just before the fall of the tyrant Rosas as a monument to the triumph of civilization over barbarity, and was accustomed to displaying it at gatherings of the most respected families. It appeared that he was still interested in politics and (in retirement) continued writing for the newspapers: if the country slows its pace, anarchy will devour it; moreover, the cultured class should take the lead, so that the backward hordes cannot reach them again. Simple, right? Pity that the matter is so complicated because of the meaning of those words: civilization and barbarity, respected families and backward hordes, changes with the generations. Don Agustín was famous; posterity, in its forgetfulness, had made him a legend. Today, no one, not even the survivors, can describe him as he was. At best: bearded, corpulent, strong. From exile he had returned definitely eccentric, but became so rich that it didn't matter. A widower without children, he fostered love among the children of his friends, perhaps because he wanted the superior class to prosper. Many marriages must have begun at his dances.

That summer night they were holding a ball. From early morning—the blue sky, cloudless, promised a distinguished assembly of stars—they decorated the patio: from orange tree to orange tree, garlands of flowers and lanterns; below a jasmine bush, the jet of a fountain; along the galleries upholstered chairs and little tables with embroidered tablecloths, each one with its candelabrum; at one side, the platform for the orchestra.

When the carriages arrived with the guests, the chariot of the sun had disappeared over the high ridge of mountains, and the mansion glowed in its own light.

A moment later a little black boy, thirteen years of age, made his appearance. Don Agustín had dressed him up as one of Rosas' soldiers: a short red jacket, a scarlet *chiripa* and a dark red headband. A dwarf buffoon from the time of Rosas! In the entourage of ladies and gentlemen . . . the former dressed in bright fabric with patriotic white and blue adornment, the latter in double-breasted jackets, tight pants and dark ties . . . the ridiculous boy in red made a burlesque out of one of the bloodiest insanities of history. He was greeted with laughter. It was (what a relief!) like the memory of a nightmare at which one can laugh only upon waking.

The orchestra seated itself—a violin, a harp, a flute, and a guitar—and the dance began. Between quadrilles and gavottes, between gavottes and minuets, the little red negro boy went from one side to the other with a tray of sweets and soft drinks, or entered the rooms to come running back with a shawl, a fan, a newspaper, or a cushion. He was already tired and sleepy.

And then the clock in the dining room joined its hands, filled its lungs and sang midnight. They heard it through the open window. "It's time!" (the parents). "It's early!" (the children). "At last!" (the little black boy). And then Don Agustín approached the orchestra and directed it to finish with a waltz.

The first measure curled into the ear, and in a rapid spiral descended to the feet, urging them to whirl. Each youthful dancer grasped his companion and spun off into space with a rush of rapture. In a turning circle, like graceful toys, the couples abandoned themselves to gaiety.

The little boy, half asleep, had to force himself not to move with the rhythm: lalalalala, lala, lala . . .

Around his inner net of nerves and blood vessels the sensations rocked within the boy, while outside the slow movements of the waltzers were barely visible through his heavy sleep-sanded eyelids, and he, half awake, half asleep, imagined that he was dancing away, lalalalala, to the hilltop, suddenly bracketed by his own yawn and the barks of Chucho, who is racing up the hill to exactly where lances and men on horseback are starting to appear, fanning out along the edge of the summit . . .

He woke from his daze (who wouldn't?) and turned his head to find Don Agustín. One of the dancers, turning his eyes in the flowing motion of the waltz, also noticed the centaurs on the high horizon, and lost the beat of the music; his partner followed his gaze and, with a cry, remained rooted to the floor. One after another the couples froze. The orchestra, absorbed in their instruments and dazzled by the lights, pounded away at the waltz until the violinist, noticing that no one was dancing, lifted his eyes, realized what was happening, and lowered his violin. The heart of the music stopped beating.

Don Agustín, like a guard among the statues in a museum, made his way through the stupefied crowd and with authority cried out, "What do you want? How dare you! Get out of here!"

A voice, like thunder, answered from the mountain, "Keep dancing. It amuses us!"

Don Agustín moved to confront them, but at the crack of a pistol he dropped. The little black boy, dressed in red, leaned over his blood-red master, and when he stood up he stared deeply into the shadows; it was certain that a lance had cut the bark from Chucho's throat.

"Keep dancing, I said!" the voice thundered. "We are watching! Music! And for anyone who doesn't dance . . . !"

Tasting death in his throat, the violinist raised his bow and the orchestra continued the waltz, now crippled from the deafness, blindness, or paralysis of the terrified guests.

In that amphitheatre, the watching gauchos, controlled and quiet, moved forward like forces stalking their prey; the dancers, now stirring about and murmuring, were phantoms in a closed world with neither present nor future. The dancing, so restrained, was little more than a succession of sounds. The horsemen must have heard only the tap-tap of the shoes on the tile floor and the swish-swish of the skirts on the turns. But perhaps they understood that the blue and white mansion, the gushing of the fountain, the lights glowing in the night, the fashionable dress, the elegance of the Viennese waltz, were all signs of a defiant civilization.

The child-buffoon, posing as one of Rosas' soldiers, was a challenge to the barbarians. The poor little fellow could not understand (only with the years do explanations become clear, yes, and the surrounding circumstances as well) that he was a burlesque, a provocation, a revenge, a trophy, and a figure capable of ceasing to be all that, and then of being no more than an object of pity, great pity.

Passing near him a young man said, in a low voice, "Get into the house. Quickly!"

But the little black boy didn't move.

"Jump, you idiot!" and the man gave him a push.

The little black boy stumbled over the body of Don Agustín, fell, and got up without losing sight of the gaucho horde that was already dismounting, descending the slope, drawing near.

The leader, also bearded, corpulent and strong, put a protective arm over the shoulders of the boy, gave an order, and waited, smiling, in the center of the vortex.

With each stab of the dagger the ponchos continued the whirl of the waltz, and screams of pain and fright mixed with the music, destroying it.

Then the gauchos returned to their horses and, as they were leaving, the voice again thundered, "Now play something pretty for the boy!"

From the platform they play . . . for the only survivor on the patio below.

Above the night, the music of the waltz.

Above the carpet of corpses below, *me.*

Ovid Told It Differently

Inés was the last soul left in the Harris bar. Her elbows on the rails, she lifted her glass and while she was emptying it in one swallow she discovered the moon.

"I know that you're watching me closely, and afterwards you'll tell on me," she murmured in English, an English with a strong Spanish accent.

If in fact it were able to spy, the eye of the moon would have seen, through the skylight of the Harris bar, in the basement of a brick building, the spirited face of a drunken woman. The reddish glow of a few candles drained the color from her mouth and from her cheeks, but, by contrast, made her large eyes and her wild hair even more black. She was one of those disturbing beauties who even at age ten anticipate the seductive woman, and at thirty-five, when they are sexually mature, evoke the spoiled child. In his recess on the other side of the rail and with his back to Inés, Harris was putting the liquor bottles back on the shelves. He was Scottish, about fifty years of age, short and broad.

"And now that you have caught me," she continued in a louder voice, "are you satisfied, Artemis?"

Harris, who on the sly had been watching the woman in the mirror, turned around. "Art what? What was that you called me?"

"I wasn't speaking to you. But to that one . . ." and she nodded at the skylight. "I am saying that Artemis has come to spy on me. Do you see her?"

"Where?"

"There."

"I don't see anyone," said Harris, who from his corner could make out only a piece of the sidewalk.

"Up there, man. Come closer. Don't you see her? Diana."

"Now it's Diana. Just now you called her by another name."

"Artemis. Diana. It's the same. The Huntress. Stepsister of Apollo. The two children of evil mothers and a dirty old man. The two of them goddesses of light."

"I don't understand."

"How could you understand! Your kingdom is the half-light, in the center of the earth," and with an ample gesture she sketched an abyss in darkness. "Once I was a creature of light. Now I've been taken captive."

Harris, who had shrugged his shoulders and now was stretching his arm toward his bottles, suddenly sniffed the promise of a deal, and approached the woman.

"So you have been taken captive?"

"Yes, and right now." She turned 360 degrees on her stool and with her finger extended drew a tremendous circle in the air.

Harris scratched his white hair. "Prisoner, eh? And right here, eh?"

"Right here."

Harris lowered his head, half-smiling at the absurdity, and swung his head from side to side as if pondering, "I don't understand, I don't understand." He heard the woman mutter, "Artemis will tell on me to my husband."

"Ah, you have a husband . . ."

"Had," sighed Ines.

"Don't worry about it. A woman like you, with that face and that figure . . ."

He would have continued opening the way. The old fellow was beginning to feel aroused. But Inés interrupted him, "In the society of man we are still husband and wife, but in the society of gods there are two siblings who want to break us up: Apollo has destroyed me, and Artemis is going to destroy my husband."

"Bad luck."

Inés blinked rapidly, squeezed her eyes shut, but could stand it no longer. She took out her handkerchief and burst into tears:

"Tears, tears! Do you know why the world is round? I'm going to tell you. Because it's an onion. It makes you cry. Sometimes scream. If I had in my throat the strength of a bird, papa would hear me in Puerto Rico. If I went to my father's house I would sink the island with the weight of my step, that's how heavy my grief is. And all because there is a worm in my heart."

Harris was not going to confuse that woman with the little whores who, not today, but any Monday at the end of the month, and specially Saturdays, would install themselves comfortably at the bar and wait for clients. Nevertheless he kept watching her, just in case. If she drowned her madness in alcohol it was a good sign. He—let's not kid ourselves—he wasn't worth very much, but she, in spite of being so young, attractive, and educated, was brought down to his level precisely by her being unhappily married, drunk, and raving. He had had more than enough of the little customers of the bar; but this was a cute little dish. Why not try your luck? After all, she was a foreigner. And with a Latin girl—everybody knows they are fabulous lovers—it would be easy going.

"Don't look at me as if I were crazy," Inés told him. "I should shut up but I can't stop. If you don't like it, don't listen. I don't know why I started to cry in front of you."

"Because . . ." Harris started. He was going to say to her, "Because you really tied one on, baby." But he said, "Because you don't feel well. It's nothing. With this heat. The worst summer ever for New York, according to the radio."

"The heat doesn't bother me. Sunlight, yes. Because you know I am a shadow. Most of the darkness in this room comes from my body. From now on, instead of making myself into a shadow at home, I'm going to let my shadowy soul hide in this den. Here I feel well: dark, all dark . . ."

"Yes," Harris approved, happy to throw out a lead. "It isn't bad here. Dark. Intimate. The two of us alone. Or am I too old?"

"You have no age, O Demon of the Bottles," she apostrophized, in a haunting voice; but in noticing that Harris had opened his mouth and left it open because he didn't know what to say, she changed her tone and added, with a superior look, "You don't understand me, Hades."

"My name is pronounced Harris. I certainly understand you. You're alone. You're sad. What I don't understand is some of your words. I am not a man for books."

"Bah! My husband is a professor and he doesn't understand me either. Tell me, when I talk you think that I'm talking like the plain drunk that I am, no?"

"Drunk? I didn't say drunk. Maybe one glass too many, but . . ."

"So serve me another," and she slid the empty glass along the bar.

"The last one, huh? It's late."

"No. Better not . . ." She recovered the glass and played with it, watching the red lights reflected there. "My husband says I'm headed right toward delirium tremens; my husband says I am a lost cause; my husband doesn't say it, but I know that one of these nights he is going to leave me."

"Didn't you tell me that you have no husband now? I thought that you . . ."

"If anyone abandons anyone it has to be my husband, because I am living in my own home, a gift from my father, the only person in the world that really loves me and . . ." A hiccough cut short the sentence ". . . I'm not abandoning anyone. I reject the bloody Apollo, and my husband is letting himself be tricked by the anemic Artemis. Apollo is in the sun, and the sun is in the grape, and cognac is in the bottle . . . Listen; to you who is the Demon of the Bottles, I will confess it. I have a bottle of cognac hidden in the hatbox, in the clothes closet. Do you know what I'm going to do when I get back home? I'm going to grab the bottle and empty it into the toilet and then—shuuufff—let the water take it to Apollo! That's what I'm going to do."

"Sure . . ." Harris said, and assuming the air of a confidant, he took her hand. "Who is he? What did you say his name was? Apollo?" The name of a negro from Alabama was what he was thinking.

"He is the one who rises in the morning, looks around, and all over the world there is light," she said, withdrawing her hand. "It is natural that in this subterranean hole you don't know him. You are the Mourner, the Dark One . . ."

"Hey! Me dark?" And the rosy-faced Harris widened his eyes so much that the oval whites appeared around the blue pupils. "It's funny that you say that, being Puerto Rican . . ."

Ines interrupted him, "I know what you're thinking: you have seen a crow fluttering around under my skin. But I am not a mulatto. I am white, Spanish. Not as white as Artemis, nor as Apollo, nor as my husband, nor as you. All blond. But I am a white Latin, see?"

And she opened her blouse below the throat.

Harris, avid, sinuous, stooped and went through under the counter and snaked toward the woman. "See? Let me see. Yes. You're white. And beautiful. What you need is to be loved. Wait a minute. It's already time to close. Come with me."

"No. I'm going, but alone. Let the moon follow me along the streets. When I stop she stops. When I walk she walks. Like that all night long. Let's see who tires first."

"Let's go, honey. I have a car at the corner."

He conducted the woman to the exit, helped her up the stairway, turned out the light and threw the bolt. Outside there was another little stairway with five more steps, and just when they arrived at the sidewalk and Harris took her by the waist he felt somebody give him a push so violent that he had to grab for the railing in order not to fall. Ines did not see this because she had started to curse the moon—the Peeping Tom—But if it had been able to spy, the eye of the moon would have seen Harris tensed up with fear at the top step.

Inés staggered, but arms caught her and steered her up the street. "Who are you? Where the Hell are you taking me?" she exclaimed, in English.

"Home," someone answered in Spanish, with a strong English accent.

"Ah, so it's you."

"Thank God I happened to be going by. I was returning home and by chance I saw you here."

"By chance, eh?"

Inés shook herself loose from the arms of her husband, placed her hands on her hips and again cursed the moon, whose light flooded the deserted street.

"Your virgin informer, Artemis, is here. Why don't you go home with her?"

And she began to cry. They walked a short way in silence, until Inés said in a low voice, "Don't you understand that you're not going to be happy with her either? She tempts you, but it's only in order to kill you with a hail of arrows."

A few blocks further on the husband scraped the lock with a key and opened the door. He carried her to the bedroom and dropped her on the bed.

"This is no bed," she protested, "it's a coffin."

And lifting her head, her finger, and her voice she added with a laugh, "Cum homo intrat lectum (hic) intrat sepulcrum. Just for you to see, Saint Bonaventure. So what are you thinking? (hic)," and she let herself fall back on the bed.

"Go to sleep. We'll talk tomorrow."

"No! Not tomorrow! Now!"

"Ah, Inés, Inés . . . Before, at least, you used to drink at home, without anyone seeing you; now you expose yourself publicly—in a bar—and you promised me . . . Now I won't be able to go out in peace, knowing that . . ."

"The fault is from your master, the accursed Apollo. Because of him I started to drink."

"All right. All right!"

"You invited him to our home. He became accustomed to coming unannounced. In my little tower of poetry he had envisioned adventures that I only dreamed of, but he understood them as real. To him as to many gringos, I was the Latin woman, passionate, sensual, exotic, who is bored by New York and always ready for an affair. That afternoon he came and you were not here. Your best friend, so he told me!"

"Please be quiet."

"It was his fault. When you entered, you surprised us. It was only once. But one bite from a snake is enough . . ."

"Forget it."

"The nights that I have spent since then! Night after night of insomnia, of boiling shame. And I started to drink. All the red sea that one carries inside rose up in one wave of madness, but blood, which is a red sea, is also red wine, and now I drink fire. I no longer exist. You prove this to me by leaving me alone."

"I have never left you alone. In any case, I don't leave you alone more than before, which shows you that things go on as if nothing had occurred. We're not children now, Inés. It would have been worse if I had shut you up, or spied on you, or tormented you with jealousy. And when I leave you alone it's not that I want to. It's that I have so much to do. I am Head of the Department . . . You ought to forget the past."

"You wouldn't have forgotten either."

"Have you ever heard the least reproach from me?"

"No. Everyone knows how civilized you are. You would never make a scene with anyone. You told me that you would pardon me, and with that you got rid of a burden and felt free. You made that gesture of kindness the way someone takes a trip around the world. And during one of the stops on the trip you made friends with that damn sister of your damn boss. Bah! Don't deny it, you fox!"

"You're unfair, but I really don't know what more to say to you. Right now the most important thing is for you to sleep. You're in no condition to talk."

Inés closed her eyes, but immediately, inside the lids, immense, black gelatinous masses started to grow, to become a feverish dizziness. She almost got sick, groaned as if waking from a nightmare, stood up rigid, and glared at her husband with all the force she had.

"Close those eyes, for God's sake!" she heard voices saying, and then someone whispering so that she would not hear, but she did. "Those eyes are seeing a rainbow of cockroaches, rats and bats . . ."

She leaned forward and screamed: "And you! What beautiful animals have you got inside? Shall we guess? Who do you think you are? Orpheus? Oh yes. In order to hear you sing the birds stop flying, fish leap from the waters; you put the sheep to sleep, you calm the dogs of death, even the trees lift up their roots to go with you, even the rocks weep! Bah! That's how you'd like to be, isn't it? Don't forget, Orpheus, the real poet is ME!"

"I know that. Now go to sleep."

"I am a poet. Or was. A precocious poet, like the almond tree. Now I am brutalized. Before, you used to tell me that all the poetry you ever learned, you, a professor of literature, had learned from me. But since you discovered that colleague, so intellectual, so erudite, you're no longer interested in my poetry, only in her opinions, her collaboration. And now it turns out that the two of you are going to make a book, just like making a child: the child that you and I could not make."

"It's just a simple textbook for students."

"I hate her. Frankly I don't know what you see in her: so academic, so cold, so lucid with her borrowed moonlight. And now your light comes from her reflected light. You'll end up by seeing the world through lunar eyes. She is using you and your name to get to publishers, just as she wanted to use me to get into this home. She is a hypocrite who spies on me and then takes stories back to you. You went out tonight to conspire with her."

"Not likely. I was at a meeting of the professors from the Department."

"And there you met her, of course, by chance!"

"By chance, no. She is a member of the staff. It's her obligation, her right, to be present at the conferences. Let me help you, Inés. Let me help you out of . . ."

"Out of that inferno where I am condemned . . . Eh, Orpheus? your poor Eurydice . . ."

"You and your mythology!"

"You'd like to kidnap me from Hell, but not to bear me sleeping in your arms, like a surrealist poet carries his dreams, but because you are afraid of the scandal in your church, in your university, in your club. If it were not for your reputation you'd be very happy to separate from me, the neurotic, the jealous one, the drunk."

The man went to the doors of the balcony, opened them wide, and looked up at the cloudless sky.

"Now it is he the moon is watching," Inés thought.

If it were able, the moon must have seen him with his hands laced at his back, and his head like the face of a castle, very serious, flaxen-haired, thin, tall, with fine lips and thick glasses.

In a little while he heard Inés taking off her clothes. He didn't want to turn his head. If he were to see her he would yield once again to her enchantment. No. He wouldn't reward her. Not tonight. Let her understand, let her repent, let her change. Yes. He must drag her out of Hell, as she herself had said. But to save her he must not turn his head, he must not look at her.

Inés, meanwhile, went to the closet and took out the hatbox. The bottle was there just as she had left it. She twisted off the cap.

He heard the squeak, looked anxiously over his shoulder and saw Inés, on her knees, raising the bottle of cognac and lasciviously putting the neck of the bottle in her mouth.

"Oh no!"

He passed by Inés, searched for his valise, and started to pack it. Inés lowered the bottle and followed him with her eyes. "Where are you going?"

Coming and going from the closet to the suitcase he did not answer. Inés got up with the bottle in her hand. "I'm asking you. Where are you going?"

"Inés, I can't take it any more. I'm leaving you in your Hell."

Inés stumbled, leaned against the wall, gave him a long look and heard herself snicker stupidly, "That tie is the one I gave you for your birthday, isn't it?" And then, "Listen. If it's because of the bottle . . . I promise you . . ."

"It's no good, Inés. You're a lost cause. Tomorrow I'll come back and get the rest of my things, and we'll talk."

The professor glanced over at the bookcase with all his books, gave a last look at his wife, and left the house.

Inés let the bottle fall and, like a doll that goes along trailing its sawdust, tried to reach him, opened the door, stepped into the street, but had to draw back and crouch down in the vestibule because— My God!—she was naked. She thought, "He said that tomorrow he would come back and we would talk. After we talk he won't leave me."

Nevertheless, she saw him moving away rapidly, as if he and the moon, two lives in one, were leaving forever.

Murder

This is the first time since I have been in the United States that I have gone down from the paradise of Harvard to the inferno of a university in the South. No need to say it will be the last time. It was an error to sign a contract with Southern College, Alabama. Of course it was my intention to stop here for a few weeks, earn a few dollars teaching a short course in summer school, and then continue on my trip to Mexico, where at least I would be able to speak Spanish. But even so, I must have been mad when I accepted the invitation. The heat is suffocating. The light hurts the eyes. The city is dirty. Men and children drag their poverty through the street, and even from the distance you can see the filth in which they live.

"There must be many suicides here," I told myself, and immediately changed my mind. "No. Instead of suicide, these people would prefer murder." Isn't it violence against others that has made the image we have of the South? Piracy in the Caribbean; lynch mobs; slave-owners that whip their slaves; gentlemen that avenge their honor fighting duels; quarrels on the river banks among the crews of the flat-boats; gangs of hooded riders turning the black nights white with terror.

I saw the same violence, although somewhat reduced, on the very day of my arrival.

Professor Hamilton, whom I had met in the park, invited me to accompany him to a beer hall, as sordid as most. We were drinking at the bar when I heard a blow and a scream. I turned and saw a man standing, furious, and, on the other side of the table, a woman in a faint, with beer and blood pouring from her hair. The brute had bashed her with a beer bottle. I rose to go toward them; from curiosity more than from compassion. I must confess, since this is a confession, that blood dripping from a real person moves me less than that from a character in a novel. In reality the appearance of blood is sudden and finds me so unprepared that my first reaction is to find out what has happened. In a novel the blood that runs is printed in red ink, and if I see it, it is because the author, with his studied strategy in skillful wording, in giving me all the antecedents, has sensitized my imagination. So more from curiosity than compassion, I approached, but Hamilton threw some money on the bar, took me by the arm and dragged me into the street.

"Don't get mixed up in it," he told me. "The police will come, and it's not good for us to be found here. Professors are not allowed to gather in these places. Moreover, who can say that the woman there didn't deserve to have her head cracked? If I complained to that man he might raise his hand against me, and then I'd have to kill him."

I looked at Hamilton, a giant with eyes of a bird of prey, and I understood that indeed he was quite capable of killing.

Professor Collins also is a violent fellow. He is married to a pretty Panamian from, he claims, a distinguished Spanish family. If I am not mistaken, in the circulatory system of the brunette, who came here as a child and now doesn't speak Spanish, are a few drops of the mulatto. Perhaps to discourage any suspicion, Collins raves against the negroes. When I expressed my desire to hear rhythmic African songs in a negro church I was dissuaded with arguments as obvious as the costume of the Ku Klux Klan. And I wouldn't be surprised if he were to belong to that secret clan, since he justified the lynching of a negro which I had just finished reading about in a local newspaper.

The others, Ford and Tracy, are more reserved, but my instinct tells me that in them also the university scholar has not tamed the animal nature. Ford, for example, admitted to me that the statistics of homicide there are higher than in other places, but he explained it using the force of logic: "Pish! In the South there are more people who deserve to be killed." Tracy, of whom I asked why Southerners were so violent, preferred, on the other hand, to offer an historical explanation: the past of slavery, the War of Secession, the defeat, the mistrust of Northern politicians who, under the pretext of reconstruction, arrived to profit from the calamity, the presence of the negro, the frontier experience in which there were always attacks, the feeling that the entire region is under interdiction, that they are pursued from outside with scorn. These things, together with new ideas, have created, in Tracy's judgment, a Southern personality with an established belief of being the victims of a hostile atmosphere and of malignant intrusions. Neither Ford nor Tracy was interested in knowing my opinion, whether logical or historical, which was somewhat less obsessive than their own.

Tracy is head of the department. From what they tell me he is a millionaire, and if he continues to teach, it is only because he likes it. Almost every night he would invite us for drinks at his home, which is stupendous. It is in the middle of a small wood. At least one can breathe there. It didn't please me to have to attend these meetings. At least not all of them. The truth is (please excuse me!) that the Southerners bore me to death. In the first place it isn't possible there to have a serious conversation. As soon as you propose an academic subject, the women protest: "Please don't talk shop!" Nor are one's colleagues desirous of risking the exposure of their intellectual mediocrity. So everybody is dedicated to frivolous entertainment. They believe this makes them look younger. What foolishness! To devote themselves to repeating the simple notions that they talked of when they were young, in those senseless prewar parties, is not to rejuvenate but to add on years. In reflecting on that past, the years double in the same way that a mirror doubles distances. The changes in the day-by-day customs are so accelerated that whoever distracts himself by casting a nostalgic glance toward his own youth, on returning to reality will no longer find youth in the same setting as before. For that reason, I . . . mix with youth? Charmed! But . . . disguised as a youth? God preserve me! Those married couples—I was the only unyoked ox—were subject to the moral tenets of their mature generation, but they wanted to entertain themselves with the frenzies of adolescents. What did they do? They played games. One night they played "Twenty Questions." Another, it was "Who am I?" And so on. On Sunday, the ninth of July—I'll never forget that patriotic date—they introduced me to a game called "Murder."

Here are the rules. On one piece of paper is written "Murderer." On another, "Detective." And these are mixed with other blank papers. Total: as many papers as players. The one who takes the slip with the word "Detective" must show it. The others retain, in silence, the little slip that luck assigned them. Thus no one knows who has received the slip of the "Murderer." The lights are turned out and the detective leaves the house. The others spread out over the house in complete darkness until the killer places his hand on the neck of someone and tightens his grip; this is the signal that the murderer has struck. The victim lets out a scream so that the detective hears, and from that moment on everyone remains in place. Everyone, that is, except the killer, who can move silently and stop in whatever spot seems least suspicious. One minute after hearing the scream, the detective enters, the lights go on; he passes through all the rooms, notes the positions of the victim and the players, has everyone return to the main room, and starts the interrogation. So since the killer is the only one who can move about after the crime, he is the only one who is permitted to lie. The detective tries to verify who has moved or lied. Finally he questions one of the suspects: "Are you the killer?" If he answers "No," the detective loses. The murderer loses if he is asked, since at that stage of the game he cannot lie and must confess. Everyone understand?

As I was saying, on that ninth of July they introduced me to "Murder." It was a night of full moon. In order to shut out its brilliance they lowered the blinds. Nine strips of paper. The one marked "detective" fell to Hamilton. He lit his pipe and, before going out into the garden, turned off the lights.

The darkness almost erased me. As if I had just awakened at midnight in the bed of one of those many hotels where I lodge on a trip through an unknown country, I did not know what I was doing there; like lying in a coffin. I had lost the notion that the room was in a house, and the house in a garden, and the garden in a suburb, and the suburb in a city, and the city in the state of Alabama. I was walking in a dream state. The thread of air that I was breathing was the totality of my world, a world which, although it was enclosing only me, I felt was absolute, that is, unlimited, and for this reason it did not seem small to me; rather it appeared that I had grown immense and filled it like a blind god. Now it was not the physical space that quietly withdraws from us, taking with it things that we don't notice. No. This space, instead of opening out away from me, fell in folds around and over me. My body was the organizing center and, like a black sun, spread in the darkness. And, as a center of movement obeying the rules of the game of "Murder," I started to walk.

First there were a few rapid steps. Danger, there was none. In sum, I recalled very well the positions of the furniture near me. Previously I had perceived the furniture as part of me; now, on the other hand, it had detached itself from me and became mere forms in my memory, and I felt it to be absent and apart, as one still feels the existence of a part of the body that has been amputated.

Later, as I was exploring areas less familiar, my steps became more cautious. Space was like a wave in time. "I have just touched the back of a chair; now there will be a little table with a potted plant that I must not knock over; next I will bump into the television set . . ." It was a succession of curves, surfaces, tops.

Finally the moment arrived when I forgot to keep walking and once again I had to learn to do it: like a baby learning to walk, I was vacillating between obstacles that both invited and repelled me.

Now I could no longer anticipate what I would encounter in my cautious journey. Set apart from their surroundings, the pieces of furniture existed only as menacing. In the depth of their lairs they lay in ambush like hedgehogs with their quills erect. Things that flee in the light of day, in the dark of night were pestering me from all sides. Thus, at the tip of every finger was an open eye. I went along feeling my way through a tactile, not a visual, space. Hands, arms, elbows, feet, legs, knees, were not enough. I grew antennas and tentacles, as a cane grows in the hands of a blind man. I wanted only to feel. Since I had fallen into a well of darkness, I hugged the walls, not in a direct walk but circulating. I was a traveler without sanctuary, surprised into an adventure I did not want, along a path that was taking me nowhere. "Bah!" I told myself, "there's no need to exaggerate! This is not a mystic experience! It's nothing more than a game!" A game, yes, but in playing it there is nothing to do, nothing to think. With action and thought abolished, space is open-ended and time is only a pastime. Space and time are born and re-born endlessly in that suspension of life, and the more one feels outside of life, the more one feels like a phantom. The game "Murder" is a simulacrum of death among the phantoms of midnight. When something touched my face I jumped. "Ah," I said to myself, "it's a leaf from a vine at the window." But my sensation was that a ghost had touched me. It was already too much. Was it that I felt myself a ghost, and that another ghost had come to put his hand on me? No sir! It was already humiliating enough that I, a mature man, was playing here like a child. No. I was not a ghost. I was a man, and the other men and women were friends who had spread out through the house. At the beginning of the game, when the lights went out, I lost the sense of being in a group, but the game itself, however solitary it seemed to be then, was collective. But in spite of having recovered the awareness of being in the company of others, I continued feeling isolated from my other companions in the game, whose steps were echoes of my own, except that I did not feel myself a blind ghost, but, in another incarnation, a nyctalopic Apache. Not Max Carrados (the blind detective created by Ernest Bramah), infallible in dark-ness, but rather Fantomas (the nyctalopic criminal invented by Allain-Souvestre), the one and only person who, in darkness, would have been able to defeat Max Carrados. I was acquiring the psychol-ogy of a delinquent. For example, when I bumped into a floor lamp, I clutched it quickly before it could fall, not with the good intention of preventing breakage, but, like the robber at night, with the stealthy impulse of avoiding the noise that might wake the sleeping owners. However, with this new psychology of the evildoer that I was acquir-ing, I figured out that the sensation which I just described of being a member of a criminal element, had been an expectation of the pun-ishment they would give me as soon as I had committed my deed. What deed? I started to consider it. I started to prepare myself. Since one cannot be immoral except in a group of human beings, I tried to place myself with the other men. And by my bringing them into mind, the room became real.

Although I saw nothing clearly, with hardly a glimmer from the moon which managed to filter through the blinds and reflect a disquieting wizardry from a mirror, and although vague anti-forms were slipping by my side and dissolving, I began to dominate the space. Then I was able to perceive my companions in the game. And I was able to distinguish the men from the women. I could not discern whether a certain presence in the darkness was Tracy or Collins, or Ford, but yes, I could distinguish the texture of a man's suit, from the texture of a woman's dress. I could hear breathing, distinguish different perfumes. The women, if I touched them, laughed nervously or, with exclamations, pretended to be frightened. Perhaps the wives of Tracy and Ford, the sillier ones, were actually frightened by the darkness, by the slow motion of the bodies, overcome, as in a resurrection of the dead, by the very idea of "Murder." Dominated by an ardent animal impulse, I felt the space keeping me from the men suddenly vanish when I was near the women: close, very close before one particular woman, of flesh and bone, whom one desired to possess.

And then the hysterical scream, like lightning, glanced off the window panes of darkness and pierced my eardrums. I thought of the rules of the game. I froze.

There was laughter. A minute later, Hamilton entered. In the doorway, standing out in silhouette against the glare of the moon, his pipe was that of Sherlock Holmes, but once the lights were turned on, the detective was a large bird of prey with cruel eyes.

I was surprised to see that, at my side, with a smile not common to corpses, Hamilton's wife was making energetic gestures at her husband, very content with being the victim. A smile of dizzying whiteness had opened her lips, so heavily painted that the red of the lipstick ran over their borders. At a distance, next to the window, was Collins. I could make out Ford in the vestibule, and his wife, with Tracy's wife, in the center of the adjoining room. Tracy and the pretty Panamian had disappeared. At least from my position I could not see them.

Hamilton observed us, measured with a glance the distances between body and body, went through the house, where he must have encountered Tracy and the Panamian, since he brought them back with him, and when he had finished his visual inspection, ordered us all to the living room.

He pursued us with questions. "After the scream did you hear anyone move?" "Just before the scream, if anyone passed did you recognize who they were?" "Ah, so you bumped into a piece of furniture . . . let's see . . . which one?" In reality he wanted to discover the murderer not by the statements of the players, but from the expressions on their faces. Be careful not to laugh too loudly. Or, the reverse, be careful not to be too serious. He pierced us with those hard eyes of a bird of prey which had impressed me so much in the beer hall, except that then he had shrugged his shoulders at the violence, and now, on the other hand he was an agent of the law.

At the end of his investigation he turned to approach me, and asked, "Are you the killer?"

In accordance with the rules I had to confess. Yes, it was I.

Hearty laughter, and then Tracy served us cocktails. A bad sign. The party would be prolonged another two hours. I made up a pretext to retire. No, no! The night is young! What . . .

"I'll take you home," Hamilton said, ending it abruptly.

"Don't bother . . ."

"No bother at all. I'll take you." And turning to Tracy, he said, "I'll be right back."

I said goodbye to the owners and the guests, and went out with Hamilton.

In order to reach my house we had to cross a park over a road that went up and down on steep hills. We were at the crest of the highest hill when Hamilton drew to a halt and asked, "Tell me. Something intrigues me. You were the killer. Why then, after committing the murder, didn't you move away from the victim in order to confuse us?"

"Well," I answered, laughing, "for various reasons. In the first place, it is expected that the murderer will flee, no? Well then, it occurred to me that by not fleeing I would cause more confusion. In the second place, I was tired and did not want to move off and take the chance of bumping into more furniture. In the third place, there's no need to take the game too seriously. It's a game, no more than a game . . ."

I was going to add, "and it shocks me that, with your years, a professor like you would give such importance to a game suitable only for students," when Hamilton again surprised me with an action that no student of that time would have done in jest. At the same instant that he questioned me, "And there was no other reason besides what you said?" with a quick motion he pulled my handkerchief from my pocket, turned on the lights of the car, and showed me the marks of lipstick, the lipstick from the lips of his wife that I had cleaned from my mouth.

The handkerchief is what put the police on the trail. They found it in Hamilton's pocket, and, taking off from there, from clue to clue, they verified that he had not driven over the cliff with the automobile on his way back to Tracy after having left me at my home, as they had believed at first, but that I, having knocked him out cold with a rock, had placed him in the car and pushed him out over the ledge. Why? Because enraged with pride, jealousy, and cocktails, Hamilton had gotten out of the car, grabbed me from my seat and punched me in the face ("Spanish rat, I'll kill you!") with the evident intention of Slam, Bang! finishing me off on the spot. When he leaned over to pick up a club from the ground to liquidate me, I had already come up with a stone in my hands.

Hamilton had forgotten that in "Murder" the detective cannot kill the killer. More in conformity with the rules of the game, I, after having murdered his wife, killed him as well. "And now tell me, Mister Commissioner, what else could I have done?"

(Signed: Edmond W. Martínez)

Glacier

I got off the train, bought *El Argentino* and looked for the announcement. There it was, even with a photo that made me look younger: "Today, at 18:30, in the School of Humanities, the eminent Professor Arturo Scholtz of the University of Innsbruck will give a dissertation on Friederich Holderlin." After the usual biographical data, it continued: "Scholtz, whose infancy and adolescence were spent in our city, settled in Europe many years ago."

Many, yes. Thirty to be exact. A long absence, above all because I was living in another climate, another language, another civilization. Nevertheless, I had hardly gone out through the enormous whale belly of the railroad station and set off walking along the Diagonal 80, when the image of Carmen appeared in my mind: fresh, delicious, so serene that it appeared sculpted for eternity out of the stuff of quietness, in contrast to her body: lively, at every step molding the air with forms of dunes, urns, and lemons.

Guided by the memory of the first love—I, twenty years of age, she eighteen—I detoured through the streets, searching for the sacred locations: the Normal School, the Church of San Ponciano, the Plaza San Martín, the Paris movie theater, the corner house where Carmen lived . . . The streets of La Plata appear straight, but in my immense nostalgia they curved, and ended up by enclosing me in an enchanted circle.

One bird—the one hundred billion birds constitute one species and the whole species is a single individual without a history—ended the song that I had heard sung thirty years back.

"I am that bird," I said to myself.

With a bird's-eye view—that of a migratory bird—I had summed up the panorama from the cathedral to the woods, to carry it with me in my head when I bid farewell to the suburb where I was born; now, perched on the familiar cobblestones, I gave it back, detail by detail. La Plata of 1960 is La Plata of 1930, except for a few changes. Sadly I accepted the changes due to time: the wasted doorway, the growth of a lime tree . . . Nostalgically I rejected the changes in space: one more skyscraper, one less garden . . . At war with progress, I demolished the new buildings and covered the wasteland with canvasses painted from memory. Carmen was triumphant in the middle of that anthological city that I was constructing with the tenderness of an antiquary. And to think that my contact with the eternal, the unforgettable Carmen lasted only as long as a dress of the season: that green silk that undulated around her when we met and that continued undulating when we parted. Scarcely a few months, intense with sentiment, but not with incidents, since in all the summer, so brief, the hours when we saw each other and talked were few.

I was timid, indecisive, awkward and so respectful that I never dared even to touch her hand. However platonic my love might have been, when with the breath of a breeze Carmen's locks were lifted toward me as if to touch my face, the joy of that possible caress was too much for my poor Plato and brought me the desire to kiss her; but I held back, lowered my eyes, and remained silent. I understood that after her first curiosity was satisfied, Carmen began to be bored. She must have considered me short of wit. To reconquer her I unfolded before her eyes the map of my future: the books I would write, the honors I would obtain. All that was of no interest to her; nor was my rhetoric, leaping from metaphor to metaphor, each more ridiculous than the last. Until one evening, not disguising the fact that she was no longer interested in me, she said goodbye. So I cursed my timidity and, from that point on, every time I accomplished one of my projects—they have now all been accomplished—I would think of some way to get even: if an opportunity were to present itself, just one, to say to Carmen, "See? I was not such an idiot after all?" The desire to prove my merit kept me in a state of perpetual expectation and so, in the restless movements of my life, Carmen was always a fixed point. I do not say that I spent my time sighing for her, but she persisted in the deepest part of me, immobile, and I, from change to change, held her in my humiliated heart like a long lament, spasmodic and drawn out, like the braying of an ass.

Evening was falling, with some tormenting grays that were forcing objects, the leaf of a tree, the bronze of a door knocker, a broken tile, to deliver up the secret of their own light. It was already the hour for the lecture. I took 7th Street and, from pure coquetry, I removed my glasses. Immediately my world became sullied from my myopia, so much so that, in entering the lobby—to make matters worse, it was very dark—fearing not to recognize among all those bulks the colleague who would be waiting for me, I again took my glasses from my pocket; but before I was able to put them on, a woman came out of nowhere, and I heard her say, "I am Carmen."

If a carriage drawn by dragons had taken me to the land of fairies I would not have been so shocked. The air was filled with wings. The universe had turned back on itself, and I repeated my past. In spite of all my regrets, I repeated my past. I lowered my eyes. As I lowered them the woman became invisible; but on the other hand, that lowering movement brought with it the image of Carmen, young and beautiful. Perhaps the actual woman who remained up there on the surface, diaphanous from her make-up, had helped the other woman to appear. I do not know. I know only that my vision was of a virginal Carmen, not abstract, but of flesh and bone, and so desirable that I felt myself ageless.

"Ah, so you don't remember me," I heard her say.

And since I remained silent, serious, withdrawn, eyes lowered, she added with the cutting tone of someone offended, "I only wanted to greet you. I'm sorry. Goodbye."

Oh Carmen! In 1930 you did not understand my timidity; you thought me shy, insignificant; you did not sense that within the adolescent that I was, there was already struggling the man that I am. Nor have you now, in 1960, understood my timidity; you believed me cold, indifferent, forgetful: you did not sense that within the man I am, there still dreams the adolescent that I was. This adolescent, presenting the image of an important man, is the person who saw you, not the Carmen of 1960, but the Carmen of 1930. You were not a projection, like an idol on a screen. You were a blending of what you were with what you are, having a common something from your past and your present and, offering a salutation in a single voice, merged into one essence.

Carmen, I will tell you a story. It happened in Austria, near where I live. Two young people in love are practicing their mountain-climbing in the province of Karten. She falls from a precipice; he, desperate, rouses the villagers to recover the body that has disappeared. A geologist explains to him that the body has fallen into the Pasterzen Glacier which, in a slow and regular movement, will slip down from the high snows: the body will travel twenty-five kilometers and reappear at the mouth of the river after thirty years. The lover waits. After thirty years he goes to the place indicated. Now he is old and ugly; and he sees his sweetheart appear, preserved by the ice in the full beauty of her youth.

Oh Carmen! Our case, has it not been the reverse? Was it not I who, thirty years ago, fell into that glacier, and today you, who could not recognize the still intact adolescent in the depth of a block of ice?

Madness Plays at Chess

He prepared the chessboard on a small table. He planned to play alone. He had not foreseen that Madness would play as well. Confined in his bachelor's home during a long illness, he had not played with another person for a long time. The truth is that even before becoming ill he had found no one with whom to play. Not even in the Club had he yet met anyone who would play with him. They had started to isolate him. Was it that they wanted to pay him back in his own coin? Perhaps, because—he could not deny it—lately he himself had fled from the others; not from misanthropy, let it be understood, but from discretion. He was withdrawing into himself in order not to become involved in the lives of others. People generally were of no interest to him. If they were chess players he looked down on them. So it is possible that his arrogance isolated him. Bah! What did that matter! He needed no one. To live with others is to accept some social unit, but for him the acceptable social unit was very small: a unit of two. And in chess this unit is so discreet that the two people scarcely know each other. They are prisoners on an enchanted little island—which is what a chessboard is—two solitary individuals who rid themselves of their souls to convert them into pawns, kings, queens, rooks, bishops, and knights of wood or ivory. They have no need to converse or even to look each other in the face. In chess the opponent has no face. One can defeat an unknown person by letter or by telegram. One can, with eyes blindfolded, or from within a dark cell, analyze a mental structure. One can eliminate fifty mediocre players in fifty simultaneous matches. Fifty mediocre players lift one hand to move only own pawn. Because they are mediocre, it is as if they were one mediocre hand.

And now, convalescing in his deserted quarters, he had finished setting up the chessboard on the little table and would test whether playing alone was essentially different from playing with another person.

While seating himself, he had already regretted that the other chair was unoccupied: he missed his opponent because he foresaw that it would be difficult for him not to win.

Generally players cast lots to see who has the privilege of opening with the white pieces. Given that he was without a partner, he would dispense with this rite and permit himself the pleasure of selecting his color for the whole day. He had never admitted it in public, but the white pieces pleased him more than the black. This for a familiar reason that the white army carried his name, Cándido White, by merest chance. But this is no joke, my friend philologers. Was the hyphenated name of the Spanish writer, Blanco-White, a joke? The initial advantage of opening the game lasts a short time, but to prove to himself that his purpose was not to take advantage of the absence of an opponent he permitted himself to win the first game in two moves: 1. P-KB4, P-K3; 2. P-KN4, Q-R5, MATE.

Very well. Playing the idiot, he had given his rival a gift of the first game. Enough of that. Now to play seriously. Again he arranged the pieces on the board. White won on the ninth move.

"There is no merit in winning that way," he said to himself. "I know what I want. I know what the other wants. I know that the other knows what I want. This resembles the dialog between a ventriloquist and his dummy. It would be better for someone else to direct Black from the other side."

No sooner said than done. He set up the pieces in the order of battle and opened the game:

First move: P-K4. He gazed around the room as if bored that it was taking so long for his slow companion to make a move. White paving stones gleamed on the black pavement. Suddenly it was the black paving stones that stood out against the white pavement. Added to the change in point of view was a reversal in perspective. Jesus' words, "In offering alms your left hand does not know what your right hand is doing," can be applied equally to both hands. Both of White's hands were ignorant of what they themselves had just done when they raised the board and gave it a half turn. Thanks to that half turn, a black pawn, in moving toward the K-4 square, felt himself directed by the arm, even by the person, who had just pushed him from behind.

White's altruistic gesture served for nothing. In spite of his good will, Black lost again.

"Ah," White said to himself, "now I know what is happening.

One head can imagine what is in another head, but posteriors have little imagination and cannot think for other posteriors. They are stuck to the chair and, with their sensations of being on the bottom, they do not permit me to forget that I, the only real person in the room, continue always on the same throne and favor the same white pieces of whom I am the lord and master. It remains to be seen if, changing the seat of my rear end, I can succeed in imagining that I am another person and that this other person can save the army of black pieces. I will install myself in the scene on the side of Black and then, like someone distracted, change over to the side of White."

He got to his feet, moved to the other side of the table, sat down there and attacked with the black pieces. Then he rose, returned to his former seat, and counterattacked, followed immediately by his again joining the blacks; thus, in going back and forth, he moved now a white piece with his right hand and now a black piece with his left. In order to emphasize the difference even more, in moving a black piece, he added to his left hand an additional motion; with the tips of his fingers he would give the piece a slight twist on its square. He never did this with his right hand. Thus the left hand and the right hand each was the captain of an opposing side. The two hands of White, although in spite of everything they resembled each other, were like two adversaries going to a masked ball, each one disguised as the other: White, one in two, two in one, sat down, got up, came and went.

No help. No way. The physical change of position helped a little, but very little. The new sensation in the buttocks on a chair of different shape and without a cushion did not manage to estrange White from himself. A pendulum, but human, he projected himself from one end of the table to the other, remembering where he came from and anticipating where he was going to. In his movements, he took with him his knowledge of the famous variations in the histories of each attack, of each defense. The second player still did not exist; he was an automaton and not self-directed. Not strange then that the end would be favorable for White, and that this would continue as long as White telepathically transmitted his own thoughts to the second player, who, without showing his hand, responded with the piece indicated. Reflected in a mirror, the advances from one side were transformed into the advances from the other side, but either or both were regulated by the same strategy from White. What was necessary was that his person, instead of being duplicated, should divide into two different personalities. The serpent Amphisbaena had a head at each end; it was necessary to cut it in two with a hatchet to have two serpents that would attack each other. But cutting a serpent in two would be much easier than cutting a chess-player in two. Chess was a confrontation of strategies, right? And each strategy had to be conceived in a brain that could not know the strategy of another wholly independent brain. Only the heterogeneity of brains permitted chess to be a game of chance, with calculations and maneuvers unforeseen. How was a single brain to know itself and not know itself at the same time; how was it to plan a threat from one side of the board, immediately forget what it had just planned, and, from the other side, elude the trap or fall into it with total ignorance of the threatening intent? A brain that gave contradictory orders to itself: "Put out the light! Turn on the light!" and pretended to guess the dark secrets of the coming movements of the pieces, when in fact those movements had already been well illuminated in past games, was a mendacious brain that, just to amuse itself, was pretending to be divided. A false division, like that of a man who, walking under the sun, might say that he is divided into a body and a shadow. Was there anything more ridiculous than a body trying to jump over its own shadow? Nevertheless, White persisted in trying to divide himself into two different personalities.

"Chess," he said to himself, "is a duel to the death between two intelligences. What I must do is to split myself apart in such a way that when the black pieces are playing, the white part of my awareness is eclipsed. To play not with myself but against myself."

One intelligence was not sufficient. Two were required. Passionately, he began to play all out. He rid himself of the single intelligence he possessed and cast it into the abyss, trusting that his unconscious, or subconscious, or anticonscious, or recounterconscious would restore it to him, multiplied. White became in turn mad, religious, childish, savage; he steeped himself in the memories of his own nightmares and hallucinations, went back to his foundations in the ancestral memory of the species and there encountered myths of divided beings, two-headed gods, which he picked over with the schizoid two-pronged mason's tool that is the cross that all men bear, and he performed incantations. Standing upright in the middle of the room, he looked about and saw everything—the ceiling with its chandelier, the walls hung with pictures, the window curtains, the little islands of furniture extended over a floor as wide as the ocean; he saw everything, everything except the body with which he was seeing. It was invisible to itself, and from that state of invisibility, seeing the tip of his nose, his chest, his legs, and above all his hands overwhelmed him with a sensation of otherness; he saw himself emerge as another person. But the other person was still himself. And yet, it wasn't. What he wanted was something more, something more. What then? Adam saw a companion materialize from his rib; Eve saw Cain emerge from her womb. Well, then, what he wanted was to see a chess companion materialize from himself. But he couldn't make him appear. The imaginary player was claiming his right to exist but still remained an obscure mass struggling in the submerged mind of White; and the submerged mind of the Other, wanting to emerge, was struggling in its turn against the octopus-like tentacles that held him prisoner in the depth of the irrational dreams. The gestation of the Other was laborious; it took place, as will be seen, in the white and black squares of the chessboard, agitated from within by the same random magic that determines the destiny of man in the chess game of his days and nights.

The opening was standard: White played alternately the white and black pieces and thus the game proceeded clearly along the lines of two plans and their ramifications, except that, in playing Black, White proposed to ignore that the awareness of the black position was deeply seated in his own mind. And he succeeded. He removed the awareness from himself and projected it into the mind of the Other person, invisible, but now capable of playing his own game. Then White committed himself body and soul to the white pieces and devised a devastating combination for checkmate on the twentieth move. He memorized the succession of moves, one by one, observed with joy that the blacks responded exactly as he had foreseen. The game appeared mechanical. Clearly the victory would be White's. But at that moment he committed an error. Instead of the nineteenth move that he had planned, he skipped ahead to the twentieth. His knight took a bishop's pawn. It was at this moment that from nothingness there blazed a brilliant morning light, a lunar mist, an opalescent cloud, gelatinous tentacles, a formless ectoplasm, a substance from another world suddenly taking the form of a hand. The hand was no more ominous than the one King Balthazar saw materialize in the air and write fatidical words on a wall. The hand—it was not the claw of an eagle, it was an eagle—fluttered over the table, came down and seized White's knight. White, giddy, impulsively moved his rook. Lifting his gaze he saw that the opposing hand had already become an arm and the arm a body. Seated in front of him, the Other smiled. Thank God it was not a mimicking monkey!

The Other was like himself: a long face, thoughtful, calm, with light blue eyes, pallid from confinement and insomnia. But he was still an inchoate, abstract form, weak as a web of dream, light as sacrificial incense. For an instant White felt urged to undo that player, to force him to commit an error even more stupid than his own, but he held back. No, no. Epic poets invented an antihero great enough to heighten the value of the hero. White would invent a powerful anti-White. He resolved to create his opponent, piece by piece, to make him credible. Since he had materialized as a body with definite characteristics, it was too late for basic changes. He had to be accepted just as he appeared. At the most, cover his paleness with a skin tanned by the sun, darken the eyes, correct his asthenia with more developed muscles. On the other hand, White had given his glands a different chemistry; he had given them the nervous chemistry that theologians call "the soul." A chemical soul which, from within, with a face similar to his own, was nevertheless producing from totally dissimilar intentions. The Other already was a man and must be baptized. White baptized him "Black." (There were precedents: in a tournament at Nuremburg in 1883, the Germans Weiss and Schwartz played to a draw; and at another in London in 1924, White defeated Black.)

The game became tense. A struggle of equal forces. The contest was between two opposing spiritual forces. White heard the drums of war beating in the enemy camp. Black's pieces, posted in a dark forest, perceived the light of dawn and finally oriented themselves. The arrogant advance of a pawn indicated that they had decided on their path, and they marched forth with flags unfolding in the wind. White, from his side, set himself to deciphering the entire strategy of Black within which the advance of the pawn had been a simple tactic. Instead of obeying, as in the beginning, the telepathic instructions that White was sending, Black made his own response. Not without surprise, White realized that Black had refused to fall into the ambush and would not withdraw. Whirlwind against cyclone in a lightning storm. Surrounded by inscrutable dangers, White began to weaken, and Black became ever more sinister. Suddenly White saw Black capture his rook and heard him say, in the most natural tone in the world, "Checkmate."

White requested a return match, but from this point on, the game became strangely irregular.

To play chess is to submit to certain rules of an activity that has no other meaning than the activity itself. If two players resolve to compete, the winning of one corresponds with the losing of the other. Each player understands with perfect logic that he must make his best possible move without concern for the annihilating effect it may produce on his rival. The only moral value which is implicit in the theory of the game is that of moral neutrality. The rules which White observed in playing with the members of his club were now, with Black, drastically changed.

The revolution started with a ridiculous rebellion on the part of

Black. He was cornered. His downfall was imminent. He had lost his bishops and, at that moment, his knights appeared to be of no use. Nevertheless, he seized a knight and moved it along a diagonal, black to black, until it came to the white queen and captured it.

"Look, my friend!" White exclaimed, unable to believe his eyes, "you didn't jump with your knight, you moved it along a diagonal as if it were a bishop . . ."

"I know that," Black replied, "But what other remedy is there? If I don't take your queen at this moment, you have me mated in three moves . . ."

"Bu . . . but," White stuttered, "a knight is a knight and a bishop is a bishop, and what you did cannot be done . . ."

"Why not? After all they are only little pieces of wood."

White was never able to recall what was said in the discussion that followed. There were arguments, counter-arguments, conciliations, changes in the regulations . . . But when play was resumed, the rules were not the same. Formerly the players directed their pieces; now two wanton demiurges were directing the players.

The Arabs called chess *ach-chitrendj*, and earlier the Persians called it *shatranj*, and before that the Hindus, *chaturanga*. In game after game, White and Black retraced the path, and, going back through time, from century to century, from millennium to millennium, returned to the remote Orient. In this voyage to the beginnings, White and Black left behind the schools of today, the tournaments of yesterday; the games between caliphs and kings, who were accustomed to resolving their differences not always by war but in games of chess; the living chess of the Hindus in which youths, sumptuously attired, took the place of the pieces on large patios laid out in squares; until chess became astronomical, then metaphysical, and they ended up in the heads of ancient divinities. The chess world became a universe in which God and the Devil contested. Vahu Manah and Akam Mana, Varuna and Mitra, Isis and Osiris, Ahura Mazdah and Ahra Manyu, Neikos and Philia, Jahwe and Satan, Ormazd and Ahriman.

Morality was now the issue.

In the time when White had gone to the Club and encountered professionals and amateurs, he had felt that he was a good Neoplatonist. He confronted moral problems with monistic solutions: a perfect God has created a perfect world; Good is the light of Being; Evil is the dark of Nothingness; we suffer pain, misery, injustice, but they are mere illusions formed out of our feelings of impotence; if we contemplate the world from within, wholly illuminated by love, we understand the marvelous hierarchy which goes from the many to the One.

All very simple, logical, true, isn't it?

But now that Black had appeared, it was necessary to confront the moral problem with a dualistic solution. At the foundation of the universe there are two contending principles: one benevolent, the other malevolent. Man is helpless to do more than ally himself at times with the light in the field of Ormazd, and at other times with the darkness in the field of Ahriman.

They struggled furiously. The pieces were mere bits of wood being moved conventionally, but White and Black now were deciding the fate of mankind and the destiny of the universe with the unconventional energy of angels and demons. A pawn could move backwards or crown himself king. A king could destroy another king or delegate this responsibility to the queen. Thus, to the individual strategies of man, western or eastern, were added various divine strategies, and the random rules made the game look like chaos.

In truth, was it chaos? White and Black were agreed that both were agents of conflicting cosmic forces, but they could not agree on the definitions of good and evil. At the moment they didn't know which was which. And the truth is that in their discussions, no less passionate than their moves, they had forgotten who was who. Neither protagonists nor deuteragonists, simply antagonists. One of them—White? Black?—took charge of the play, invented the rules for every move, and at all times moved at will. The other waited patiently for the right occasion to intervene suddenly with a move that blocked, detoured, annulled or countered the previous move so that the universal squaring of the cosmos was changed once again. Was it an agent of God who dominated the game with an orderly parade of pieces? Was it an agent of the devil who randomly imposed change? Or the reverse? In any case, while White and Black, indifferent to anything except their own pieces, attacked each other along straight lines, columns, diagonals, in reality their ambiguous dialectic was compelling the men of the whole world to escape from one trap only to fall into another, not knowing, no more than demiurges know, whether life was happiness interrupted by unpredictable pain, or unhappiness interrupted by random pleasure.

"Checkmate!" exclaimed a stentorian voice, pronouncing it with the intonation of a Persian Manichee: "*Shah, mat!*"

The loser rose up angrily and looked out of the window, down along the street.

The street, and the people who were at that moment in it, represented the pieces on one of the chessboards that White and Black had played. That board covered Buenos Aires between Barracas and Flores, and between Recoleta and Belgrano. And as a result of the kind of chess they had played, all the men—good or evil—advanced from Palermo with the knight (horse) of Garibaldi, from Retiro with the English rook (tower), with the bishop of the Plaza de Mayo, with pawns (peasants) from all the city slums, with an ugly little king, a demagogue from the Casa Rosada, and a little queen who was administering vengeance from the Caja de Justicia y Previsión.

From the window, the player who had lost started to scream at the men in the street, "I am not guilty! I am doing what I can! The other one is Evil! He breaks the rules, but he wins! Run, all you chessmen! Leave the board before it is too late!

The people started gathering below the window. Some laughed, others cursed. Still others looked at him, dumbly.

A policeman approached. "What is going on here? You sir, you are creating public disorder."

"Not me, no! It is He! It is He!" the man exclaimed, pointing inside the room.

The policeman rose up on his toes, looked in through the window, and saw no one.

"Who?"

"White! He is the Evil One! I am Black!"

SELECTIONS FROM

Klein's Bottle (1971)

Esteco: Submerged City

The torrential rain of summer erased the plain and the mountain range. Alí Assán turned away from the window and returned to the front desk where, awaiting him, open, was the college textbook. Although on vacation and in charge of Los Alamitos, his father's inn, he had to prepare for his examinations, out there in remote Buenos Aires. He had already begun to study when he heard an automobile motor. A moment later a man entered. With a valise in his hand and a curse on his lips he inspected the place, asked if the bed had bedbugs, rented a room—his signature: Isaac Noah—and shut his door on Assán's nose. Assán returned to the front desk, but still was unable to continue studying because another man entered, with a blond beard and entirely drenched from the rain. He carried no valise but a backpack hanging from his shoulders. He shook off the water that poured from him; "I'm raining," he said, laughing, rented the only remaining room—his signature: Diego Duffy—and asked for a towel "to disguise myself as Mahatma Gandhi while my clothes are drying."

"They came in to find shelter from the deluge," Assán thought.

He was not used to that class of guest, one with the air of an international capitalist, the other a bohemian tourist. Separated from the main group of houses by a few aspens which his father had planted, the inn, unpretentious, served the farmer and his wagon, never people from a big city.

An hour later Noah and Duffy met in the dining room and, without saying a word to each other, looked out of the same window. For a few minutes it appeared that not even the deluge was sufficient to get them talking. Apparently they had nothing to say to each other. Suddenly their two heads came together and they were talking in a low tone. Then, looking at them out of the corner of his eye, Assán thought, "Careful! Appearances are deceiving! They surreptitiously made an appointment to meet here. Why? I must find out."

And in order to learn what they were talking about, he sat down at the next table and pretended to be absorbed in his book. What he heard served to confirm his first supposition: they had come in to find shelter from the deluge and until that moment neither one had known of the existence of the other.

Duffy was youthful and talkative. Without anybody asking, he brought out a diffuse autobiography with little phrases such as these: "I travel by going in circles around myself"; "I'm a vagabond who collects impossible horizons . . ."

Noah was mature, dark, taciturn. He pressed his lips together to hold back insults, but the corners of his mouth, so pinched, revealed all the resentment he did not express in words. Having been questioned by Duffy as to what he did for a living, he muttered that they had ordered him to travel from city to city to organize aid for Israel.

"Ah," Duffy exclaimed, "so you are also a poet. Israel is a dream."

"That was before," Noah answered, with a sour gesture. "Today it is a state at war. For a dream, I wouldn't take a step. I am a realist, a man of action."

The rain stopped and the heat began to swell up with gusto. When Noah announced that he would leave on the following morning and travel through the village of Pacana Ucu, Assán was about to say something, but remained silent. Only when Duffy offered to accompany Noah did Assán lift his eyes from his physics book and warn them:

"Pardon me, gentlemen. This is none of my business, but be careful. Here we had only a cloudburst, but in the mountains the cloudbursts come together and you have floods."

"I don't care," Noah snorted. "I'm leaving early tomorrow."

"And I with you," Duffy said.

"It rained heavily on the upper slopes," Assán insisted.

And Duffy: "So much the better if there are torrents. Columns of water, arches of water, walls of water . . . Water spouts, canals, troughs . . . I won't see the rocks that may be there; the only thing that will be visible, suspended in the air, will be a trembling palace of crystal."

During the night the sky was filled with stars. Right at dawn, Noah awakened Duffy; they had their breakfast together and, with a basket of food and drink that Assán had prepared for them, they left for the mountains.

Duffy gazed over the landscape and it was as if that dune, that tree, that hill were all the successive letters of a Word which, once formed, took possession of him and obliged him to talk. From that time on, in an incessant monologue, he transformed each thing, each event into a metaphor: "the night carried off the stars stuck in its tail like burrs"; "the silent explosion of the dawn had blown the colors of the rainbow into pieces"; "the pampas sweated drops of gold"; "a flowering shrub was still bowing to the archangel who had just passed"; "they had pushed the mountains high into the air against their will, and what they really wanted was to throw themselves down on the ground and rest . . ."

Noah, cursing inside himself at that charlatan, pressed his lips together and examined the steep slopes of the rocky pass. From time to time he would bring the car to a stop, consult the map, and then continue on. One one occasion—about two hours had passed—he could stand it no longer:

"You talk so much that I'm distracted. Because of you, I may become confused and we'll get lost."

Duffy responded to the driver's bad humor with a burst of laughter and continued making metaphors. Hours later he was still talking. "Riding in the car we miss much of the beauty. All we see is what is framed in the windshield and the little windows. On foot we would see . . ."

"You want to get out?" Noah interrupted him with a cold glance that said, "to me it makes no difference what you do; if you're such a poet get out and leave me alone." He slowed the car down as if in truth he would stop and leave him there. But after that threat, satisfied that he had taught him a lesson, he stepped again on the accelerator and added, "Without the car we would see more but we wouldn't get anywhere."

"Don't you believe it," Duffy said, laughing, "the advantage of living on a round planet is that each one of its points can be the beginning or the end of a voyage, as one wishes. On a terrestrial globe every complete voyage consists in starting at one place and finishing at the same place. This can also be done by staying right where one is."

"Profound, profound . . . But you know? I'm a very busy man."

Duffy was about to answer him when Noah again interrupted him, this time speaking to himself, "Something's wrong. Even going slowly we should reach Pacana Ucu before noon. The sun is already high and there is no sign of civilization."

"And what does it matter? This piece of the planet is at the end of the world and nevertheless it has the aspect of being the beginning of the world. Like a second creation. All my life I've wanted to discover America but as I arrived late, Columbus had already discovered it for me. If by some miracle the world is once again young, perhaps I too will be a great Discoverer . . ."

Noah frowned over the thought that was working at him, and said, "We should already have met some highway, some post, some ranch . . . Where the devil is Pacana Ucu?"

"Where the devil lost his shirt, I suppose. But don't worry about it. Nature hides from people a flower at the peak of a mountain and a shell at the bottom of the sea; it hides stalactites in caves and designs in the middle of the mahogany tree. Why is it strange that it hides a village from us?"

"Yes. Talk, have fun . . . If we are lost . . ." and his lips drew tight.

"Bah! All men are lost. Some are lost men. Because of these reckless fools, whole cities are lost as well."

"You like to hear yourself talk, eh? although no one understands you. Isn't that so?"

"I'm referring to cities like Esteco. Have you heard of it?"

Noah shrugged his shoulders.

"They say it's around here somewhere," Duffy continued with a wave of the hand so vague that he could have been indicating that plain or the whole province. "It was a luxurious city, with buildings of gold and silver. The inhabitants let themselves be corrupted and one fine day the earth opened and swallowed them, houses and all."

"Look, you're wasting my time. Tell somebody else about it. The only cities that are important to me are real ones. You're a dreamer, a visionary. That city must be one of those impossibilities that, as you told me, you are searching for on I don't know what horizons."

"Yes and no. Esteco is a moralistic legend which has spoiled the memory of the real city that disappeared. Although you don't believe me, I'm going to tell you the legend: 'Once upon a time there was a city . . .' But seriously, the city did sink into a lake. Every one hundred years it emerges for only a few hours, from twilight to twilight, to submerge once again for another century. During those hours, a most beautiful maiden comes out from the city, which is on an island, and walks across the waters of the lake, arrives at the shore, and enters our world. Imagine that I, by pure chance, pass by at this moment, and it's my turn to greet her . . ."

"You're a humorist or you're mad. From thinking so much about apparitions, finally you'll make them appear to you. One of these days you'll sit down on a chair that isn't there and hurt yourself."

When Duffy began referring to the Chronicle of the Indies, Noah was no longer paying him any attention.

It was noon. By that time they should have arrived at Pacana Ucu, but all that could be seen were ravines, dunes, red granite cornices, and heaps of sunbaked stone.

"Hummm! What have they put in the basket for us?" Duffy said.

"I thought all this talking was because you were hungry."

"Ha, Ha! Look, if sometime you happen to smile, who knows, maybe you might be nice."

Duffy put his hand in the basket and took out a turnover. From its blackish dough, suggestions of green leaf and ruby-colored flowers were showing. He looked at it suspiciously and said, "You know something? The Arab wants me to eat this garbage and to kill you. An assassin (or *hashshashin*) is someone who eats hashish."

And he ate the turnover.

"Look!" he said immediately, "a little bottle of red wine!"

"In this heat? Take a look to see if that Moslem also put in a little bottle of water."

"Yes."

They stopped in a clearing and ate. If they had had eggs they could have fried them on the hood of the car, which was burning like fire. Duffy took the bottle of wine and Noah the bottle of water. They threw the empty basket on the back seat and departed. Duffy tilted back the bottle like an angel with a trumpet and then, in his Irish tenor voice, he sang, "Let Erin remember the days of old."

The road branched. Noah hesitated. He glanced at the map and, in a rage, threw it to the floor. Then he decided. He veered over to the side and started to follow the curve around. On one of the turns, at his right, he heard the sound of water. Somewhere, probably behind the hill they had just left behind, there had to be a cascade or a river or various streams coming together. He drove down into a streambed which scarcely wet the tires; and only when it had become impossible to back up because there was not enough space to maneuver, did he realize that the stream was rising menacingly. He accelerated in the hope of finding an exit, a stretch of high ground, any possible escape. Duffy looked back.

"The waters are chasing us! The nymphs are chasing Hylas and Hermaphrodite. Whee!" he exclaimed, drunk with wine and myth.

As they were driving down, Duffy, through a cleft in the rock, managed to discern a plain: misty, white, verdant, golden, moving . . . Moving? Moving because of a little breeze rocking the cat-tails; or from the rolling mists floating over the lagoons; or from the coming and going of messages between the male earth and the womanly sky; or from the rapidity of the car's descent. A moving plain. Noah didn't see it; he was looking through the rear-view mirror at the tongues of the rising current, and he cursed and braked the car. It stopped, trembling. They had let themselves become trapped in a sand pit. It was necessary to climb out at a bend in the stream. Duffy, stumbling, got out of the car and climbed up over a few rocks to the cleft where he had glimpsed the plain. For an instant he remained transfixed, and then, turning toward Noah, he cried, "Come! Look! The enchanted city! It's just emerged! Palaces of gold!"

"Forget the fairy tales. There are no palaces in Pacana Ucu."

"This is not Pacana Ucu. Don't fool yourself. We've already passed Pacana Ucu; we left it behind. We've crossed over a ridge and now we're stopped at this big wall of stone. I'm telling you that through that breach I see the enchanted city."

"You're drunk. You're crazier than a goat. Come down here and help."

"Help with what?"

"Push, push! Can't you see that the car is stuck?"

"It's useless," Duffy cried. "Get out. Right now. The torrent will sweep it away. Here's the way out. This way . . ."

The water leaped forward, crested, smashed against the rock and fell back on itself.

"Come on! Push!" Noah called.

"Useless . . . But what are you doing?"

Noah, seeing that the water was rising and was already at the height of the doors, closed the windows.

"Don't close them!" Duffy shouted. "The pressure of the water won't let you open the door from inside. Don't be stubborn. Leave the car, for God's sake. Now!!!"

Noah did not hear Duffy. And Duffy did not hear Noah any longer, but for another reason. It was ecstasy. The enchanted city which he saw on the other side fascinated him. For a few moments he had fought over two realities: the disaster, which demanded action, and the golden reality which was inviting him to dream. For a few moments he had felt himself on the border between the two. A poet is like that. A poet wants to give himself over body and soul to the poem that he is writing and suddenly, from outside, he is distracted by the voice of a moral obligation. This had happened many times to Duffy; and it had just happened once again. But not now, not now! The beauty of the poem triumphed over the moral obligation. The rushing current turned the car over, with Noah inside. Muddy water covered it. The only thing visible, like a little island of death, was the shell of the car-body; and in the plain, in the middle of the lake, there rose up the great island of life, with its prodigious city. Duffy abandoned reality, of no vital interest to him. On the other hand, what was of vital interest to him was the adventure that was being offered him. Outside himself, filled with awe, hypnotized, he gazed at the enchanted city. A thought that is extended beyond the limits of thought itself is a window through which we can look out over a mysterious dimension; in the empty space where normally nothing is seen, suddenly an extraordinary memory flowers; extraordinary because, although a memory, it comes to us from the future. Through the open window of his senses and also through the rocks around him, Duffy was seeing a mystical transparency and, in its depth, the enchanted city. He made his way through the cleft in the rocks. The sandy beach burned like an oven. Far off in the center of the island, he saw a castle with clouded towers. That portentous architecture was reflected in the azure lake. The same royal pinnacles that reached up to the sky were reflected, inverted, in the mirror of the water. It extended across the dune, beneath the implacable sun. From that city, recently risen, a beautiful maiden would come forth. And, in fact, he managed to make out someone coming to meet him, walking over the water. He lifted his arms and fainted onto the sand.

When he recovered his senses and half-opened his eyes, a face was bending over him. Not that of the beautiful maiden; that of Alí Assán.

Duffy, feverish, told all that had happened, detail by detail.

"How can I be at the inn," he asked. "Who brought me here? Because . . ."

The face of Assán twisted up in something like a sob, and his body crumpled over at the waist as if in a sudden pain. With his head hanging over his knees he gave out a few choking sounds. Only when he lifted his face did it become clear that he was not really suffering; his breath, held in before, burst out in convulsive laughter.

Duffy looked at him, astonished and very serious:

"Noah drowned. That is no joke."

Assán swallowed his laughter, but Duffy, noting the urge to laugh still gleaming in his eyes, remembered an episode in the Book of Esther: the Arab Amán, in spite of his riches, cannot be happy while the Jew Mardocheo is kneeling like a beggar at the door of the king; perhaps that Arab would have been happy if they had assured him that the Jew was dead. Duffy had to discard that suspicion when Assán said to him:

"They've already gone to recover the body. Poor fellow! Forgive me for laughing, but isn't it funny? Both of you made mistakes. The realist, Noah, died because he was convinced that he had crossed a large distance, and all that time he had circled round and round the same spot, without leaving here, and he was unable to discover reality, he, the realist! And the same for you, who, moreover, believed you were seeing an enchanted city. You saw a mirage. What you saw was this group of buildings, with the Inn and the aspens. Or better, the mirage of all this. A strange mirage, but I too saw it once, on a torrid day like this one, after a flood. The atmosphere, unstable from the different temperatures and densities, warps the rays of light and along a vertical axis produces refractions that place the earth in the sky and the sky down on earth and enlarge, draw together, invert, duplicate, and distort everything. You were the one who believed in the enchanted city, you are the one who was saved."

Eyes (Mine, Peering Up from the Cellar)

I was fifteen years old. During the siesta hour I used to go down to the cellar, settle myself on a bench, and look up through the yawning skylight to the level of the walkway at the corner of 12th and 54th streets. The prize for my persistence came to me when a girl—Berta Arreola, for example—stepped up onto the streetcar. With eyes like little holes in the ground, I peered up and saw the marvel of those silky legs that, when raised to the step, revealed sudden glimpses of dark mysteries.

That afternoon the legs that were up against the bars of the skylight belonged to a man. At first I feared they would block my view in case a woman were to appear. Since none came, I entertained myself imagining what Sherlock Holmes would make of it if all he was able to observe were those black pants of English cloth, well pressed, pearl gray spats—the latest fashion in 1925—shiny new shoes, and an elegant cane with a tortoiseshell knob like the one Papa has. I didn't manage to reconstruct the complete personality of the man because I was distracted by a blind man who, from the sidewalk in front, was getting ready to step into the street. Acid or fire had eaten away his eyes, his nose, his mouth, and only one ear appeared to function since, with an inclination of the head, he advanced it in order to hear better. He was listening for danger but there was none. In that street in La Plata there was scarcely any traffic. At most, a boy on a bicycle. Automobiles? If one were to pass, it would be the event of the day. On the cobblestones, the horseshoes and the carriage wheels made such a clatter that not even from there did one have to fear an unexpected collison. As for the streetcar, every half hour it would announce its arrival from afar in resounding steel.

If the face of the blind man, ashen and scarred, was repugnant to me, his rags filled me with pity. The old man crossed the path, stepped on the rails, with his white cane felt for the mouth of the sewer—perhaps from there a rat was spying on him as I was—stepped up onto the curb, advanced to the wall of the house; I could no longer see his torso and, in the picture frame of the skylight, there remained only his tattered pants, alongside those well-pressed pants of the person who was already there, motionless. Leaning his back against the wall, the blind man must have brushed the other with his arm since I heard him excuse himself in a voice of misery, "Ah, forgive me. When one is blind . . ."

"It's nothing," responded the man in spats, roughly.

"A poor blind man . . . as you see me now, who was once healthy and hard-working. What changes life brings! Pardon me sir, but I'm dying of hunger . . . Couldn't you give me alms, for the love of God?"

The blind man had an Andalusian accent.

There was a pause. I thought that the man in spats must have been looking for change. He must have given it to him—probably it was not change but a bill—since the voice of misery now was singing out, "Thank you sir, thank you! May God repay you. If I didn't really need it, I wouldn't have bothered you, believe me. Thank you sir, thank you."

"That's all right."

Whether he needed to talk or wanted another favor, the blind man continued his quavering sighs and tremors. "It is very sad to live this way. Blind, alone, and unable to work."

Another pause.

"The afternoon is beautiful, isn't it, sir? Wouldn't you say it's beautiful? I only smell it. The odor of the sun."

I tried to picture in my mind the ruin of his face, but was able only to visualize black holes in melting wax. That blind man had retained not even the form of the hollows where his eyes were. Blind, absolutely blind. The truth is that there—some of us more, some of us less—we were all blind.

1) The blind man absolutely, totally did not see either the gentleman at his side, or me.

2) The gentleman saw the blind man but since he was unable to see me, he was relatively or partially blind.

3) I, from my hiding-place did not see the face of the gentleman, and as to the face of the blind man—if one could call that seared crust a 'face'—the impression that it had produced on me was so repellent that I erased it from my memory.

So sight was not a bridge between us. We lacked the face to face contact, that eye contact which makes one known while wishing to know another. One's glance is searching but also revealing. It gets information and it gives it. It discovers and informs. The sequential flow of years that each person has lived is reflected in the corresponding traces in each face. At a glance, it is possible to understand a physiognomy as a reader understands the synoptic page in a history text. That glance, as I have already said, is usually reciprocal. Individuals who look at each other mutually know with whom they are dealing. It is an immediate apprehension of individuality. But the blind man does not see the deep, permanent interior of the soul as it is fixed in one's appearance. On the contrary, in order to know his neighbors, he has to wait for them to speak and learn about them from what he hears them say, in words that slip by, slow, broken, deceiving and always insufficient.

The man, absolutely and totally blind, waited for the other to speak and listened to what he said.

"Was it long ago that you lost your sight?"

"Fifteen years, sir. At the time of the fire in the Blomberg Laboratories. I don't know if the gentleman remembers, but it was a famous fire . . ."

I was listening to that conversation in the same way that, I suppose, any blind man listens. As I was unable to see either their faces or their gestures, the meaning of their words reached me like the musical expression of a duet between an oboe and a bassoon. It seemed to me that the oboe of the blind man carried a tone of pride, as if the fame of the fire conferred a kind of distinction on him. I knew about that fire. Mama had told me that on the night I was born she saw through the window, up against the sky, the brilliant glow of the fire. So I was not surprised that the man in spats had heard of it.

"Yes, yes," he said. "I know. A gas explosion. The laboratories burned like paper. Twenty or more deaths. Some survived with horrible burns. Some were blinded . . ."

"The last thing I saw," the blind man interrupted, "was those men who were trampling each other and screaming and looking among the flames for an exit. There were very few doors or windows through which to escape. It was a frenzy of beasts. Some fell, others ran over them. I remember that one of the bosses, a so-called doctor in chemistry, was trying to escape through a skylight and already had his head out when a worker grabbed his legs. 'Let me go first!' the worker shouted, and with one pull he dragged him down from there, climbed up over his body, and kicked downward with his feet to heave himself on through. Nuts! It didn't do him any good because another explosion burned his face and he became one of those who were left blind from that cursed fire."

"He deserved it!" exclaimed the man in spats. "God punished

him. To use brute force at the expense of his neighbor's life was an infamy."

"Who knows. Maybe anyone in his place would have done the same."

"Not anyone, no. At least, not I."

"Certainly not you, sir. But that man must have been crazy from fear. Also he was a laborer, poorly paid, exploited by the bosses; and the other man was a boss."

"That has nothing to do with it. Workers, bosses: they are all men."

There was a silence; and after that another voice, the voice of the blind man:

"I don't want to argue with you, sir. You're right. There are no workers or bosses, only people. But if all men are equal, neither is any man worse than another. No one is always moral, no one is always immoral. In life everything is very mixed up, sir. And there are moments . . ."

"Nonsense! What that man did was an outrage, an unjustifiable barbarity."

"Yes, no argument. The gentleman is right to be indignant. It was a barbarity. And what remorse he must have suffered afterwards!"

The blind man scratched his calf with the tip of a shoe. Weren't they going to talk any more? Ah, yes. The voice of the blind man returned, now more than ever with an Andalusian slur, "Listen, sir. With a beggar, the more he has suffered, the more they offer him. You have given me a peso because I am blind. I'm going to tell you a secret so that you'll know that the blindness is not all my misfortune. To anyone else, not a word. To you, yes. Your indignation proves that you are a decent person and you'll understand the horror of my existence. I am a blind man, but a tormented blind man, sir. The story that I told you, I told in reverse. Now I'm going to straighten it out so that you'll have more pity for me. Scorn me if you wish, but have pity on me: I was that worker."

"I already knew that," the one with the spats said, in a hollow voice. "I was the boss and you are the one who pulled me down from the skylight and climbed up over me to save yourself."

I saw the legs of the blind man move away from the legs of the other; what a pity that I did not see from below how that sideways movement was translated up above in the burned face of the blind man!

"My God! You! I thought you had died! Look how things turn out . . . I don't know what to say to you . . ." Suddenly the voice of the oboe rose up angrily, "But . . . Damn!! I was blinded and you were saved. And all this time you, to show off your generosity, gave me a peso, let me talk and talk, laughing at me, enjoying yourself at seeing me blind . . ."

"That's the way things are. Suffer!" the bassoon answered in a voice that appeared to have opened wide in a smile of vengeance.

A shaking of iron on iron invaded the silence and was becoming more and more strident. The streetcar arrived and stopped in front of the house. The blind man remained up against my skylight and the other stepped out. Now, for the first time, I was able to see his whole body. He advanced toward the streetcar, holding out his cane: he too was blind.

The Gold Doubloon

A little girl nine years old, with her fist held out, comes running up from the beach. "Mommy! Daddy!"

ટે

Each island has a personality and each person is an island. The island and its islander.

ટે

The island breathes, sings, laughs, changes expression. No one could mistake it for another. It has a beach, curves like a woman's hip, palm trees that talk with the wind, a sea with peacock plumage and, in the hours of the ebbing tide, a grotto emerges, sculpted by the waves. It is a gold doubloon: a blind god who might run the tip of his finger across the coin would feel the raised form of an antique effigy; seen through the eyes of a man, those reliefs are hills and valleys. Twisting banisters of granite lead up to the house at the top of the green slope. Two hundred years ago, pirates burned the fortress. On its ruins, one hundred years ago, smugglers rebuilt it. And ten years ago, this islander remodeled it for his own home. Now, from his window he sees the little girl come running up from the beach.

"Mommy! Daddy!"

ટે

The islander is an old man, as isolated as his island. He has the mark of a sailor. His skin is like those stones that brighten when they are touched through the water by the sun. In his eyes, a constant sea-blue gleam; his hair, white and wavy foam; his mouth, busy with a pipe; and he looks indeed like the captain of the ship of his own bony and muscular body, with that pipe like a smoking chimney. He is nearing eighty years of age—for him there remains neither relative nor friend—but he holds himself as erect as a bottle of whiskey. He is rich. He has bought the house, has remodeled it, and lives there alone, at the edge of this world and of the world of the fairies. He knows that that border, although magical, mingles with a more vulgar reality. For a mystic, the mystery always stands waiting a few steps ahead of him. And suddenly, in the symphony of the morning light, he has marked the appearance of one of the fairies. She comes running up from the beach like a tiny planet, untouched by gravity. "Mommy! Daddy!"

The Old Man—an island within an island—leaves his window and starts to descend, content with the good result of his plan.

ঌ

The Old Man is an old professor who has retired from the university and from the universe. A reader of the Bible (a good North American!), he is cured by Ecclesiastes of his vanities. His past as a luminary in the sciences is for him an almost forgotten novel. More vivid are his memories of his childhood, of those Easters when he searched for the treasures which his grandfather, with a novelist's imagination, distributed in the hiding-places of the mansion. This year, with the presentiment that, on a day least expected, another player of games would hide him as well, like a thing, in a tomb, the Old Man let it be known, without much publicity, that he would rent out two rooms. The terms of the contract, very strict, contributed to his fame as an eccentric that he had already acquired along the coast. First, he would rent only to a married couple, students with a daughter. Second, the daughter had to be less than ten years old. Third, so that the summer dwellers would vary, they could never stay more than two months, and only once.

The first experiment was successful. He rented the two rooms to a married couple: he, a poet; she, a poetess; and the daughter, a poem. All that the Old Man desires is to have at his side a little girl who will save him from the depressing empty hours. He has the heart of a grandfather, always available, a heart softened by a second childhood. It is possible that the little girl's parents might be exhausted at the end of the day: so many cares, so many precautions, what if illness comes, what if there is an accident! The parents will tolerate even her mischief because, in spite of the bother, the little girl is enchanting. Old people like himself enjoy only the enchantment, without anxiety, without responsibility. If the child were to come crying, he would stay up above; let the parents take care of consoling her. But the little girl came up ecstatic, with her fist extended. "Mommy! Daddy!"

ॐ

The married students—he, the poet; she, the poetess—do not know that the Old Man is an old professor. They cannot see his books—many of which he wrote himself—because they are packed away in a secret attic; it was constructed during the time of the smugglers, and to enter it one would have to discover the door disguised as one of the wall panels. Also in the attic, the Old Man kept his private little museum. At least in the beginning. But during this year he changed his plan. It would be better, he said to himself, to get rid of the valuable collection. And remembering how his grandfather on the Easter treasure hunts of his childhood had scattered his collection over his land, placing precious stones under ordinary stones, nailing an ancient dagger into the entrails of a rotten tree, burying a verdigrised mask in a ditch, hiding amphoras among rocks, strange concha shells and coral in the grass, gold coins in the fingers of the sand . . .

ॐ

The girl comes calling, "Mommy! Daddy!" And she holds out her fist.
The parents approach. The Old Man too. The girl opens her fist: a gold doubloon.
"Mommy! Daddy! I found a treasure! I found a treasure!"
The Old Man pretends surprise. Behind his beard, he smiles.

Bats

Can I imagine the situation of a man who, feeling responsible for a woman's death, must prove in court that it is a case of suicide and not of homicide? Yes. And I'm going to tell you why I can imagine it.

When I visited Buenos Aires and was welcomed in Argentores, a lady approached me with a cocktail in her hand, speaking to me in English. It must have been evident to her that her name ("My name is Gloria Dahl") meant nothing to me, since she decided to offer me her credentials: she had been a television star, she had retired, and now was directing an experimental theater, she . . .

I lifted my glass as if I was going to drink to her health and interrupted her, "Pardon me for not having recognized your name but . . . you understand . . . one is often ignorant . . . in the United States it is difficult to hear about what is happening on Argentine television . . . pardon me . . ."

She forgave me magnanimously, we touched glasses, and toasted ourselves with generous swallows.

Her move from actress to director did not surprise me; what can an actress do who cannot get directors to cast her in the star role, except to assume the role of director herself and assign roles to younger stars? It is not that Gloria Dahl was old (for me, at least, she was not; she could scarcely have been over forty), but her heaviness was the kind that television tubes don't accept; even before going on the screen she looked inflated, as if in a distorting mirror. She must have been very conscious of her deterioration since she lamented quickly, "If you could only have seen me in my good days!" Of that former beauty only her eyes remained; as for her figure, imagination would have had to strain itself to conjure up a slender actress from those rolls of flesh. The most charitable thing that could be said of Gloria Dahl was that she had an airy plumpness, with the liveliness of a flying balloon. And in fact, a person of good will could have praised her for the grace with which she lifted her turned-up nose as if searching for the sky; the agility with which she walked on tiptoe as if waltzing; the delicacy with which she moved her little fingers as if playing a harp. She was ingenious—even in English she invented puns—and since she flattered me by telling me that my stories were stupendous, I stayed by her side. At one point she proposed to me that I should profit from my visit to Buenos Aires: together we should adapt one of my stories for the theater. The project interested me, as much for vanity as for any other reason.

For another hour I watched her drink cocktail after cocktail (was her puffiness that of an alcoholic?), and I too consumed my monthly quota. Now the party was ending. I prepared to say goodbye. In order that we might continue our conversation some other day, I gave Gloria the card from the hotel where I was staying, with my room number. She glanced at it and exclaimed, "But we're neighbors. The apartment building where I live is right next to your hotel."

So I offered to take her along with me in my taxi. She accepted. And when the car turned sharply, Gloria overflowed onto me. "Oh, I am crushing you under my weight," she said, trying to straighten up.

Traveling in a taxi with a woman, any woman, a man tends toward gallantry, so I answered, with a tongue already thick, "To die, crushed like this, would be a pleasure."

"Ha, ha! Are you serious?"

"She can't believe that," I thought; and in one of those leaps of imagination, perhaps due to the heat which made me curse the formal clothes I was wearing and want to undress and take a shower as soon as possible, I imagined how happy clothed statues would be if they could walk around nude through the streets that summer in Buenos Aires. From the images of beautiful goddesses and courtesans I came, I don't know how, to Gloria Dahl, and said to her (thinking "She cannot believe this"), "In the history of painting there are very few thin ladies, isn't that so? There must be some reason for it. The most impressive are the plump Rubens ladies."

Suddenly my memory brought up the picture of a harem, not with the nudes separated, but grouped in a single nude mass, round and rosy; and maliciously I added, "I know in what exact spot you are painted in *The Turkish Bath* by Ingres."

The poor thing squeezed my hand gratefully.

No need to say it: that body said nothing to mine.

We got out at the corner. Before we said goodbye, she lifted her head, looked up to the top of the skyscraper, and said, "I live up there; up at the top, you see? the top floor. Do you see that large window?"

So I counted the floors of my hotel, made a mental picture of the distribution of rooms and hallways, calculated which would be my window and showed it to her. Her window and my window were opposite each other.

"Good," she said, "we'll arrive there at about the same time. As soon as we arrive each of us should turn the light on and off a few times. What do you think? That will be our way to say good night."

I laughed. I could have said, "Listen. I, fiftyish, and you, fortyish, we're too old for those games." But I didn't. I obeyed (I should call myself Peter the Pushover) and, like fireflies, we flashed each other luminous signals, and went to bed. I, at least, fell asleep immediately, since although I hadn't drunk as much as Gloria, I had drunk more than I'm accustomed to.

The telephone wakened me. I turned on the light; three o'clock in the morning!

"Hi!"

And I heard the voice of Gloria Dahl, "Go to the window and look over here."

She was sending me firefly messages. I hid my ill humor and when she told me to come up to her room, at once, right away, immediately, that very instant, I tried to protest: it was late, this was not the right time, it would be better to arrange a meeting for another time, perhaps we could dine together on Thursday . . .

No good. No, sir. She advised me that from the moment when we parted she had been working on the dramatization of my story, she needed my opinion and if we didn't strike while the iron was hot, then all right, the project would go no further. That this was the way she was: impulsive . . .

She gave me instructions. The street door would be closed. I should push button 20-A at the phonoelectric calling-board. She, from above, would ask who it was and, after a buzzing signal which sounded like a cricket, the lock on the door would open.

"Thank you," I said, "for the lesson in Argentine technology."

With ill will, but hiding it, I—Peter the Pushover!—dressed and went out.

I just said: "went out," but my sensation was not of going out. Between my room and Gloria's the space was all interior, as in a nightmare or in a prison. Because of my slight familiarity with the streets of Buenos Aires, the strangeness of the call, my sleepiness, my hangover, the night, and my neurosis or whatever it was, I didn't feel that I had left the hotel, walked around in the city, and found the apartment building, but that I was groping through an architectural fantasy drawn by the Piranesi of the *Carceri d'Invenzione*. Floors, houses, hallways, stairs, avenues, balconies, columns, patios, arches, walls, interpenetrating each other and weaving an imaginary city, soft as smoke, hard as crystal. I was about to push the bronze button of the electric door in an enormous entrance with black iron bars, when I saw a human doorman approaching from the rear of the lobby. Through the wrought iron, he studied me carefully and, when he realized that I was a foreigner, courteously but firmly submitted me to a kind of examination. It was past three in the morning, who was I, whom did I wish to see, was I expected . . . I don't know the customs in Buenos Aires, so I accepted an interrogation that, in New York, would have been impertinent. Finally he said, "Just push the button"; I pushed it, Gloria answered, and only then did the doorman open the door. He wished me good night once again, and I went up.

The only light was the far-off light of the elevator. The door of 20-A was ajar. A voice came from the darkness, "Does it bother you that I'm not turning on the light? I want to show you something."

A hand led me to the window, open to the thick night.

"Those are my bats," Gloria said.

I heard them before I saw them. I heard little squeaks and the noise of rags flapping in the wind. Then I saw. My eyes were open but what I saw seemed to be not outside of me, but inside, underneath my eyelids. They were like the dark moving spots that, when we are sleeping, make us dream. They were umbrellas in a storm, shadows of madness, mourning drapes, wing-beats of death. They were whirling rapidly, rapidly, so rapidly that, in order for me to catch with a glance even one of those black slashes that I knew to be flying rats, my eyes moved horizontally, followed a slash, turned back, followed another slash and never managed to quite make out its form.

Gloria draped her arm over my shoulder (I shuddered) and when out of courtesy I replied by grasping her waist, I realized that she had undressed and was wearing only a robe. My hand slipped along the silk and, although the silk was less disagreeable to the touch than the flesh over which the silk was sliding, I had the impression that I was touching the wing of a bat. Luckily I did not have to remove my hand, since she left me and went to get some drinks. She returned and we started to drink in the darkness, continuously glancing out through the window at the night and the bats. Suddenly she screwed a kiss on me, and, pulling me by the hands, led me to the bed where she collapsed, more drunk than erotic.

I—Peter the Pushover—undressed and, when I went to get into bed, I observed that Gloria, in spite of the heat, had covered herself with the sheet. I too had to get under the sheet and I embraced her with the hope that I might feel some desire.

"Don't handle me," she said, and started to cry.

Between hiccoughs and sobs she told me about her life. She had gone to study dramatic art in the United States on a scholarship. She fell in love with a fellow student who went off to the Korean War. There he was decorated with a medal on his chest, a bloody metal. So she stayed behind without a man but with a child in her belly. The child was born dead. (I suspect that Gloria aborted him.) Because of her nerves, she started sucking into her mouth, like a newborn child, all the comestibles in the world. So much ballast was needed to weigh down her anxiety, that she became fat. In addition, she started drinking like a madwoman. A failure in everything—even in two attempts at suicide—she returned to Argentina, now only a shade of what she had been.

"One of these nights I am going to throw myself out the window . . ."

While she continued with her drunken sobbing, I very slowly got into my clothes. When she noticed, she screamed at me, indignant, "What are you doing? Are you going to leave like that? What do you think I am, a tramp? Come on. Get into bed."

I protested as well as I could. Truthfully, it was grotesque. What was worse, I, who was at least dizzy if not drunk did not feel lucid like a writer who is thrown by chance into a sordid adventure and knows how to profit from the circumstances in order to write a story, but felt rather like a character in a story written by another writer, much less compassionate, who was making me look ridiculous. That writer was having fun making me take off my clothes again. All right. I had to end it once and for all and get out of there. I wanted to open her robe and caress myself with her breasts. In the darkness it was the only way I could get myself in a condition to possess her. She wouldn't let me. What kind of a monster was she? Lower down she opened her legs, but higher up she covered herself with the sheet and with her robe, and so that I couldn't see her, she took my head and held my mouth down on hers. I was sweating, but her sweat was melted fat. I lost whatever small desire I had pulled together. I got up, this time without pretense, and once again put on my clothes. I suppose that from the bed she must have followed my movements with the night vision of a vampire since when I arrived at the door, I heard her scream at me, "If you go, I swear to you, I'll throw myself out of that window!"

"Goodbye," I answered.

The last thing I saw was that she ran to the window and crouched, sketching the position for a leap into a night in which all the stars had shaken loose and been changed into bats.

I closed the door, took the elevator, went down the twenty floors in a state of confusion. Everything seemed absurd, unreal. They had trapped me in a bad story written by a bad writer. Gloria, doubtless, down there, spread out all over the pavement. What could I do? Just ignore that mass of flesh and blood? What a scandal! The doorman would accuse me. He would say that I killed her and fled. The police. The embassy. The press. My family . . . My head was sick from a poison worse than alcohol. I was observing things, but barely, without distinguishing between what I was perceiving and what I was imagining. Once in the lobby, I could make out the dawn at a distance through the bars of the large door and I almost tiptoed along, more ghost than man. I was horrified at myself, and my horror consisted of wanting to rid myself of what I imagined that I was inevitably going to see. I was unreal. Or I existed, yes, but altered by the assault from all sides of unnerving thoughts. I had disintegrated, my consciousness broken into bits and pieces. Each piece of my consciousness entertained something different; one piece perceiving, another imagining, another fearing. And I saw what one piece of myself feared. I was hallucinating without closing my eyes or looking away, and when I looked through the bars of the door into the dim dark of the street, through the dim darkness of my mind, I saw Gloria splattered out on the pavement. In the highest apartment of the building, Gloria remained still crowned with bats. Now all the bats were a single bat, and the dim early light was the membrane of a vast wing. That single bat was holding between its claws the cloth of the dawn, unfolded like a cape in a gothic novel; Gloria, spattered over the asphalt, was just that, a scene from a gothic novel, and it was also the hollow formed from her absent body. My imagination had externalized her image, and the image, in the circular flight of a boomerang, had returned to enter into my eyes. I breathed again, in relief.

The Eyes of the Dragon

At the end of the course of study in the School of Philosophy and Letters no one could avoid taking "Methodology." One of the requirements of the program was to substitute for a professor and for two weeks to teach as much as you could to students at the secondary level. It fell to me to teach in a good quality high school, and an older colleague warned me that the students there were trained to be aggressive.

So I went to my first class with my nerves on edge. My body was a complete collection of symptoms of fear: a knot in the throat, heart palpitations, a heavy weight in the pit of the stomach, cold sweat, fever, nausea, diarrhea.

In the professors' lounge was an old man, alone, with white hair, slouched against the window. We greeted each other in silence with a slight nod of the head; he continued reading a newspaper, and I, standing, began reviewing my notes.

Suddenly I realized that although I thought I was being quiet, while reading I had been circling around on the carpet and probably reciting out loud the sentences with which I would start my teaching career. Could I have been bothering the elderly gentleman? I looked at him out of the corner of my eye. The newspaper was now completely covering his face.

Ten minutes to eleven. It was still early. Perhaps it would be prudent to go in a few minutes ahead of time and take a look at the empty room; even the most experienced of actors doesn't perform without first familiarizing himself with the stage, right? On the other hand—and I drew back a step—it was not prudent to mix into the life of the school. After all, the students were scarcely younger than I. If they saw me wandering along the halls, idle, indecisive, perhaps they'd think I was one of them and wouldn't treat me with respect. I pictured the humiliation: a big fellow in the fifth year takes me by the arm, real friendly, and waving two fingers in front of my face to ask for a cigarette, shouts at me in a familiar way, enough to destroy the reputation of the most pedantic professor. "You know what's happening, buddy? You know that today we have a substitute teacher, very green, very green. If you want to have a little fun, sit in the last row."

I gathered my strength and tried not to worry. Embarrassment in your first class is natural. Don't they say that even the great Kant was so nervous that he was almost unable to speak? But let's not imagine embarrassing scenes with students who don't recognize you as a professor . . . Moreover, I thought, that must have already occurred many times in the history of education and, for that reason, was less likely to be repeated. And if it happened again, what's wrong with that? It would just be a joke! So let's get on with it! I resolved to leave the teachers' lounge. I opened the door and saw, along the corridor, as if through an artery, the hot, red life of youth circulating, and I was afraid of being young. I drew back, again shut myself up in the teachers' lounge, leaned against the door, and felt my heart beating as if I had just saved myself by a hair from a mortal danger. When I looked up, I saw that, over the unfolded newspaper, the eyes of the elderly man were observing me. He lowered the newspaper and I saw that he was not laughing at me; his mouth, softened by the whiteness of his mustache and beard, started to move and then I noticed that he was saying something to me, "Once upon a time . . ."

What! Was the old man going to tell me a story? What did I need with a fairy tale?

"Once upon a time there was a Chinese painter who, very slowly, was painting a vast mural. One day, one line; a few days later, another, and another, and another . . . People were asking: what is he painting? a thing? various things? Until he painted some eyes. Then they saw that what he had been painting was a dragon; and the marvelous dragon, now completed, took off from the wall and flew up to his heaven."

There was a silence.

"Did you like it?" he asked me.

"Yes, the little story of the dragon who flew away. Very poetic." And I looked at my watch: five minutes were left before class.

"That dragon flew away, but look out for the other one, the dragon who, once formed, throws himself on you and eats you up."

I understood that the little old man, not content with having invented a story, now wanted to convert it into a parable. That is how pedagogues ruin stories: instead of leaving them alone they box them into a real situation and cancel them out with a moral.

"You're going to give your first class. You have no experience. You're young. You're vulnerable. As soon as you enter the classroom the students, like the Chinese painter, will start to paint a dragon. One student is going to ask you a question that no one can answer, another is going to argue about his opinion; there is another who is always loudly dropping all his books and papers on the floor, and another who is taken by a violent fit of coughing or by a sudden desire to confess something, or to make a pun that turns out to be offensive. And there will always be the one who throws chalk at the blackboard . . . To sum it up: watch out. If you don't stop those provocations with cleverness, good humor, and firmness, each one of them will paint in another stroke of the dragon. Any unanswered defiance will take the form of a claw, a tail, a wing, a snout . . . Until suddenly someone will flaunt his disrespect with a couple of jokes: those are the eyes of the dragon. Now the dragon is complete. Nothing in the world will be able to save you now, my friend."

I entered the classroom; from the height of the platform I considered the monster that would create a monster, and before a hair of him could be drawn—so that no such hair could ever be drawn—with the air of a professor who had already been through the fire, I began my lecture:

"Once upon a time, a Chinese painter . . ."

William Faulkner Saw a Ghost, and Then . . .

Leopoldo Morey was an Argentinian from Patagonia. It would be hard to find someone who was more of a Southerner. He wandered northward and got his doctorate in economic science at the University of Buenos Aires. He continued climbing the parallels—Lima, Bogotá, Mexico—and now, in North America, he was invited to give a series of lectures at the southern University of Mississippi. That's the way it goes: after so much traveling, in the South again. His colleagues in Mississippi, impressed by his scientific contributions—notable above all because, according to *Who's Who*, this learned man was not yet thirty-five years old—had invited him with the secret intention of offering him a permanent post in the department of economics. All that remained was to meet him and sound him out. They took for granted that he would be a serious professional. That's what is expected of an economist. They could not have foreseen, since they had invited him sight unseen, that the economist would turn out to be an eccentric, enchanted with literature and disenchanted with science: imaginative, waggish, impulsive. Because of his tendency to act scandalously even in the most sophisticated social gatherings, one might say of him what Oscar Wilde said of the scandalous Frank Harris, "He has been received in all the great houses—once." The same with Morey; he was received at the great University of Mississippi . . . once. The story that follows explains why.

His lectures turned out spectacularly for him. His audience applauded, highly satisfied. Every classroom is a theater and the actor, Morey, had played his professor's role with solemnity. Once the short course was ended, he had to stay in Oxford two days more because his plane was leaving on a Saturday; and since by chance the university was going to celebrate he knew not what special event, he was invited to a banquet. With nothing else to do, he spent Friday taking a walk.

Morey knew the region only through the novels of William Faulkner. After getting information from brochures, it was easy for him to imagine that if Faulkner himself, who died in 1962, were to accompany him on this walk in 1972, he would not have recognized the area, so many were the changes. Since he wrote his trilogy of the Snopes family in fabulous Yoknapatawpha—*The Hamlet, The Town, The Mansion*—the population had doubled, the schools had grown, stores and factories had invaded the streets, elegant brick houses had replaced the sordid wooden huts. The cotton fields now were pastures and the negroes would no longer rent themselves out cheaply to milk a cow or gather eggs in a henhouse. In former times the farmers would arrive in Oxford in mule-wagons; now, in cars and buses. Formerly, hunters pursued raccoons and opossums by night in a neighboring wood, and foxes by day in the green undulations of the field; festivals—with a musical background of yelping dogs—that now were ended. Those who still were interested in hunting, crowded into an automobile and had to restrain the impatience of their shotguns during a long ride.

Yes, many changes. And Morey himself was changing. One after another, he was losing his masks (the first to fall was that of the professor) and he was losing even his sense of being real.

"What am I doing here?" he asked himself.

Men and women from that geographical area had been transposed by Faulkner into his fiction; in life half-dead beneath the crosses of the church, and now wholly dead beneath the crosses of the cemetery, they still survived as shades in Faulkner's inferno, with names like Compson, Coldfield, Sartoris, Stevens, and Snopes. But Morey?

What was Morey doing there? Morey, a foreigner, did not belong in Mississippi. Mississippi entered into the world of the novel, but he was not a fictional character. Nevertheless, what he had in front of him was not a horizon open to the future, but a past enclosed in books. He was not a free man; he was a trapped animal: the reader. And he was walking with the strange sensation that seeing is reading. The substance of the buildings, the natural landscapes, were to him less perceptions than images evoked in the writings of Faulkner that he had read. The earth and all that inhabit it are not words, but once observed by a writer of genius are installed in the language and from that point on are purely verbal and exist as words encoded in letters. Faulkner had presented a society in ruins: old southern families dissolving in an ambience of brutality and violence. Morey, on the border between reality and fiction, at times stumbled into physical objects that were not in Faulkner's fiction; at other times, confused, he stopped seeing them, and merely noted their absence. Threads of time from various skeins, as in the labyrinthine prose of Faulkner, enmeshed him in the labyrinths of memory. Men of flesh and bone faded away into eternity, and spectres were embodied in stories. It was like drunkenness. He needed no other. But unfortunately he chose another, and because of that, the university never invited him back. What happened?

Morey followed unmapped paths, the kind that lose themselves at the edge of the world and lead nowhere. Suddenly, in a cluster of trees, he made out a broken-down store, solitary and dirty. He was feeling so dazed that for a moment he doubted his own eyes. "What if this is a mirage," he said, "and in a few more steps I discover that the earth has ended and I step off into nothingness?"

Nevertheless, the afternoon sun was real, his thirst was real, and he entered the store to get a drink. It was deserted. After much calling, an old man with a white beard stepped out from between two bushes, limping; he approached, wearing a green hat pulled down to his eyebrows, scraped the mud off one shoe and, in calm silence, inquired with his expression what was wanted. When he learned that Morey was Argentinian and had come very far to see the place where Faulkner had drunk and written, he went to the back of the store and returned with bottles of whiskey and Coca-Cola. They sat down and the ceremony began, a rite more complicated than a creole tea: two swallows of whiskey followed by one swallow of Coca-Cola, and the bottles coming and going between the Mississippian and the Patagonian.

The old man—Mr. Daniels—stuck out his chin as if defying anyone to pull his beard, and said, "Ah, I knew him well. I never read his books. What do you expect? I am not a man for reading." He let out a laugh. "I'm a bottle man! Don't tell anyone, but when I was young I smuggled moonshine. Faulkner was one of my clients. That is, before Mississippi legalized the sale. Faulkner? He always seemed to me half crazy."

He shook his head, laughing so that the Argentinian would know that he was speaking in jest; but just in case, he added, "I'm saying this as a friend. He was always absentminded. You could walk up to him until you almost touched his face and he wouldn't pay you the slightest attention. He was quiet and shy, hiding himself behind a wooden face. In Oxford, have you seen Mr. Hall's smithy at the foot of the hill, a block from the courthouse? Ask Mr. Hall. He used to shoe Faulkner's horses. He was a good rider, believe me, but in his last years he began to lose his balance. He was always falling off. They say that his falls from the horse were the first symptom of his illness. I thought he fell off only because he was absentminded. He was a good man, but strange. He'd come dressed sloppily, unshaven, his hair uncombed, his hands filthy—the hands of a farmer, not of a writer—and with his eyes half-hidden under the dirt on his glasses. At times he'd sit down here on the very spot where you are, and I'd talk with him just as I'm talking with you. Suddenly he just disappeared. Can you imagine? He was gone in the blink of an eye, without saying a word. He never said hello to anyone. He went around like a ghost. I don't know, but it seems to me that he believed in ghosts. He liked to tell children stories about hauntings, on Halloween nights, around a bonfire. He told me one of them, and you can kill me but I am sure that he believed it. You want me to tell it to you? All right, I'll tell it to you."

And he told it to me.

With all that, after so much mixing of whiskey and Coca-Cola, Morey was over the edge. He left for the banquet with a drunkenness which increased, and along the way he took the time to visit Rowan Oak, the two-story mansion at the edge of town that Faulkner had bought in 1930. After the story of hauntings that he had heard from Mr. Daniels, he couldn't go to Oxford without seeing the mansion first.

It was an ancient building constructed in 1848. It rose at the end of an avenue of cedars, surrounded by stables (he saw a blind bay horse), gardens (he saw a rosebush eaten by ants), and orchards (he saw a broken pear tree struggling against death). The university preserved the house exactly as he had left it: here was his typewriter, ready; and his pipe beside it; and, carved in mahogany, a Don Quixote. But what interested Morey, because of Mr. Daniels' ghost story,

was a balcony and a magnolia tree, both ghost-like. Tall columns
rose up into the air, white, white, white, and the balcony, with the
teeth of the balustrade, smiled at the tree, twinkling with flowers,
that stood in front of it. It smiled, and its smile was macabre. Morey
understood the mute hostility between the balcony and the magnolia; without hesitation he drew away from the balcony and approached the magnolia. It was the hour of dusk and a brisk wind was
blowing over the red forge of the sunset. Some alchemist was trying
to manufacture gold, and for a few minutes he succeeded, but suddenly the gold broke down into silver and the silver into lead until
by chance the laboratory of the night again produced gold, this time
in the form of the moon. Under its light the tree grew larger. By
stretching out its limbs and twigs, it would have been able to touch
all the points in space; at least its flowers were pointing exactly to
the openings where the first stars were peeping through. Meanwhile
the magnolias took the place of stars in the sky, low down. Rather,
in a chamber of mirrors, Morey corrected himself—since all the
magnolias were mere reflections of a single magnolia which, filled
with wind, turned its neck like a woman's head and murmured un-
intelligible words. Then he remembered the ghost story that Faulkner had told to Mr. Daniels, Mr. Daniels to him, and that he now felt
the need to tell to another; and he imagined that the tree was a
votive lamp, lit for some dead woman in a secret cemetery. With a
magnolia flower in each hand he continued stumbling toward the
university. Finally he found the dining hall. And, to make matters
worse, he was late.

They had decorated the immense hall with flags that were unknown to Morey. Four lines of tables formed the M of Mississippi. A
fifth table, set apart, served as the head table. Glass, china, and
metal shone on the tablecloths. Bunches of flowers overflowed the
vases. The ladies' party gowns radiated color. The gentlemen in dark
suits remained silent and circumspect. Morey, seated in the place assigned to him, placed on each side of his plate one of the magnolias
that he had brought with him. He ate with discretion and drank
with abandon. Suddenly the Master of Ceremonies arose and started
his speech. Morey did not know what he said because instead of listening to him he began to watch the grimace his mouth made in tilt-
ing up to the right cheek and down to the left, duplicating the two
theatrical masks: Comedy and Tragedy. Morey jumped when the
Master of Ceremonies, nailing him with his eyes, zap! with a toast
turned the banquet over to him.

He was the guest of honor and he didn't know it!

"Well . . . they could have told me," he grunted.

With applause they urged him to speak. He got up with difficulty.

"This time," he stuttered in an English that would have left Benjy, the idiot of *The Sound and the Fury*, open-mouthed, "this time famous southern courtesy has played you a bad joke. You have made a mistake. You believe that you are honoring an important person. Who? Me? It can't be me. I don't exist. In any case I would be the ghost of that person."

Scarcely had he pronounced the word "ghost" than a cold shiver ran along the tables and twenty-nine faces were left frozen. The eyes formed part of those blocks of ice, but were threatening to pop out.

"It would be better to say thank you and sit down," he thought.

He couldn't remain silent; as in nightmares he felt free of inhibitions and at the same time compelled to utter the words that were thronging in his mouth.

"I have just left an old store where I was chatting with an old friend of William Faulkner. That storekeeper told me something that he had heard from Faulkner. Something that occurred in the mansion that many, I mean many years later, Faulkner himself would occupy, and which today is a sanctuary maintained by this distinguished (hic!) university. During the Civil War a beautiful young lady from the Confederacy fell in love with an officer from the enemy Union. This could not be. The family was opposed and she threw herself head first over the balcony. They buried her close to where she landed, at the foot of the magnolia tree. Faulkner told the storekeeper that he had seen with his own eyes the suicide's stricken soul, in torment as she rose up out of her tomb and circled around the tree. Well then, ladies and gentlemen (hic!), I have just gone through William Faulkner's mansion. And I tell you that I, too, saw the ghost of the beautiful Southern belle. First there was a trembling in the air; then, shimmering silk, and a blur, and a form, and a spirit becoming flesh; and finally a nude girl—because garments do not become ghostly as people do, right?—and her breasts were two more magnolias, beneath the tree made bright by the moon. She guessed my wish, plucked two more and gave them to me. Don't say that I am lying: I brought them with me from the other world, and here they are . . ."

Morey lifted the magnolias from the table and held them to his chest. "It was love at first sight. She didn't say a word to me. Why should she? Her expression spoke for her. She looked at me, she smiled. Pale, beautiful; the difference in age—she was more than a century older—was not visible. And we knew we were betrothed. She, a ghost; and I, also a ghost; the ghost of an economist whom you believe you are honoring. In all sincerity, I want to tell you, here and now, that she and I will go off together, at midnight. I hope that it doesn't disturb you that a foreign ghost is kidnapping your local ghost. Comfort yourselves by thinking that I'm a southerner too. What irony! I, a South American, am more a southerner than you (hic!)."

And he fell back onto his chair.

No applause, not a word, not a sigh.

Head down, eyes closed, he just managed to think, "They must be studying the intruder: is he a clown, is he crazy?"

With his eyes closed, he was caught up by a violent nausea. It flipped him over, lifted him up, dropped him down into a dark sea. He opened his eyes in order to fix his gaze on something unmoving. There was nothing that did not move. And the fifty-eight persons (now he was seeing them double) were disintegrating. Their faces were falling apart like masks. One would drop and another would immediately reappear below it, and in turn would fall and be re-placed, in a cascade of face-masks.

William Faulkner had always looked down on his teachers in Mis-sissippi. With the same contempt, Morey again stood up and with his thick tongue shouted at them: "I know, I know why you're not applauding me. You want to punish me because I'm an impostor. Yes. I am an impostor. So what? You're impostors too. In this meet-ing you're pretending to be professors. Professors? Ha! You're not professors. You are the real, the only ghosts in this room. You amuse yourselves once each year conjuring up a real man to speak to you of the world of men. You have conjured up a poor guy, an economist. And what enrages you is that that real man wanted to pass for one of you . . ."

And his nausea spewed out in vomit.

That is why we received him—once.

Nalé Roxlo and the Suicide of Judas

In July of 1964 Conrado Nalé Roxlo told me the plot of a play he had never had the courage to write. "I wouldn't want to offend a friend of mine who is very religious." The last time I was with him in 1969, he had not yet written it. A few days ago—in July of 1971—I received news of his death. I do not know if he had left among his papers so much as a sketch of that plot. In case he did not, I will attempt to tell it just as I remember it.

Bethlehem. Shepherds and shepherdesses have gathered together to celebrate the birth of Jesus. Dances, carols. Suddenly a shepherd sees a serpent fleeing like a black bolt of lightning. They run to pursue it with sticks and stones but a dreadful scream from the house leaves them astonished. The diabolical serpent had bitten the newborn babe, and Mary had just discovered him, dead. Now Joseph is the only one who knows about this, since Mary has become crazed with grief and is embracing the corpse as if her son were alive. When the kings of the Magi arrive to worship the awaited redeemer of mankind, Joseph tells them of the tragedy. The Magi kings search for a child to replace him. They find a beggar woman who bore a child at the same time as Mary and they make a deal with her: the beggar woman will give the crazed Mary her child and will take away the body of the Child of God to bury it somewhere in the vicinity; in exchange she is promised that her own child, brought up by Mary and Joseph, will become the king of the Jews. The beggar woman accepts. The years pass. Jesus grows up in Nazareth, humble, sweet, and full of charity. Now he is thirty years of age and is preparing to proclaim the good news. He goes into the desert, rejects the temptation of power, travels many times between Galilee and Judea followed always by twelve loyal disciples: one of them, Judas. Convinced that he is the Messiah announced by the prophets, Jesus turns the world upside down. What the Pharisees judge to be good is evil, what they judge to be evil is good. He is now the incarnate word of the kingdom of God and those who accept him will bring heaven to earth. The suspicious authorities—Jews, Romans—conspire to kill him. One day, in Jerusalem, the old beggar woman meets him, ties the threads together and, with a heart in agony, understands that this Jesus, suffering and in danger, is her own son. They had promised her that he would be more powerful than a king, and she sees him a beggar like herself. A mob of fishermen, farmers, prostitutes, unstable, possessed, simple-minded, foolish, and seditious people surround him and praise him, but the decent people scorn him. The Magi, then, have not done what they promised. So she approaches Jesus and tells him the secret of the exchange of the dead child for the living one. "You are not a supernatural son of God but the natural child of my whorish womb; it is not your mission to sacrifice yourself for mankind; save yourself because for you there will be no resurrection."

Jesus feels relieved of the weight of his divinity. That night he dines with his friends and, for the first time, enjoys himself as a man, with wine, with women. Then, after the others have left,

Judas, who is the intellectual of the group, reproaches him for his frivolity. So Jesus has learned that he is not the Messiah? No matter. The true Messiah will come another time. Or he won't come. Meanwhile, Jesus, an exceptional man, must give a new meaning to his life, a human meaning, yes, and a noble one. Now that he is no longer a messenger from the celestial Kingdom of God, let him be an agent of progress in the terrestrial kingdom of men of goodwill. In the course of the discussion, Jesus is overtaken by a crisis of conscience. He feels that he is usurping someone else's role, but if he refuses to be an impostor, he will be a nobody. He exists as an impostor or he does not exist at all. He is not the Son of God, but the men of the world believe that he is. They need him, their salvation depends on him. Thus he decides, piously, to lie. He will continue to preach as if blessed with authority; he will seek his own death, of which the prophets speak, as if mankind will be redeemed by his death. But that is not what Judas had counseled him. Now Judas reproaches him for his sin against truth, a sin more deadly than the sins of that night of wine and women. He denounces him before the priests and the gentiles. When they arrest Jesus and crucify him, Judas commits suicide because he understands his error: the love of Jesus for mankind that made him turn himself into a mere imposter is in itself a divine quality.

A Famous Conversion in the XIVth Century

Giannotto di Civigni, a Paris businessman, proposed to save the soul of his very rich friend Abraham and, for that purpose, begged him to abjure his error (Judaism) and embrace the truth (Christianity).

"Judaism is the error? Christianity is the truth? I don't see why," Abraham replied.

"It is evident," Giannotto explained, "that the church is prospering while the synagogue decays."

One hundred and one times Abraham refused to deny his religion, but since Giannotto kept on insisting, in the end he said, "You are very desirous that I become a Christian, and I would like to please you except that first I would like to go to Rome to know the person you call the Vicar of God on Earth, to assure myself that his habits— and those of his cardinals—are better than those of the Jews."

When he heard this, Giannotto, who had been in Rome, became alarmed. Ah, his efforts to convert the Jew were lost; if he went to the Court of the Pope and saw the evil and the sordidness of the clergy, what would happen? Not only would the Jew not become a

Christian, but on the contrary, if he were already a Christian, in all likelihood he would become a Jew.

"Don't go to Rome. Why run the risk of such a journey? If you doubt my word, you can consult those who know more than I, the theologians of Paris . . . You don't need to go to Rome."

The cautious and subtle Abraham did not give in, and left for Rome. When he returned he informed Giannotto:

"God is kinder to these Christians than they deserve. In the Roman clergy I saw neither sanctity nor devotion, only lust, avarice, gluttony, untruthfulness, pride, and even worse things. I believe that the devil is using the Pope and his cardinals and prelates in order to destroy the Christian religion. But since this is not happening, and at every moment the church is becoming more widespread and conspicuous, I have to admit that the Holy Spirit is protecting it. I have resolved, therefore, to become a Christian."

The maiden Neifile thus ended her story (it is the second story in the first volume of the *Decameron* of Boccaccio). She omitted—voluntarily?—Giannotto's reaction to the attitude of Abraham. After the celebration which followed the baptism of Abraham in Notre Dame de Paris, Giannotto summed it up:

"The Jew Abraham becomes a Christian, not because Christianity is better than Judaism, but rather because for him, the God who is sustaining the Church continues being the God of the Jews. It could have occurred only to Yahveh (Abraham must have been thinking) to protect a corrupt church and permit its expansion. Yahveh would have good reasons. Perhaps Abraham has guessed them and is entering the church in order to make it worse."

Anchored in Brazil

From the bridge the man with blue eyes measured the round horizon of the sea: a disk depressed in the middle by the weight of the ship.

The *Cuba Liberty*, a freighter built in 1944 for wartime convoy duty, was in 1947 already an iron wreck, all of it dirty. The sailors—they had become sailors only to avoid military service—worked as little as possible. They moved in the air with the slowness of divers in the water. The heads shouted and laughed without rousing the arms and legs from their lethargy. An undisciplined crowd without fear of their captain, mean and drunken, paralyzed on his bridge. They had just sailed from Buenos Aires, bound for New Orleans, and were sailing through a burning January.

The man with blue eyes, exhausted from the heat, tired and sleepy, at midnight went down to his bunk. In spite of the vibration of the machinery and the swinging of the ship, he managed to go to sleep, naked in a sea of sweat. He dreamed of waves, waves, waves. On the following day he looked out the porthole and saw the Brazilian city of Santos, spread out along the coast. He went up on deck. The *Cuba Liberty*, crowned with gulls, was passing along a line of fifty motionless ships. Flags of many nations colored the morning. There was no room at the dock and they had to drop anchor far from the port. The coffee would be loaded when the other North American ship left. If, in his bunk, the man with blue eyes had been a piece of meat in the oven, on deck he was a piece of meat on the grill. He went back and forth searching for a shady spot, but scarcely had he found it than he lost it again since the ship swung around its anchor and the rays of the sun struck from all sides. At dusk a launch took the crew ashore. Although recently bathed, they were still streaming sweat: as if the moon had started to do the work of the sun! An avenue of towering palms promised other secret beauties, but at first sight Santos was ugly and poor; even the hilltop "el Cerro"—its best feature—had been spoiled by the casino with which they had covered it like a hat. The man with blue eyes continued along the streets where crews from all of the ships mixed together. He was looking with curiosity into an ugly little shop when he heard behind him, "Hey, Johnny . . ."

He pretended not to hear.

"Hey, lanky," he heard then, "what ship do you come from?"

He turned his eyes—the same color as his white pants and blue shirt—and, with a forced smile, answered the little wiseguy, "From *Cuba Liberty*, and you?"

"Ah, you're from Argentina, or Uruguay?"

"Argentina."

"Let's shake. I'm from the *Paraná*. Over there is a bunch of I don't know how many Argentinians. The guys are waiting for me. Do you want to come? We'll have some fun, buddy. So . . ."

The fun started in a bar and ended in a whorehouse. With all the whores, perhaps choosing the best parts of each, one might be able to form a lovely lady. A drunk opened the blouse of a negress and showed a marvel of two very firm breasts, but the face, with the wide nostrils and missing teeth, was that of a monkey. Mulatto eyes—green as olives, serene, limpid, beautiful, and soft—had a charming sleepy look, but the woman's body was that of a hippopotamus. If only it were possible to match these lips with that nose, these thighs with that hair, this bust with that waist, this smile with that gaze! The men and women drank, danced, and at times a pair, now without music, strayed away to the side where the little bedrooms were. The fellow with the blue eyes drank aguardiente along with the others and joked with his companions as if they were lifelong friends. He was like a basketball player well-matched with his team: they threw him a joke and zap! he tossed it at the basket and made a goal. They invited a few women over. A little negress sat down at the side of the man with blue eyes.

"You have such delicate hands, eh?" the little negress said.

"Shush!" he whispered, and put his hand under the table to caress a thigh.

"Aye, you have a sailor's body but not a sailor's hands."

"Shush, shush . . ."

And turning to the others he said, "Do you understand Portuguese, guys? They seem to whistle every time they talk. As if they're going to spit at you."

He was one of them. He sang a maxixe, danced a samba, and went to bed with the little negress. When the fight started between his group and a few North Americans, he was a victorious windmill of fists. The bottles had already begun hitting the mirrors when the police separated the gangs, and the Argentinians went out arm in arm singing; they carried the man with blue eyes over them like a flag.

"A few days ago, when a few sailors from a cargo ship believed me to be one of them, it was the greatest honor as a human being that I have ever received," Professor Alexander Dugan said to a colleague on his arrival at Harvard University.

A Heart Outlined

Montaigne (*Essays*, II, 13) relates that the Emperor Adrian ordered the doctor to indicate around the nipple the precise spot where the person charged with killing him must strike.

In the story *En la señal* by Luigi Pirandello, a girl, ill in the hospital, has the nurse outline for her the position of the heart, and afterwards, just there, drives in a stiletto.

In Colombia, real life contributes three situations to this literary tradition: one tragic, one tragicomic, and the third, comic.

The tragic situation was that of the poet José Asunción Silva. In the evening of the twenty-third of May, 1896, he asked his doctor to trace on his chest, with a dermographic marker, the form of the heart. There, some hours later, he discharged a bullet.

The tragicomic situation was that of Colonel Aureliano Buendía.

Having been asked where the exact location of the heart was, his doctor listened to his heart and traced a tiny circle on his skin. Into this tiny circle, days later, the colonel shot his pistol; but he didn't die. The doctor had traced for him "the unique point through which a bullet could pass without injury to a single vital center" (Gabriel García Márquez, *Cien años de soledad*).

The comic situation is that of a university student who started to write verses imitating Silva and, again imitating Silva, wanted to end his life. He visited the glorious tomb, SOON I WILL BE WITH YOU! inscribed on the marble, in front of a mirror painted his heart on his chest, and announced to a friend that he would commit suicide. The friend—Germán Arciniegas, who told me this story—without losing a minute told the father about the boy. The father, a good peasant from Antioquia, in turn wrote a letter to his son:

"I am told that you are going to imitate Silva also in the manner of his death. I respect your privacy. Everyone has the right to do what pleases him most. All that I would ask of you, if you are still determined, is that you do it before the first of July, the date on which I must pay for the second semester at the university, since it would be absurd . . ."

The boy changed his mind.

SELECTIONS FROM

Two Women and One Julián

(1982)

Prologue

Looking backward is dangerous: Lot's wife was turned into salt.
Orpheus lost Eurydice, Collin de Plancy discovered that his guardian angel was the devil himself, Alejo Zaro was swallowed by his
past; and I, in taking a retrospective look down the path I have followed, run the danger of becoming discouraged and abandoning my
career as a writer. One never arrives at fame which is always one
step ahead! (Even Achilles abandoned his race as soon as he realized
that the tricky Zenon of Elea had obliged him to pursue an impossible tortoise.)

Looking backward, I prepared the edition of my complete narratives, but in this third volume there is a glance forward: I refer to
the unedited stories of *Two Women and One Julián*. The path ahead
is still open. I continue following it, with the desire to plot new
adventures.

Enrique Anderson-Imbert

The Fallen Hippogriff

The hippogriff that Perceval, waking, saw on the roof was more
deformed than that in Ariosto's *Orlando Furioso*. The front, eagle-
like (wings, beak and two feathered legs), and the back, lion-shaped
(tail and two furry legs), had features of the griffin. But what Perceval
saw was a hippogriff, fathered by a griffin and a mare; it has inherited, in addition to the lineaments of eagle and lion from its father,

the equine eyes from its mother. Except for those extraordinary eyes that shone like mirrors of jet, the animal recalled the customary figure from a gothic bestiary. Was it an eagle with the body of a lion, or a lion with the head of an eagle? Difficult to decide, since the stiff way in which it raised its forefeet was like a bird of prey, whereas the lazy elasticity of the hindlegs was that of a feline. It didn't seem possible that the four legs could move in harmony. Nevertheless, the animal advanced toward Perceval with perfect elegance. Now it stretched out the left wing, now the right, and the feathers brushing across the ridges of the tiles produced the sound of a guitar being strummed. In spite of the fact that the beast had fixed him with its gaze, Perceval was not afraid. On the contrary, he thought, "How exciting! When it comes closer I'm going to see myself in the convex mirror of its eyes." He was not afraid because, in a strange rush of sympathy, he had understood that the hippogriff, weary of flying from the depths of the centuries, was telling him of its desire to find rest on his roof. And, indeed, it hid its head beneath a wing and dropped off to sleep as if blessed; evidently it was confident that ancient gods would protect its sleep. Even crouched down, it was enormous. With the hippogriff on it, the roof, formerly vast, now appeared small.

Perceval lived on the tenth floor, but due to the heat on that summer night, he had carried his cot up onto the roof. He went down to his apartment, put on his clothes and from the cafe at the corner telephoned the secretary of the newspaper where he worked. The secretary was not grateful for the call; what possible news could be so important for him to be awakened at such a time? When Perceval told him about the hippogriff, the secretary exploded: was this a joke? or was Perceval drugged, drunk, or mad? The discussion turned more and more violent. No. The secretary would not send a photographer to take a picture of a hippogriff. No. The secretary would not publish a single line about the presence of a hippogriff in "the city next to the motionless river," in the city "where runs the great lion-colored river." All right, all right! Agreed! Since that's the way it was, he, Perceval, resigned his position as a reporter and was going to offer his services to the rival newspaper where surely there would not be a secretary so stupid as not to take advantage of a scoop, unique in the annals of journalism, concerning a live hippogriff on the roof. But the editor-in-chief of the rival newspaper was no less stupid. When Perceval declared, "I have a hippogriff on the roof," the chief could not resist a joke and asked him, "On which roof, this one?" Meanwhile, in a friendly way, he began to tap his forehead.

Everybody in the room burst out laughing and Perceval left, cursing them. He wandered around the streets without being able to calm down. Finally, he went into the church. In the church there can't be unbelievers. In the church they believe in the supernatural. Without doubt, Father Erro, the famous medievalist, would be able to advise him.

"My son," Father Erro murmured, "I am a theologist, not a teratologist. If you were to speak to me of a griffin, I could tell you that, in the good times, it was the emblem of Jesus Christ: the lion because he reigns on earth, and the eagle because—like the resurrection—he soars up to heaven. But as to the hippogriff you refer to, I can say nothing, only that during the bad times it was mounted by knightly heroes in romances."

Perceval did not wish to argue, but the medievalist left him disillusioned. To whom could he reveal his secret? Not to the government, capable of calling his guest an undesirable alien as justification for shooting him. Very well, he would go directly to his neighbors. He would tell them that the most fabulous of creatures had come to the port city. He would urge them to be compassionate. But hours went by and no neighbor was convinced that the hippogriff existed. It was already night when Perceval, overwhelmed by so much disbelief, withdrew to his rooftop for consolation. The hippogriff, seeing him appear at the top of the stairs, drew itself up, stretched out its wings and, in one leap, perched on the railing. Immobile, it was a statue of itself. An admirable monument! Perceval gazed at it with pride. After all, it was his! He climbed up as best he could and perched at its side. He looked up above, he looked down below. Above, the stars suggested the lights of another city; below, the city lights suggested the stars of another heaven. Human ants were parading along the avenue. He shouted at them, "Hey! hey! Look up here, at the hippogriff. Do you believe me now?"

It was enough for only one passerby to hear him and stop to scan the sky, for a crowd to gather around, with faces uplifted, mouths open and eyes bright.

"Do you see the hippogriff? Do you see it?" Perceval yelled.

The hippogriff bent its neck and, with its head hanging out over the precipice, observed the crowd frozen on the asphalt. The viewers, in turn, looked from the asphalt at the top of the building, but were only able to distinguish, against the starry vault, the silhouette of a solitary man, shouting with all his strength, like a carnival barker, "Look! Look at the hippogriff!"

A boy laughed. "He's crazy."

A lady murmured, "The poor fellow is going to commit suicide."

A man protested, "There's never a policeman around when you need him."

A policeman was already telephoning to headquarters. After a while the patrol arrived. Officers in blue uniforms made their way through the crowd, ran into the house, and broke through onto the roof. The man stayed up where he was.

"Get down from there," the officer said to him.

Perceval turned around, surprised.

"Ah, you came. Good. Now you have proof that I am not lying. Gentlemen, permit me to present to you the hippogriff."

For a few seconds, the hippogriff drew itself up into the posture of "lion rampant," but then immediately dropped down on all fours and crowed—caw, caw, caw—and saluted them with the tuft of his tail.

"Do you see how gentle it is?"

The officer insisted, "Come down, buddy. We don't want you to fall. Afterwards you can tell us about the hippogriff. Come down."

"But what's wrong with you? Don't you see him? Are you blind?"

"Come down, buddy."

Unwillingly, the officer began to move toward the railing. Perceval stopped him with an outburst, "Stop! You're not going to call me a madman!"

He has clasped the neck of the eagle, has raised himself onto the back of the lion. "Let's go!" says Perceval. The hippogriff unfolds its wings and launches out into space. The instant expands. A second is like an hour. Time dissolves into eternity. With his soul stretched to the limit, Perceval longs to fly. So urgent is his desire to soar up to heaven that, like Astolfo—the rider of the first hippogriff—he cares nothing for the earth. But to the ground is exactly where the hippogriff is plunging with its claws extended. To ask it to change direction, Perceval leans out over the feathery neck. The hippogriff lifts its head and turns it to the side. It is then that Perceval sees deep into the eye of the mare—the jet mirror—and realizes that the lights of Buenos Aires are coming up toward him at the dizzying speed of a fall.

Two Women and One Julián

Ever since her betrothed was killed in an airplane accident just on the eve of their marriage, Delia Pirán had lived withdrawn from the world. Twenty-five years of solitude in a chalet lost among the parks of Bella Vista! So as not to become completely mad, she amused herself solving mathematical problems in a magazine of "mental exercises" to which she had subscribed.

While she enjoyed good health this was sufficient in itself, but her body had started to fail—whether from a cold, whether from the heart, whether from the nerves—and in a notice in *La Prensa* she solicited the company of a lady to help her, not as a servant, but as a friend.

A widow appeared, Silvina Campos, and they became friends immediately. Both were fifty years old. Neither had any family. If one had lost her sweetheart, the other had lost her husband. And even the differences between them were compensated for. The taciturn Delia knew how to listen, and Silvina, the eloquent, needed to be heard. As soon as she began listening, Delia hung on every word. How easily the sentences rolled out! After dinner Silvina was accustomed to tell her stories. The great surprise was when Silvina confessed that some of the stories were her own inventions. What?! She made up her own stories? Yes. Silvina wrote stories. Did she publish them? No, not yet, but she was writing them. A writer in the house! What luxury! What an honor!

The language of numbers, since it was exact, did not daunt Delia; on the other hand, the language of learning, of the fine arts, frightened her with its hypnotic power. Wasn't it frightening that with a few illogical words, ambiguous, over-used, a writer could hypnotize his readers to the point of making them forget themselves and live only as he wished them to live? She begged Silvina, then, to explain to her with what tricks and witchery she had composed this or that story. Thus the wakeful evenings sounded like sessions in a literary workshop. The disciple listened to the master with evident admiration at at times with secret envy.

"You," said Delia, "always speak of the art of weaving plots, and I understand that plots are very important, but what about characters? Aren't the characters also important?"

"Of course, but I don't know how to create characters. If I knew how, I would write novels, not stories."

"So it is that difficult to create characters?"

"Oh yes. Most difficult. That is where I fail."

The "I fail," reflected in a mirror as the inverted form of "would I fail?" aroused in Delia the desire to emulate her friend, to collaborate with her, to prove to Silvina and to herself that she was capable of imagining a character. When Silvina went to bed, Delia entered the guest room, which had an odor of death, opened the window to

air it, and made the bed. Afterwards she unrolled a rug, placed wire
hangers in the closet, brought a lamp down from the attic and stood
it beside an easy chair. The room was a toy; and a little girl—a little
girl fifty years old—was playing house. The next morning Delia
went out without saying where she was going, and returned with a
package.

"See what I bought," she said to Silvina.

Silvina opened the package and found herself looking at a couple
of men's shirts. Delia, like a child who gives her playmate a hint to
help her figure out a riddle, added, "I chose the color and the exact
size: sixteen at the neck."

"You bought them for some relative?"

"You know very well that I don't have any relatives."

"For whom, then?"

"That," Delia answered softly, "that is what we must decide: for
whom?"

Silvina smiled. Could Delia be challenging her? A challenge to
see who was the more imaginative?

"Ah, Delia. Now I get it. It's a game, right?"

"You must judge. If it's a game, now it's your turn."

There was no doubt about it. Delia wanted to play, but not in jest,
as serious people do, but seriously, the way people who are joking do.
Exaggerating the expression of grave complicity that little girls assume when they are conspiring in some mischief, Silvina pretended
to look for someplace where she could put the shirts. As if the game
of shirts consisted of discovering not hidden objects, but the best
place for hiding them.

"Now I know," she said, "the shirts must go in the room . . . his
room . . ." and she searched Delia's face to judge the effect of the em-
phatic "his room."

Delia did not change her expression and, with the voice of a stu-
dious child who is tutoring an unprepared classmate for her examinations, she inquired, "In whose room?"

Silvina, without hesitation, gave him a name, "Julián's."

"Very well, but before you go into Julián's room you must knock
on the door, mustn't you?"

Silvina had ascertained the nature of the game: she must give up
what before she had considered reality. And she decided to accept
the terms of the competition. After all she, not Delia, was the writer
whose specialty was fiction. So she left the living room, carrying the
shirts, and went up the stairs. On one side, Delia's bedroom; on the
other side, her own; between them, the guest room. It had to be
there. It was not going to be upstairs, in the attic filled with old fur-

niture. Silvina knocked on the door, loudly, so that Delia would hear down below that she was respecting the rules of the game ("She won't beat me!"), and entered.

Minutes later, when she came down, she told Delia, "Julián wasn't there. I stored the shirts in the bureau."

"Very well. Why don't you put a few of those detective and mystery novels that you like so much in Julián's room? He'll like them too. Choose them carefully, eh."

Silvina was beginning to doubt that Delia was playing. When someone in a party is joking and pretends to be crazy, he holds in his eyes a tiny spark of irony so that his friends know that if he wishes he can recover his senses in a jiffy. Silvina did not see that signal in Delia's eyes.

The next day Delia went out and returned two hours later with another package. She revealed its contents, article by article, in front of Silvina:

"An electric razor. Soap. Handkerchiefs with a **J** embroidered on them. And this red tie with white dots. What do you think? Perfect to go with the black eyes of a young man twenty-five years old, right?"

"We're a couple of silly old ladies," Silvina thought, but did not dare to say so in case Delia was really ill and fast becoming mad. She merely suggested to her, so that she would not throw away her money, that as long as she was buying things, she could buy them at discount sales. The suggestion was counter-productive. Delia's imagination was caught up in a plan of extravagant spending, not of saving. Julián had been born already with twenty-five years on him, but he was naked, and Delia wanted to clothe him from head to foot. She went immediately to Harrod's and bought him a suit—the measurements were those of a model athlete—as well as shoes, socks, pyjamas, and underwear. Silvina, silently, helped her unpack the purchases and place them in the drawers in Julián's room; silently because she believed she had guessed the drama going on inside Delia. A spectre named Julián had come to fill the empty place of a past love. He was the substitute for the lost lover.

One fine day, that imaginary man who, until then, had been simply "Julián," acquired a last name. Silvina read it on the envelope of a letter that arrived in the morning: "Mr. Julián del Valle, Esq!" Delia was sending letters to a fictional person. This was the limit! Silvina abandoned the game.

"Delia, dear Delia. You have beaten me. I, even with all the words in the dictionary, never knew how to create a character. You created one with a wardrobe; you filled all those empty clothes with a

Julián. It isn't wise to continue this game. Julián doesn't exist. Do you understand?"

Delia answered with icy calm, "Of course I understand. You are assuming the right to decide when a person exists and when he does not exist. By the same right I could say that you are not a widow because the man who died did not exist."

Silvina felt herself struck in the most painful part of her soul: in the memory of the death of her beloved Alfredo. To hide her anguish, she left the living room and went to cry in the basement, where there was a room for washing and ironing. Delia did not have time to apologize because at that moment she heard a noise on the floor above. Someone was walking around in Julián's room. She went up, opened the door, and saw a young man. "Julián," she murmured, about to faint.

The young man who was about to escape through the window, stopped upon seeing the woman, and studied her strange expression.

"What did you say? Julián? Did you call me Julián?"

"Julián," Delia repeated in the smothered voice of a person speaking in a dream.

"You're frightened. Calm down."

"I prepared this room for Julián."

The young man took a step toward her, still studying her, "And naturally you were expecting to find Julián here."

The echo, "Julián . . ."

The young man took another step forward. "How she's exaggerating," he thought. "She has the expression of an actress making believe that she sees a supernatural apparition."

"You saw me and you said, "Julián." But you said it more as if you were asking yourself, 'Could it be Julián?' You mean that you haven't seen Julián for a long time, isn't that true? You might not be able to recognize him even if you saw him . . . Maybe you've never seen him . . . So who is Julián?"

The echo, "Julián."

"My God! You're going on as if you're in a state of shock. Or do you really believe that I'm Julián? Tell me, what's going on here? A scene from a play? A mystery?"

He laughed. He had white teeth, even and strong—and parodying a bow from a seventeenth century comedy, he said, "Madam, this room is not mine and I am not Julián. I, although of good family, live in a poor tenement. I'm a thief. And at this moment I'd be a murderer too if you, instead of confusing me with a certain Julián, had started to scream. Then I would have had no other choice than to strangle you. But don't be frightened. I came only to steal."

A boy of bad character, yes, but of fascinating beauty and graceful movements; how could he have been turned into a criminal? She asked him, and the boy, with the affected indifference of an actor in the role of a cynic, gave his autobiography: poverty, misfortune, selfishness, poor judgment, vanity, bohemian tendencies, drugs, theater (he had failed in the theater). In sum, the life of a lost soul; and Delia, now recovered from her fright, felt pity. Pity and also—incredibly for her, an old maid—a kind of maternal love, since if she had married that lover who crashed on the eve of the wedding, she would have had a son twenty-five years old, perhaps also a good-looking boy. She gave him money and went with him to the door. Leaving her, the boy said, "My real name I can't give you, but just call me Julián. I like that."

Silvina learned of the adventure because on the following day, answering a ring at the door, she admitted a boy into the house ("Tell the lady of the house that Julián wants to see her") and after Delia came to meet him, she heard them talking. With a disconcerting boldness, the young man demanded more money. And the ecstatic expression with which Delia, the sorcerer's apprentice, contemplated that demon! What was all this? Good heavens! Could it be that Delia, unconsciously, in the same way that she had drawn the image of a fictitious person from the mold of her dead sweetheart, now was replacing him with a gigolo? The gigolo had the physique of an Adonis, one had to admit it. Silvina could not remember any movie actor who looked like him, but without doubt his arrogant manner made one think of a future actor. And Silvina was right in associating his beauty with an actor's because at this point the boy said that he had taken small parts in a few plays, but that in the last year he had not found work, and how could he ask for work in these rags? He needed to buy some clothes. Delia told him to go up "to the other Julián's room" and to deck himself out in the suit and all the other clothing that he found there. When the young man climbed the stairs and went directly into the guest room as if it were his own, Silvina couldn't hold herself back any longer, and reproached Delia for her conduct. There was an explosive exchange of words. Silvina, feeling herself treated like a servant, ran up to her room and a few moments later came down with a suitcase in her hand. Before leaving the house, she managed to see the boy beside Delia, very elegant in "the other Julián's suit," looking at her mockingly.

On Sunday evening Julián appeared with a mousy little girl, fifteen years old, thin and timid.

"I want you to meet my sister Alberta."

"Pleased to meet you," Delia said.

The little girl looked at her sideways and silently nodded her head.

"We come at a bad time, right? It must be the dinner hour."

"I've already eaten."

"Alberta hasn't. Would there be anything left? Even if it's only bread and cheese? Alberta is dying of hunger."

Delia let them in and gave them something to eat.

"This chalet is too big for just one person alone," Julián commented when they had finished eating.

Delia felt she heard a tone of reproach in Julián's voice: her chalet was a spacious island in which she as an old maid lived comfortably while in the city entire families lodged in one room. And in the reproach she sensed a vague menace: some day or other a violent emigration from over-populated Buenos Aires, a people's revolution, a confiscatory decree, would sweep away her privileges. Now afraid, very much afraid, she heard Julián say, "You must be living on your income or with a good pension. You have more than enough money, don't you?"

Why had the brother and sister come? What did they want? She, having a weak character, could not defend herself. Nevertheless, when Julián ordered Alberta to clear the table and wash the dishes, Delia gathered her strength and opposed it, "No. Leave it, leave it. It's too late."

They didn't move. Delia waited a moment, and again insisted, "All right. Now it's time for you to go."

Julián, as if he had not heard, said, "Alberta could help you with the house chores."

"No, thank you. She's too young. I need an older person. Like Silvina Campos, the lady who left yesterday."

"But Alberta would help you for nothing. Beginning tomorrow morning, she'll come to help you. You need her."

"No. I said no. Please go."

"You live so alone. Someone has to be with you. Alberta can take the room that Silvina Campos had before she left."

Delia protested and was about to say, "If you don't go I'm going to call the police," when Alberta turned up the whites of her eyes and fell flat on the floor. Julián picked her up in his arms, took her to Silvina's room and put her on the bed.

From that moment on, events happened rapidly. Very early on Monday, Julián arrived, accompanied by a man with lively eyes and a red nose, whom he introduced as a doctor. The supposed doctor pretended to examine Alberta and said that in the condition she was in, it would be impossible to move her. Julián, to care for his poor little sister, decided, without more ado, to occupy the guest room. Delia tried to use the telephone to denounce the imposition, but they had already disconnected it. She tried to escape, but the doors were locked and the keys had disappeared.

"I'm going to have you all put in jail!"

"Don't get excited," Julián advised her, "think about death, which is worse."

On Tuesday Julián opened the door to his parents who were coming to ask after the health of their daughter. The pair of them—Manuela and Augustín; they wouldn't give a last name—were humble, respectful and well-mannered. They stayed in Alberta's room only an hour. They returned on Wednesday, stayed for two hours, and used the bathroom. On Thursday they prolonged their visit. Manuela went to the kitchen and prepared dinner for all. By Friday the family had taken possession of the whole house. Also at dinner was the fake doctor, who turned out to be an uncle.

Delia called Manuela aside and said to her, "You must go. I'm very ill. I beg you to go."

"Oh, I'm very sorry, my dear, but it isn't possible!" Manuela answered with sincere regrets. "We're all of us very grateful for all that you've done for us, but you know, Alberta, the poor thing . . . If we take her from here, she will die. Also, we don't have anywhere to go. I've wanted to speak to you about that. My husband and I have lost the rooms we had in a family hotel. We are going to have to settle in some little corner in this house."

She understood. Delia understood. In a second she saw everything that was going to happen. The vision of it all, then dizziness, then a faint. She recovered her senses in her bedroom, where they had placed her on the bed.

"What are those noises?" she asked Manuela, who was beside her applying a compress soaked in cologne to her forehead.

"Nothing. Just my son bringing down furniture from the attic. He's going to set up a bed for my husband and me in the living room."

Indignant, Delia tried to stand up, but the deliberate dominating force with which Manuela held her down proved to her that she was a prisoner. At that moment Julián entered.

"Are you feeling better?"

Delia turned her face away.

"What! You're afraid of me? It's because you still consider me a stranger. And even though, in an effort to please you, I've adopted the name of Julián. Do you realize what that means, Miss Pirán? . . . Delia, if you don't mind. With me here you don't need to concern yourself with anything. I'm in charge of taking care of your interests. I'm your butler. If you need anything, here's a little bell to ring. We're at your service."

Going out with his mother, Julián locked the door from the outside. Irony. Delia, who at the beginning had rejoiced at the captivating beauty of the young man, was now his captive. Except that the beauty of Julián finally had revealed to her its secret: it was the beauty of Lucifer.

In the days that followed—three, four? sleeping badly, she had lost count—Delia observed that the invaders were having a very good time, judging from the sounds of dishes, bottles, and glasses, the bursts of laughter and one or another drinking song. They were like gypsies. They did not give the impression that they were planning to murder her. On the contrary they took good care of her. The father looked in to offer her the newspaper. The uncle took her pulse. Manuela attended to all her needs, even bathing her. Alberta brought her food. Delia was in her own home, but at moments it seemed to her that she was in a sanatorium or a hotel; she had been kidnapped, but at moments her kidnappers seemed to be nurses or servants. The worst of the band was Julián. He had ordered that if Delia did not sign checks in his name ("to take care of the expenses of the house"), he would not give her anything to eat. Delia began to believe that Julián was a maniac from the theater who had convinced his family, also crazy, that they should improvise a "happening," without a script, but with a theme, that of a rich house invaded by poor people. He had chosen her house as a stage and Delia as protagonist and spectator at the same time. When the play was finished, would the actors disband?

One day she heard knocks, voices, cries, footsteps. The door of the room crashed open, forced by a tremendous shove, and two policemen broke in. Behind them, like a chess piece that for many moves has been inactive but suddenly moves and wins the game, Silvina entered, embraced Delia, and on hearing her sobs, said to her, "Everything is all right. Everything is fine. They've already caught those thieves."

"Silvina, Silvina . . . how did you learn what was happening in this house?"

"Through a presentiment. Two friends talk about novels. It occurs to one of them to create a character. The character becomes real, presents himself to the author and demands money. A classical theme. I thought, if I were to write a story around the situation of the autonomous character, what ending would I give it? Logically, that the will power of the character destroys the will power of the author . . . Now, dear, you and I are going to write this novel that we have just finished living."

"We are going to write it? It should be you, you are a writer, because you . . ."

"No. We two are going to write it. I'm good only for the plot; but you? Who, tell me, who is better than you in creating a character? Eh?"

Delia, between tears, had to laugh.

One X and Two Unknowns

Since I retired from the university I have used my winters to learn about the north and my summers to learn about the south. "It's a shame," I told myself last year, "that at my age I still don't know the lakes of Río Negro." And I decided to visit them.

I arrived at the hotel during the night, so sleepy that I didn't pause to appreciate the delicacy with which the clear water, behind the black mass of the wood, defined the silhouette of a birch tree.

In the morning when I was going to the dining room for breakfast, I saw a girl about twenty years old stretched out on a divan in a little room at the end of the corridor. She was wearing a robe and slippers, from which I inferred that she had just left her room so that the maid could finish cleaning it. Her hair, long and tousled, fell as if on the way to a total collapse. Her eyes were closed and sunken. Her pallor—accentuated by a mole on the left cheek—was sickly. She made a pained movement and, with her left hand, covered her forehead from temple to temple, murmuring, "What a cursed headache!"

The following day—I, from the top of the hotel, contemplating the sky, the wood, the lake—saw her again. She appeared quite different. Well dressed, well made-up, smiling and scintillating, she passed by my side and went down to find a place among the flowers of the garden.

"Who is that?" I asked the manager.

"I believe it is Celia. Celia Lugones."

Ah, the short story writer! I too, in my good period, knew how to write stories, so that the young lady interested me, and since old age carries certain privileges, I went down to the garden and without more ado addressed her, "Are you feeling better?"

She turned around with the haughtiness of a queen, but upon

seeing me—seeing an old man—she answered with the condescension that one reserves for a grandfather, "Better than when? I always feel well."

"Yesterday morning when I saw you in the little corridor room, you appeared not to be feeling well . . ."

"Ah," she said, laughing, "you have confused me with my sister, Delia. Without doubt you saw her having one of her attacks of migraine. I'm Celia. In spite of differences in character, we are an extreme case of identical twins. We were born from the same egg and we look as though one of us is real and the other is her mirror image."

"Identical identical twins? Hmmm!" I know nothing about twins, but I pretended to. "The young lady that I saw yesterday had a mole on her left cheek. If you were as identical as you say, one sister would have it on the left and the other on the right cheek. Don't try to fool me. You are the same one that I saw yesterday."

She looked at me in silence. I thought she would become angry, but she laughed. "Very well, if you say so . . . So I have no twin sister. Very well. Let it be. But in any case, the woman you saw yesterday was not I. Better said, was not my real self. I have two personalities. The other woman is a depressive, filled with anxiety. I am not. She does not know what I do, nor do I know what she does. Something separates us into two parts and each part lives on its own. I am schizoid."

"Don't show off. Schizoid you're not."

In order to lead her on, I expounded on psychology and added, with aplomb, as if I knew what I was talking about, "You are referring to your two selves as if they were living in separate bodies, ignorant of each other. That is not possible."

Celia lowered her head, without doubt in order to hide her smile, and when she looked up, she had put on a smile of comic seriousness, "Good, now I see that you cannot be fooled. I lied with a credible lie; now I'm going to be truthful with an incredible truth. What is happening to me is not of this world. It is something supernatural. You say that I do not have a twin sister nor a double personality . . . As you wish; but in a certain sense I am both one and two since I am possessed by an evil force. I am a person possessed."

To converse with a person who is a liar and an artist with words is like witnessing, as in *La verdad sospechosa* by Alarcón, the spectacle of the transformation of a lie into a story. With a certain pleasure, then, I sat back in my theater seat to hear the famous storyteller, Celia Lugones, tell her third lie, now neither biological nor psychological, but metaphysical:

"There is evil spread all over the world," she started. "Each one gets his share. What is difficult is to imagine which share is given to someone else. Let us see if you and I are capable of imagining that. Let us take as an example: I see the evil in the form of a blot. If I am facing the lake, the blot is like a floating island that sometimes approaches me and sometimes recedes. If I am in my room, it is like a spark that grows to the point of blinding me or diminishes to the size of a pinpoint. The evil is not always visible. Days pass, weeks, without my seeing it, but I cannot escape from it. It follows me everywhere. It has followed me to this hotel. It is here."

Crossing her arms in the form of an X she lifted each hand to the opposite shoulder and, shaking as from a chill, she explored with her eyes some region of the air. She continued: "When the blot appears, I feel that it is taking away my strength, that the closer it approaches me, the weaker I feel. It is a parasite that is feeding on me. It is sucking out the juices of my life. If I am not careful, one of these days I will die of anemia and then be changed into a ghost. But I fight against it. I see it coming and I go out to face it down. The blot of evil advances toward me, and from far away casts its shadow on me, and I advance toward it and force it to take my form. We assume the same posture, like two duelists. We are two: the blot of evil that is possessing me, and I, the woman possessed. But I am also the evil, and the evil is also the woman. We are equal. I see her and I see me, here and there, coming and going, as when I am walking toward the mirror in which I am seeing myself."

With a tightening of the lips, a narrowing of the eyes, and a shake of the head, she manifested her dissatisfaction with what she had just said and, in effect, corrected herself: "That comparison with the mirror is not correct, because the inversion to which I refer does not occur in space but in time, and for this reason it would be more appropriate to compare it with turning over an hourglass. The deposit of sand in the upper glass is being changed slowly into the pile of sand in the lower glass. The hourglass has the form of an X, and the X is the mystic symbol of the intercommunication between heaven and hell."

In saying "between heaven and hell," Celia undid the small X which she had formed with her crossed arms, but formed it again as a large X when she spread her legs, lifted her arms, and in that posture I imagined her nude, like the famous figure of Marco Vitruvio, drawn in the form of an X inside a square inside a circle, with the navel at the center. Then Celia relaxed her pose and continued with her story.

"When in my change I arrive at that point where the two lines of the X cross, I have a prescience of salvation. Below, a lifeless woman, possessed. Above, a living woman, free. And from hell, she passes to heaven. After the evil effect of a stroke of lightning which penetrates the head and blows it apart, not feeling it any more is a benediction that creates a second head, this one sane. Yesterday you saw a young lady almost dead. How do you see her now, after the journey through salvation? Animated and very alive, right?"

I wanted to applaud, as at the theater. The girl knew how to lie, that was certain. With a mischievous smile she said goodbye and went off in the direction of the lake. It was a pleasure to see her walk, so light-footed. I was thinking about the gift that she had left me: the gift of her third lie.

"What an imagination she has, that Celia Lugones!" I said to myself. "All that fantastic story about a supernatural evil only to hide the natural origin of her illness. Since she doesn't care to admit that her suffering is commonplace, Celia adorns her symptoms with extraordinary mysteries. The fluctuating blot is a simple migraine, and the journey through the X with which it is cured is the effect of a common aspirin."

She hadn't gone fifty yards when she stopped, like someone who hears a voice, turned her head toward the trees, hesitated for a moment, and entered the wood. I lost sight of her. From curiosity— what voice could have taken her from her path?—I went after her. I didn't find her immediately. The diffuse light which filtered through the foliage was like that which, filtering through the eyelids, makes the sleeper dream about himself all alone in a strange and empty world. Having wandered so much around and about among the trees, I no longer knew whether I was going forwards or backwards. In one of my turns, I finally found Celia: she came from behind one tree to slip behind another. I nearly called to her. I stopped myself in time because it occurred to me that Celia might be approaching a furtive rendezvous. Again I lost sight of her. Either she was playing hide-and-seek, or the other who was playing was the wood itself. I detoured around fallen trunks. I lost my way. I reversed my direction. Perhaps I retraced my steps. I hurried, zigzagging. From one angle of my zigzag I saw the Celia whom I had seen hunched over in the little room of the hotel. The same Celia, seen for the second time. Or was I seeing two different girls searching for each other in the wood? I stumbled over a trunk and fell. When I looked up it seemed to me that, far over there, two different girls had come together face to face, as in a mirror. If in fact there were two, the girl with her back to me was hiding the one facing her. She covered her so completely that I would not have suspected her existence were it not that the hair of the hidden girl could be seen around the hair of the girl with her back to me, as the corona of the sun can be seen in an eclipse. The two girls melted away into a single shadow in the wood. The exact spot of their disappearance was marked by two trees whose trunks crossed to form a large **X**: I visualized the skull and cross-bones on a pirate flag, on the label of a bottle of poison, on the illustration of a memento mori. And then I heard a werewolf's howl. Finally, after another turn, I reached the spot and saw Celia. She was alone, rigid, as if carved from the tree against which she was leaning, pallid as a wax doll, with her eyes closed and her mouth open in a grimace.

"What has happened, Celia?"

"Don't call me Celia; my name is Delia."

"Come on, Celia! Do you still want to play the game of masks? Only a moment ago you told me . . ."

"I? I have never spoken with you before, sir."

I thought, this is the fourth lie: the fourth tip of the **X**.

She asked me to accompany her to the hotel because the pain was blinding, and I took her by the arm. We spoke not a word more. I wanted to say to her, "You who are a storyteller, why don't you write a story about all this?", but I remained quiet. What the devil! Why shouldn't I write it myself? After all, I too, in my better moments, was a storyteller. But the true reason why I stayed quiet was that it would have been cruel to insinuate to Celia in the state she was in, that she was a liar.

Ah, but that much of a liar she was not. How wrong I was! The girl had not lied to me. In any case, her lying was reduced to switching masks. Because on the whole, all that she had told me turned out to be true. There were, in truth, two twins. In truth, one of them believed herself to be only half of a split personality. Truthfully, this schizoid half was possessed. Truthfully, evil was everywhere. I learned this in the most tragic manner possible. That same night I was awakened by voices and noises. I put on my robe and, alarmed, went out into the corridor. The manager, along with three or four employees, was looking into the interior of a room. When he saw me, he approached me gesticulating in disgust. "Horrible, sir, horrible! It is the first time that a thing like this has ever happened in my hotel. One sister has killed the other."

"Which? Celia Lugones?"

"Or Delia. No one knows. Here they are, the living one staring at the dead one. Look into the room if you wish. The police have not yet been able to identify them. I can't tell them apart. Perhaps if you . . ."

Forever Sweetheart

Tired of driving for hours and hours in the rain along the curves of the sierra, I decided to spend the night in the first little hotel that I found. This turned out better than I expected. The hotel keeper, from Córdoba, with a big gray mustache, came out to meet me, saying "I'm the owner, Hilario Jiménez, at your service." He must have liked me since right away he called me "my son" and invited me to have a few drinks. "The cognac is the only thing that's dry today," he told me. In a few moments I learned that he was a retired professor ("from sheer boredom I invested my savings in this little hotel") and he learned that I was an editor of a newspaper ("I am traveling all over the country in search of unusual stories").

With that, a man of about fifty appeared at the end of the corridor, like Don Hilario but extravagant-looking, perhaps because of his British air; his face, clean-shaven, respectful, smiling, rotund, and rosy, had an expression of gentle madness. He lifted his eyes from the book which he was reading (I thought of Hamlet) and approached us with elastic steps like those of a boy (I thought of Lawrence Olivier in the role of Hamlet). The contrast of a head with the gray of fifty years and a torso with the vigor of thirty made me uneasy: that man, by means of some atrocious operation, had succeeded in taking possession of either the face or the body of some other person. Don Hilario introduced me, "Eduard Woolf, this young man is Héctor Ordóñez. Just look how things happen! Here we have gathered three professionals, all literary."

"Ah, you're a professor, like him?" Woolf asked me.

"No. That business about being a literary professional is Don Hilario's little joke. I'm a journalist, and lucky to be one. But you are a professor, aren't you?"

"No, I'm not. But I'm going to be one very soon. I need only one more course for my degree."

What! At retirement age he still had to pass an examination? What supercareer would that be in which an old man still has to be examined?

Deep down in my perplexity, the vague image of a face started to form, a very fine face, very like the weathered face of Woolf; a face that I had never seen in living expressiveness, but which, nevertheless, I believed I recognized. Before the image became clear in my memory, Don Hilario changed the conversation (had he realized my perplexity and did he fear that I might interrogate Woolf?), but even had he not changed the conversation, I would not have been able to force myself to recover the lost memory because suddenly I saw a woman so attractive that from that moment on nothing was more important than my pure admiration of her. I didn't see her come in; I saw her standing motionless in the same place in the corridor where Woolf had appeared. She was clothed entirely in white, as if she had materialized from the white wall behind her. Her features harmonized with such perfection that it was evident that they had not passed through the chubby fullness of infancy nor would they pass through the thinning wrinkles of old age. That woman was born already completely perfect. And like the fairies, she was ageless. I knew immediately that I would love her. Serious, calm, reserved, proud, distant, she held her gaze on me, and I on her, and we sustained our gazes, and I swore that I would not be the first to drop mine. The man has to dominate, has to conquer, right? I was expecting Don Hilario to introduce us. But he did not, and finally it was I who lowered my eyes because her severe look pierced me, as if she was giving me a reproof. The warning look of a schoolteacher who says wordlessly to a child in her class, "Watch out that you do not misbehave! Watch out that you do not commit an indiscretion!"

Woolf, without having made the least gesture of greeting, of recognition, not even of having noticed her, said to us, "Well, I'm going to my studies. Within a week I'll be presenting myself before the examining board for Greek. I must be well prepared. I'll see you later."

He made a quick turn into the corridor and, I suppose, went on to his room. The woman, who had moved aside to let him pass, turned again to fix me with that schoolteacher's stare ("Watch out!") and, without saying a word, left in the same direction. And I, obeying the law of good form, continued the action initiated by those two bodies that disappeared one after the other: I picked up my valise and followed them.

Before I reached the room that Don Hilario had indicated to me, my brain lit up and I remembered who Woolf was. His insistence that he had to take an examination to finish his course of study still left me perplexed, but at least that vague image of a face that I had seen and yet not seen gradually became clear. I had seen that face in newspaper photographs; photographs on the occasion of a prize, a lecture, a voyage . . . So I returned along the corridor and, on the pretext of asking Don Hilario to have me awakened at seven in the morning, since I had to reach Córdoba before noon, I again took up the conversation with him and tried to draw him out. "Tell me, Woolf was a famous professor, right?'

"Ah, you recognized him, eh? I hope you're not thinking of interviewing him. Please, just this once forget that you are a journalist hunting for material. Leave him alone."

"Don't be alarmed. It's just that suddenly I remembered that face. Although older, it is the same face that I once saw in the newspapers. Afterward, I stopped seeing his photograph, and it's been years since I've heard his name. It's not that I considered him dead; I merely had forgotten him. What happened to him? Because I see that he's studying for an examination . . ."

"I'm going to tell you what happened, but not so that you can repeat it elsewhere, eh? Woolf and I were classmates. He achieved a position at the university and I, on the other hand, remained a professor at the secondary level. When he became ill, I brought him with me every year to pass the summer here."

"And?" I had to nudge him because Don Hilario was stuck in a pause. "You were going to tell me what happened with Professor Woolf."

"Ah, yes. A traumatic event. One of his former students, a rascal who was working as a student assistant, had taken notes in his classes and given them to him to read so that he might see if they were well done and accurate. The kind-hearted Woolf not only read the notes but also corrected them, amplified them, and with annotations in the margin suggested a new organization of themes. A couple of years later that shameless fellow published a book: it was an arrangement of Woolf's notes! The plagiarism was brutal; nowhere was Woolf mentioned. Even worse, a first-year student who had just finished reading the book, hearing Woolf's lectures, recognized certain ideas and started the rumor that Woolf had plagiarized the book. Can you imagine? Woolf learned of this and went to ask for an explanation from his former student. He ran to catch a bus, already underway. He caught it, but collapsed into his seat and lost consciousness. Imagine! The emotional shock, the chase . . . He recovered his senses, but was not the same as before. He was in a state of confusion. He could no longer distinguish the borderline between the real and the unreal. Even in those moments when he appeared to have his feet on the ground, he was floating along in who knows what other dimension. He was between two lights, like a drunken man, like an amnesiac, like a man lost."

Don Hilario stopped abruptly, and then with a little nervous laugh unfitting to the occasion, came out with this incongruity: "A professor of Roman law always initiated his course with this genial declaration: 'The Law, in Rome, began by not existing . . .'"

"And?"

"And nothing. All things begin by not existing. Woolf's career began by not existing and terminated, after a jump backward, by starting again with nonexistence."

"Please, Don Hilario, don't speak to me in such difficult terms! Just tell me that Woolf forgot about his career as a professor."

"All right. He forgot it. He remembers his years as a student up until one week before the examination in Greek that would give him the title of professor. That's all he remembers: that he needs one week more to get his degree. And he goes on preparing himself day after day. Each day he starts studying again because he's forgotten the Greek he studied the day before. One week more, one week more! He's like a needle on a scratched record: he can't get out of the groove. He studies and forgets, studies and forgets. It's the nightmare of the person who wants to run, but can't move. In his case he is immobilized in time."

Still ruminating over the words of Don Hilario, I went again to my room. I lay on my bed, turned out the light, and evoked the image of the silent woman. Tall, slender, pale, with large green eyes that looked at me without blinking. Who could she be? His daughter? His nurse? If his nurse, she was carrying her duties not like a weight on her back but like a star on her forehead. Who could she be? It was too late now to return to the lobby and ask Don Hilario to tell me about her.

Through the wall I heard the low sound of Woolf's voice. Was he reciting in Greek? Was he perhaps giving someone a lesson? That low sound was covered by another more powerful, the sound of the rain which had returned with renewed force. I dreamed that the future was presenting me with sweethearts who were copies of the woman: tall, slender, pale, with large green eyes that gazed at me without blinking.

The following morning I breakfasted early and when, with Don Hilario, I went to look for my automobile I saw that Woolf, standing at the back of the garage, was marveling at the ornament on the hood as if it were the prow of a Greek ship.

"Ah," he said, "you're leaving? What a pity! One week more and you would have had a scoop by publishing in your newspaper the important news that I received my degree."

And he winked at Don Hilario.

As I drew near him to offer my hand I discovered the woman; she had been at Woolf's side all the time, except that she was hidden by the car. She looked at me again with that intense gaze of the previous day, sustained, serene. On this occasion, Woolf did not ignore her presence. On the contrary. "I would like," he told me, "to introduce you to my fiancée." Not his daughter, not his nurse; his "fiancée," he said. I opened my mouth in surprise. First, the old man was studying Greek like a student, and now it turned out that, also like a student, he was giving himself the luxury of having a fiancée whom I, much younger than he, would have wanted for myself!

She acknowledged me with a slight nod of her head and fixed her eyes on me, again with that schoolteacher look that warns a child "watch what you do, watch out!" while she confirmed Woolf's words in a voice hollow with loneliness, "Yes, I'm his fiancée. We'll be married next week, after Eduard passes his examination and gets his degree."

A little later, Don Hilario informed me that she was not his fiancée but his wife, and she was the same age as Woolf.

"The same age? Then she is more than twenty years older than I!"

Incredible. Not a single wrinkle, not a single gray hair . . . A healthy complexion? Cosmetics? Plastic surgery?

No, no. Nothing so prosaic. Here something poetic must be occurring. What do I know! Something like the story of that monk who after hearing the brief magical song of a bird, remained transfixed in ecstasy, not noticing that three centuries were passing through his cloister and changing it to a ruin. Or the story of the magic portrait able to picture the progressive decadence and corruption of its subject while he, changeless, always showed a clean and shining face. Or like the story of the paradisiacal atmosphere at the top of a mountain, that guaranteed eternal youth to whoever breathed it. Or like the story of that magic mirror through which fled the years of whoever was looking into it. Thus I understood the miracle. Woolf's consciousness had stopped at a moment in time, holding his beautiful wife in suspense, and not letting her age. That was it. That was the way it had to be.

The Alleluia of the Dying

Isaac Kornblit went to visit Rodrigo Alvarez, who had just left the hospital. He found him haggard but very happy to be living once again in his home.

"So you were able to see him and hear him up until the last moment?" he asked him. "What a privilege, although sad, to be next to the great Jacob Stein at the hour of his death! What did he say? Because I suppose he retained his lucidity to the end."

"Yes, of course," Alvarez answered, "but don't imagine that he was very profound with me. But yes, he knew how to tell a story."

"What story? The history of Israel?"

"No, just a story."

"What do you mean?"

"Well, I've already told you. When they took me to the hospital, they put me in the same room where they were caring for Stein. A night table separated our beds. He was much more ill than I, but I was much more depressed than he. Probably he knew that he was going to die and that I was suffering from nothing very serious. If so, his conduct was very laudable because he overcame his own suffering, and, in order to encourage me, kept talking to me. I had no desire for conversation and so that he would leave me alone (pardon me, I know that for you Jews, Jacob Stein is an outstanding Zionist, but for me he was nobody; I scarcely recalled that he had been a professor of history in Israel) I warned him that if he wanted to talk, he should talk, but I was not going to answer him because I was feeling ill and also because, like Azorín, when I had something to say, I wrote it down and didn't need to talk. At that point, Stein started to philosophize on the subject of the oral and the written. It surprised me that, being Jewish (and I suppose that for the Jews the Bible carries some weight), he would say that books were harmful to mankind. He repeated the argument of the Egyptian Ammon in the little story that Plato, in the *Phaedrus*, puts in the mouth of Socrates: that the written word, unlike the spoken word, weakens the memory of the reader and makes him mentally lazy. I limited myself to answering him, I believe rudely, that my eyes were more useful to me than my ears and that what was offensive to me in that hospital was that I could close my eyes but not my ears. He was untouched by this and continued provoking me in order to force me to talk. At this point I let slip that I had written one or two stories in my time, and Stein asked me if I was certain that those stories of mine were not based on some oral tradition. Because, he added, he had located the source in folklore of many of today's stories that were trying to pass as original writing. Did he want to make me doubt the originality of my stories? On the night table was a book. Stein showed it to me. It was written in Hebrew characters. He leafed through it. I knew (that ignorant I am not!) that Hebrew is read backwards but it seemed to me a little infantile that so old a man would turn the pages from the back to the front. 'It is,' he told me with a sparkle of mischief in his eye, 'an anthology of Israeli stories. You see. They are written down, so according to your theory they must be good.' He smiled mischievously and gazed at me through ironic little eyes. 'Why the devil is he smiling and looking at me this way?' I thought. He added, 'If you wish, I will sum up one of them for you.' Without waiting for my answer, he started to relate a story that I've never been able to forget because of the joyfulness with which he told it. When I awoke the following day, the bed beside me was empty. They explained to me that Stein had taken a severe turn for the worse at midnight and that in the early morning he had died. I was sincerely sorry. I thought of the story he had told me, he, the dying man, in order to encourage me, who suffered from nothing really serious. And I cast a glance at the night table. The Hebrew book was still there. Since no one claimed it, I took it with me. It is with me now."

Kornblit sighed, "Poor Stein! And tell me, what was that story that impressed you so?"

"It was a story about two soldiers in the 1967 war between Israel and Egypt."

"Please, tell it to me."

"In the room of a military hospital there are two beds: one alongside the window and the other in a corner. When they bring in the soldier, David, the bed near the window is already occupied by the soldier, Samuel. The latter, in spite of the gravity of his wounds, is an optimist. He greets his new companion in misfortune and, seeing him very depressed, tries to encourage and even amuse him. Since from his bed he can look out through the window, Samuel describes to David all that he sees: a captain who slips on a banana peel and falls, a dog that will not return the ball to a child, beautiful nurses who cross the garden with their skirts lifted by the wind . . . David listens to the description of this interminable parade of scenes. Days pass. David's health improves. Samuel, on the other hand, gets worse and dies. That night they carry David to the bed Samuel occupied, and David's bed is taken by another wounded man. David waits impatiently all night long because in the morning they will lift the blind and he will be able to look out the window, see the interesting things that are happening in the garden, and cheer up the new soldier as Samuel had cheered him up. The nurse opens the blind. David, eager, looks out and sees that there is no such garden: two meters from the window there is a large wall obliterating the whole view. And how can he now cheer up the new wounded man if he, David, does not have Samuel's imagination?"

There was a long silence from which Kornblit finally emerged with a low sound. "Hummm! What a coincidence! The two soldiers in the story, wounded and in a hospital. Stein and you, also in the hospital, ill. Quite symmetrical, don't you agree? Excuse me for being so suspicious, but will you let me see the book from which that story was taken?"

"Certainly. There it is, on the bureau."

Kornblit got up, went to get the book, examined it, and burst out laughing.

"What are you laughing at?"

"This book, my dear Alvarez, is not an anthology of stories: it is an archeological treatise entitled *The Third Wall of Jerusalem*."

"Are you trying to tell me that the story he told me was not there?"

"I suspect not there nor anywhere. Possibly Stein wanted to entertain you, and knowing that you have more respect for a book than for conversation, he pretended that the story he told you was written down. Have you noticed the curious coincidence? The soldier who claims to be looking through the blocked window and is enlivening his companion with lies is the 'double' of the Jacob Stein who amused you by pretending that he was reading a story from an archeological work. He made up the story of the two soldiers especially to coincide with the situation of the two of you, stretched out in the hospital room. Who knows for what purpose."

"That is possible. However that may be, it pleased me. I still go on enjoying the garden just as Samuel described it to David. I can see the beautiful nurses with their legs exposed by the wind, as if they were showing them to me at this very moment. What a pity that the oral story has not been written down."

"Why do you regret that it doesn't exist? If you enjoyed it, even though only once, it is sufficient, no? That it does not exist as literature . . . Very well. All the more reason why you should make it exist. Write it. Write the story that he told you, if only to prove that you are not as inhibited as David, so unimaginative that he was unable to console his fellow man as Samuel had consoled him. The story could start as follows: 'Isaac Kornblit went to visit Rodrigo Alvarez who had just left the hospital. He found him haggard but very happy to be living once again in his home.'"

Kornblit and Alvarez burst into laughter, like children.

Juancito Chingolo

Adelina knows that sooner or later Lucas is going to leave her. Forty years of marriage; forty years of love, loyalty, and sacrifice; and suddenly a letter, discovered by chance, from an unknown woman, confirms for her the suspicion that sooner or later he is going to abandon her.

She understands and is resigned. She is old and ill. Lucas, on the other hand, has remained strong and handsome, every day more famous. When he abandons her, what is she going to do, alone, in this little house on the outskirts of the city?

It is spring. Her sadness, her anguish, do not allow her to sleep. At four in the morning she hears the sound of a bird. On the following day again. And again. It is a whistle, a warble, and a trill. When she gets up to prepare Lucas his breakfast, Adelina looks around for the bird. There are many. Some on the roof of the garage, others in the apple tree, others on the wires, but she recognizes her own. It is a tiny bird with an expressive crest. Now it has perched on the kitchen window sill. It moves in little jumps, feet together. With a wing it brushes the window screen. It is daring. What a funny little beak. It tips its head to one side. It looks at her with black and shining eyes. She smiles at it, speaks to it, and the little bird flies away.

She tells Lucas about it. "I have a friend. It visits me every morning. Its name is Juancito Chingolo. Look at it over there on the telephone pole. How do you like that? A friend with wings!"

Lucas goes out into the garden. He sees the little bird that Adelina points out for him. He also sees other birds that are flying around the house. He hears the incessant, universal chirping. He turns to Adelina and says, "Don't be silly. How stupid to choose a bird and call it a friend! One bird is like another. Maybe the bird that you saw that first morning has died and this is the one that replaced it. All birds are the same, and the song of one is the song of the whole species. The bird that you see is the same one that Eve saw. It cannot be your friend for the simple reason that Juancito Chingolo doesn't exist."

After destroying that friendship, the only one that remained for poor Adelina, Lucas packs his bags—with one in each hand he looks like a bird dragging its broken wings—and leaves her.

The Last Glances

The man looks around him. He goes into the bathroom. He washes his hands. The soap has a perfume of violets. When he turns off the faucet, the water keeps on dripping. He dries himself. He hangs his towel on the left side of the rack; the right side is for his wife. He closes the bathroom door so as not to hear the dripping. Once again he is in the bedroom. He puts on a clean shirt, the one with French cuffs. He has to search for his cuff-links. The wall is papered with designs of little shepherds and little shepherdesses. A few couples disappear under the picture of *The Lovers* by Picasso, but further on, where the doorframe cuts off one edge of the paper, many little shepherds are alone, without their girls. He enters his study, stops at the desk. Each one of the drawers of that piece of furniture as big as a building is a home where things live. In one of those drawers, the blades of the scissors must continue hating each other, as always. With his hand, he caresses the spines of his books. A beetle, which has fallen on its back on a shelf of the bookcase, desperately waves its little feet. He turns it over with a pencil. It is four in the afternoon. He enters the drawing room. The curtains are red. In the corner where the sun reaches them, the red softens into rose. Now almost at the door, he turns around. He looks at two armchairs that are facing each other and appear to be arguing, still. He goes out. Down the stairs. He counts fifteen steps. Weren't there fourteen? He almost turns to count them again. But now it is unimportant. Nothing is important. He crosses the front walk and, before turning toward the police station, he looks at the window of his own bedroom. There, inside, he has left his wife with a dagger driven into her heart.

The Palm Tree

"I was married, very young, in Florence, to an old man from the Polish nobility. Although he was very kind, there was no love in our marriage. A few years later we had to settle in Caracas and then I began to hear flattery: that my face . . . that my figure . . . In Latin America, men believe themselves obliged to conquer women. I confess that their flirtation flattered me but—I?—no flirting, not a smile or glance that anyone might misinterpret. Not once did I think of betraying my husband. When he suggested to me that we sleep in separate rooms—for some time the poor fellow hadn't been able to do anything—my bedroom, which in truth had never been a romantic place—began to serve as a reading room. I walked up the three floors and stretched out on the bed to read, read, and read. Sometimes I would interrupt my reading to listen to the sound of the wind in the branches of the palm tree that was growing in the garden, just beneath my window. It was growing with tropical rapidity. In Florence I had never seen a tree with such enormous wings. Years passed. The palm tree continued rising. One night I noticed that it was approaching my window and stretching up to offer me its branch of palm leaves. Another night we started to converse, I from above. I heard it reproach me for not daring to live. That palm tree turned out to be a convincing matchmaker! Because of it, something happened inside me. Suddenly I felt a wild desire to live. I needed to enjoy a more beautiful style of life than I had known. Curiosity tormented me. I could no longer control myself. And one night I made a decision. 'When the palm tree reaches my window,' I told myself, 'I will take a lover.'"

This is what the Florentine girl, Gina, told me, while the wind sang in the top of the palm tree, quite visible in the center of the bedroom window.

SELECTIONS FROM

The Size of the Witches (1985)

The Size of the Witches

When her brother, the mathematician Andrés Dolan, abandoned his country in order to settle for good in the United States, taking with him his wife and children, Dolly Dolan was left as mistress of the paternal mansion.

The people of the neighborhood could not imagine how much Dolly would suffer at finding herself alone. They scarcely knew her, since she was intimate with no one, and who could know that in that adult person, so mature, so serious, so self-sufficient, there beat the tiny heart of a child! They classified her as an eccentric—she who had been the center of the family—because they were of the opinion that a female without a male is unbalanced. Her rough character, reserved conduct, and dull dress suggested to them a hidden war against the male, resulting from a lack of femininity. They would see her returning from the Calvinist church, mannish, setting the pace with her large feet and carrying a Bible in her large hands. Their attention was drawn especially to the enormity of her hands, and, in noticing that her ring finger did not carry the ring of the usual womanly woman, they smiled maliciously, enjoying the grotesque quality of an elderly termagant and virgin. But Dolly's virginity, like her tiny heart, was not that of an old maid but that of a child.

And now the brother and his family had gone to North America!

For many months she wept as she walked through the empty rooms. She missed her little nieces and nephews. Now she had no one to entertain with fairy tales. Especially, she missed John, eight years old, to whom, in addition to telling stories, she would give stories to read, and then would talk them over with him: the habit of a former teacher! Influenced by her, John had constructed a little puppet theater and had just started to perform scenes that he himself had invented, when that cursed North American university took their father away, and with him all the others. All the others except Dolly, because she would be crazy to leave Buenos Aires.

Now the little puppet theater was stored away in the attic. When Dolly saw it again—she had gone up to put a hat in the trunk—her heart contracted with nostalgia. Certainly the ray of sunlight that filtered through the skylight brought out the lively colors of the stage, of the backdrop and the decorations, but it also revealed the agony of the puppets hanging from the flies. Floppy, floppy. They had nothing left but skin. They looked dead. Nevertheless, as soon as Dolly put her hands inside the dolls as if they were gloves—an index finger for each head and the thumbs and little fingers for the corresponding arms—eyes of glass thanked her for bringing them back to life. She thought about John and his favorite puppets, made to fit his little hands, and a wave of tenderness brought her relief from her loneliness.

The neighbors remembered that the old maid of more than sixty years had been a teacher—they continued calling her Miss Dolly—and so they were not surprised to receive invitations to a children's party in a puppet theater.

The children arrived, some of them accompanied by their parents, but Dolly separated the two with the authority of a cashier separating copper from silver coins.

"The show is only for the children. You can watch from the back. Let the children, alone, sit in groups of the same age."

One mother, offended, gestured to another as if to say, "You see? She still thinks she's at school!" And the other, with an equally expressive gesture, nodded as if saying, "Yes, she likes to give orders."

Dolly was not, in fact, authoritarian, but appeared so because she was of Scottish descent, more strict than the Creole, and especially because of her imposing bony frame. The strategy of addressing children and adults with her arms crossed in order to hide her over-large hands, conferred on her a false aspect of arrogance.

When the children were seated on the carpet, Miss Dolly judged it necessary to prepare them with an explanation. They were going to see, she told them, how the witch Jezebel kidnapped children, but they should not be frightened because everything was going to happen in an imaginary world that had nothing to do with the world in which they were living. It was all inside a crystal ball. No one could get inside it and no one could get out. A stage is like a page in a storybook; neither the black letters nor the colorful actors can escape from the scene. The witches that they were going to see were harmless: they were perfectly well-behaved. So nobody should be afraid.

The same mother as before whispered to the other, "You see? With that explanation the teacher has ruined the fun. Children love to be frightened."

And the other whispered back, "Do you think they understood?"

"My little Enrique, perhaps yes . . ."

"Your little Enrique must be a genius . . ."

"I don't know. But he is unusual. Perhaps he understood . . ."

Shush! Miss Dolly bowed and disappeared behind the frame of painted cardboard.

Already in her hiding place, Miss Dolly had taken down the empty skin of Jezebel, and with her own hands, long and bony, she straightened up the skeleton. There was still time to peek out at the audience through a small opening. The children were waiting with their faces lifted and their mouths half open. Over one of those faces, drawn to it by its likeness, appeared the face of John, the absent one.

What? How? And it came to her suddenly, like lightning . . . that out in the front row was her nephew. No, of course it was not John. But the two were freckled, red-headed, and blue-eyed. The boy who was there was impressively quiet. "John," she said, invoking the absent one, "I am dedicating this performance to you."

Very well. Get started. She plugged in the electric cord with its little purple lights, and drew back the curtain.

The full, bright, diffuse, and silky tone of the afternoon was rent like a very fine cloth, and the hollow of the breach was filled with the violet light of a forbidden hour, the light that the sleepless child sees in that hour when his mother has put him to bed to go right to sleep, but he cannot. The prettiest color was not in the curtains, or in the enamels, the wigs, Miss Dolly's ornaments and flowers, but in the purple reflections touching and waking all the objects lying hidden in the shadows of that cave.

Suddenly the children felt that the space to which they were accustomed had been taken over by another space that came out of nowhere. They would not have been able to describe it then (only one of them, many years later, would attempt to do this, in a tale about witches) but yes, they felt the shock of the encounter of the two different spaces, like two persons walking with their eyes down who bump into each other and look up surprised to meet another person like themselves but unknown. The real room and the unreal scene, a confrontation of objects of true proportions with other objects of unreal proportions, was shocking for an instant; but only for an instant, because the dizzy illusion demolished the real room, and the unreal scene took over absolutely, and all its forms and figures were triumphant. The children settled down in a new dimension and—oh, how marvelous!—an immense dark night extended before their eyes.

High up—the moon.

In the distance—a castle.

At one side—the forest.

On the other side—the mountain.

Nothing more.

In that space whose illusory vastness was now familiar, a witch leaned out over the children, shook her head and fixed them in her gaze. She made several leaps as if trying to fly, but an arm from hell was holding her from below. She turned rigid and in a shrill voice announced that she would enter the castle and kidnap the princess. She let out a screech of laughter so hair-raising that the children shook with fear. But not the quiet boy. Not the freckled boy, the red-head, he of the blue eyes. Not the boy who looked like John. Far from becoming afraid, he stood up. No mother could have stopped him. He came up, grabbed the witch's hair and gave it a tremendous pull.

Hair and clothes fell off and in the middle of the stage a colossal naked hand remained. It was not a hand that might belong to just anybody and be capable of adjusting eyeglasses, or taking a book, or shaking hands—as when Miss Dolly was walking around the room. No. In a setting outside of the room, the hand was (how absurd!) alive, free, independent, isolated. And yes, colossal.

The bold little Enrique Anderson, at first so intrepid in the presence of the witch, now drew back, terrified of those fingers which are as large as the castle, the forest, the mountain. The fingers of a foreign god who is meddling in our universe, and who, with a snap of a finger can send the moon to the devil.

The Tomb

They had announced that a storm would break, but he had not believed that it would be so fierce. Although well sheltered in the bus, Renato heard the storm crashing down and felt uneasy. Like all people who wear glasses, he would have liked to see, see, see more and more, but he could not see anything because it was night and the deluge blocked the view through the small windowpanes. In addition, because of the water that rushed over the windshield, from his seat in front, he was scarcely able to see the few meters of road that appeared in the beam of the headlights and then immediately disappeared under the wheels.

Did he do the right thing in not staying on in the hotel at San Nicolas? Well, it was too late now for regrets. A couple of hours more and he would be in Buenos Aires. At the moment of departure, a presentiment of death had moved him deeply. Now he shook off that fear with a resigned shrug of his shoulders: "After all, life has no meaning; we're born to die; fate plays with us." For example, a good move by fate was that the splendid Alexandrina had consented to be his wife; but a bad, a very bad move was that Alexandrina did not return the love that he offered her. We're born in order to die, we win in order to lose. What possibilities did he, a poor man, have with which to defend himself against the whims of the Great Roulette Wheel? "None," he continued, reflecting, "but just by making the attempt, at least one should be able to strengthen his character. If one behaved with integrity, one could cause the absurdity of the world to appear to be unjust."

It was unjust that he should desire Alexandrina and that she should not desire him. In the beginning, he wanted to believe that the restraint in her demonstrations of affection was due to her Nordic blood, to her family upbringing, to her reserved character; and he even wanted to believe that she was disciplining herself not to permit her emotions to disturb the serene beauty of her face or the elegance of her bearing; but soon he had to admit that more than merely inexpressive, his wife was cold, and that her frigidity (don't be deceived!) was an absence of love. Perhaps he had not been inspiring during the honeymoon. Perhaps, due to the nuptial disenchantment, the romantic memory of an adolescent sweetheart had returned to capture Alexandrina's soul, taking his place in her heart. However that might be, of one thing he was sure: Alexandrina would never let herself be touched by another man. Unfaithful to him? Never. Absolutely never. Unthinkable.

Nevertheless he thought about it when, on his business trip, he had to stop at a hotel in San Nicolás. It was a mere idea, suggested by an old tale—older than Boccaccio—of a woman who amuses herself while her husband is traveling; but the truth is that Renato decided to return immediately to his home. He had always advised Alexandrina of the date of his return. This time he did not tell her. He would surprise her. It would be like returning from afar, after a long absence.

One passenger was snoring at his side, and probably the others were sleeping as well. In spite of being tired, he was unable even to doze. The storm continued whipping the windowpanes. Already in Buenos Aires, they were approaching the Plaza de Miserere when, in

taking a curve, the bus skidded on a coating of mud from an empty
lot, crashed against the wreckage of a demolished building, and fell
into the excavation. Renato lost consciousness for a few seconds
and, when he came to, found himself in the rain, on foot next to a
corpse.

It took a moment for him to realize what had happened. He lifted
his hand to his face: his glasses had flown off, leaving him with his
vision blurred. A sensation of coming out of a cloud. Where was he?
What was he doing there? He heard voices, screams, groans; he saw
bodies trapped, and other bodies, that, like worms, by twisting and
turning, managed to get out through the openings of the overturned
bus, but he had nothing to do with those people. He had no compassion for the pain of the others because he had none himself. Was he
dreaming? The darkness of the early morning was that of eyes that
are closed. In just a moment, he would wake up . . .

No, it was not an awakening. It was more like his mind was clearing up. When he understood that it was not a matter of a nightmare
but of an accident, and that he had escaped from death by mere
chance, he had already walked a block away. He was another person.
Instead of returning to the site of the crash to help the injured, he
kept going. A lack of human kindness unworthy of him. He would
have liked to explain himself to the people who were rapidly hurry-
ing toward the disaster, but they passed by without paying him any
heed. Something strange was depriving him of all willingness to
help anyone. He felt detached . . . apathetic, inert, weightless. He
didn't even need to make an effort to walk, since the wind was carrying him along.

He turned a corner and, without his glasses, made out the window of his bedroom, wide as a television screen. On that screen his
jealous mind projected the scene of infidelity that he had imagined
in San Nicolás, with Alexandrina and a lover. A giggle sounded in
the deserted street. Alarmed, he squinted into the shadows. No one.
The person who had giggled must have been himself. He must have
laughed without knowing it. Laughed because his jealousy, baseless,
was as comical as monkeys in a mirage, appearing to walk on air.
There was no reason either for jealousy or resentment. Alexandrina
could be cold, frigid, but not unfaithful. In every couple there is one
person who loves and another who lets himself be loved, that was
all. He, who loved her, would have to teach her how to love. Perhaps
a second honeymoon . . .

With confidence in himself, with much hope in his heart, he
entered his house, stepping heavily, not on tiptoe, not like that
husband who in the old tale returned to confirm his dishonor. He
wanted so much to tell Alexandrina about the accident, he wanted

so much that she, finding him weak with fatigue, soaking wet, soiled with mud and even blood, would comfort him. It didn't matter if he made noise. On the contrary. If she was asleep, let her wake up, let her wake up.

He stopped in the bedroom doorway. In the half-light, the sheets traced the outline of a block of marble which, with its smooth curve, suggested the statue which the Supreme Sculptor would carve from it. And from that latent statue a lovely form already had emerged, the head of Alexandrina, turned toward the window. The statue did not move. Renato coughed. Nothing. He undressed and threw aside the wet clothing with a feigned exclamation of disgust. His wife did not stir. At last he spoke, "Alexandrina, do you hear me? Sweetheart, do you know what just happened to me?"

Useless. She didn't hear him. He put on his pyjamas and took a few steps alongside the bed. He managed to see that Alexandrina had her eyes open, but that she was not looking at him. To force her to see him he had to interpose himself between her and the window.

"Alexandrina," he murmured.

As if his own body were intercepting the little light that filtered in from the street, Alexandrina's eyes began to close and then shut completely, like bluebells when the light leaves them.

Was it possible that Alexandrina did not see him, did not hear him? Renato remembered a story that he had read in a magazine many years before. A man who had crashed in his car, continued through the city, not realizing that he had left his broken corpse in the wreckage and now was an invisible, inaudible, and intangible ghost.

This was not the case. He was not dead. He slipped in between the sheets and touched a bare arm.

"Don't keep me awake," Alexandrina said, "I'm very tired."

The sheets were a shroud. The bed, a tomb. Alexandrina and he, side by side, although rigid as the stones of a sepulchre, were not dead. No. But the marriage was.

Baby Bear

(Gilberto Viscarra Waxon returns from Dartmouth College in the United States, where he has spent a year teaching history.)

How ironic! Just when in that other country which was not his own, they had distinguished him with academic honors, in his own country a dictator had fired him from the University of the Andes.

(While the airplane, with the joy of a bird, flies in full sunlight over the cordillera, Gilberto's thoughts, with the torpidity of a serpent, slide down into a black depression.)

Poor Homeland! So in need of aid. But he . . . How was he going to help it? Without the authority which a university position would lend to his political opinions, with what weapons could he fight?

ट॰

Once in the airport, he noticed the change. The setting, formerly friendly, festive, touristic, was now an ominous barracks with soldiers ready for war. The Colonel had started by firing him. Would the next blow be to put him in prison? The loss of his salary was of little importance—after all, he enjoyed a comfortable income—but if they locked him up, how would his wife and son react? His wife had never gone along with him in his ideas. The poor thing was stupid. It was certain that, if worse came to worst, Ernestina would not know how to explain to her son why his father was in jail.

"Anything to declare, sir?" the customs official had just finished asking. No. Nothing. Not even a gift for his wife or child. The truth: he was not much attached to his family. For him, the marriage was a burden. He should not have married. They were not suited for each other. Differences appeared very quickly. He, without a drop of mixed blood; he, with distinguished Creole ancestors; he, cultivated and intelligent. If, at least, Ernestina were to give him the satisfaction of admitting, in some way, however modestly, the inferiority of her race, her family, her upbringing; but she, imperturbable, appeared to lack the gray cells necessary to distinguish the inferior from the superior.

As for the child, business and travel had not given him the time to play with him, to assist in the unfolding of his personality, in effect, to take him into his heart. In his paternal feelings there was more curiosity and expectation than tenderness. To relieve a bothersome sense of guilt, he had hit upon a theory. Tenderness, he theorized to himself, is nothing more than a state of feeling: bland, amorphous, inert, and momentary. On the other hand, curiosity about the future of a child and alertness to the first manifestations of character, in order to develop it, are concerns more noble than mere feelings, are more—how to say it?—more intellectual; and he, what was he if not an intellectual? Tenderness leaves one in the same place. Curiosity, on the other hand, moves one on into science; expectancy always accompanies one who struggles for a better world . . . He was right. Nevertheless a sense of guilt continued bothering him.

After the customs inspection, Gilberto carried his luggage to the lobby and, among the people there waiting for the passengers, he distinguished his wife and son. Ernestina leaned over Manucho, said something in his ear, and pushed him toward his father. As if he had been wound up like a toy, Manucho ran toward his father with his little arms open wide.

They embraced.

"How tall you are!" said Gilberto.

Tall, yes, for his six years; but his gaze was so empty that Gilberto feared the child's intelligence had not developed along with his body. A blank look, innocent, tranquil, impassive, that went through him as if he were made of air. "Who can have been the ancestor?" Gilberto asked himself. "Surely on his mother's side, generations back, they carried the genes of those eyes and passed them on to this child. Those eyes, like a statue that looks without seeing, are certainly not mine." He would have liked to see himself in his son. A physical resemblance between the two would have carried with it, perhaps, a mental similarity, with the possibility that sometime the son might extend the life of his father in the same direction. But in Manucho he saw only the shadow of Ernestina's family.

Half an hour later, Gilberto was driving the car toward the foothills.

You look very well. You too. Do I look a little fat? Well, a little. You didn't write very often. Didn't you get my postcard? Yes, but . . . Any news? None. And . . . how are you? OK. And how are things going? All right. And for you? OK too.

The flower of conversation! To change the record, Gilberto turned to Manucho, but he kept his head down and, although he was moving his lips, what he said could not be heard. He was speaking to himself. Only when they had finished eating dinner, was Gilberto able to understand a sentence. He understood the words but not the meaning. The sentence was: "Baby Bear wants more ice cream."

"Very well," his mother answered, "you go to bed and I'll bring it up to you."

As soon as they were alone, Gilberto commented to Ernestina: "How formal, eh? Manucho speaks in the third person, like an oriental king. Since when does he refer to himself as 'Baby Bear'?"

"No, no. He isn't Baby Bear. Baby Bear is a friend."

"Ah, a doll . . ."

"No. A real little bear, but invisible. They are inseparable. They talk to each other all day long."

"Strange, because Manucho gives me the impression of being taciturn, silent, you could even say retarded."

"Not at all. Right now he is shy. He has to get accustomed to seeing you. Wait a few days. You'll hear him. He never stops talking with Baby Bear."

"And aren't you afraid that all those fantasies are bad for him?"

"No. Why?"

"Well . . . some lives remain mired in the imagination . . . It is never too late to draw a child out of his confusion and develop his intelligence . . ."

"And isn't imagination a part of intelligence? I mean . . . I don't know . . . You should know . . ."

The last words were tentative and respectful, but the first words had implied Gilberto's lack of common sense by means of a well-aimed observation—"Isn't imagination a part of intelligence?"—and it irritated him to be bested on his own territory. He wasn't ready to permit Ernestina, poor little Ernestina, to lecture him, him of all people.

"Yes," he replied, forcing a smile, "of course I know about it. This is a case of eidetic imagery, very common among children. In adults as well, the act of confabulation causes us to project around us imaginary speaking companions. It was in this way, with fictitious characters, that novels were constructed. Not only novels. I know that this will shock your religious sentiments, but mankind, much earlier than this, also speaking to imaginary gods, established religion. You understand me? Or not?"

"Of course I understand you. I am not that stupid. What you are saying about the novel and religion is very interesting. They used their imaginations intelligently, right?"

"You see? You don't understand me . . . The imagination of primitive man, not yet controlled by judgment, peopled the world with supernatural beings. It was peopled, but now it must be unpeopled. We must unpeople the world of phantoms and gods, of dreams and superstitions in order that the imagination can serve for more than religion and poetry. Imagination in the service of intelligence. That's where we are. Where reason controls the imagination. So don't come at me with 'Imagination is a part of intelligence.' I know that. And I know that a child, your child (and mine of course) repeats the prehistoric phase of human development."

"That I certainly do not understand."

"No matter. Forget it. All that I am saying is that it worries me that the child likes to speak with a bear."

"With Baby Bear."

"Imagining a human friend, that's all right. But a bear! There aren't any bears here!"

"There's Baby Bear . . . now."

His discourse had been for nothing. Ernestina was unimpressed. On the contrary, she lifted her head, raised her finger, and warned him: "Don't even think of denying the existence of Baby Bear. That would certainly harm Manucho. Ever since you went away, we have been accustomed to speaking of Baby Bear as a living person."

"Ah. You too. I see. A willful hallucination. Folie à deux."

"And what would you have? We must amuse ourselves somehow. We are always alone. We went to the movies; we saw a film where Jimmy Stewart made friends with Harvey, a six-foot rabbit, invisible to everybody but him . . ."

"Bah!"

The following day Gilberto was standing in front of a bookcase, consulting a treatise by Keynes, when the little voice of Manucho reached him.

"Papa."

"What?"

"You're standing on Baby Bear. It hurts him. Please move your foot."

He scrutinized the face of the child to see if he could find some spark of humor, some sign that he was joking, but since he saw nothing but a mystical gravity, he wanted to challenge him: "Are you pretending to be dumb or are you really dumb?" That was all he needed, that the child should turn out to be a fool! You never know what hereditary defects or surprising potentialities are developing in the brain of a child. The question is, has it stopped at this point or is it developing? Manucho gazed at his father with a leaden stare, lidless eyes, eyes resigned to contemplating an infinite metaphysical mist.

At that moment, Ernestina entered. Rapidly, Gilberto moved his foot and Manucho, with the flash of a smile, thanked him for releasing Baby Bear.

"This afternoon I'm going to pay a visit to my friend Lara," Gilberto announced to Ernestina. "I suppose he is still in charge of *Los Andes* . . . Yes? . . . So much the better. I'm going to propose a column in which, under the pretext of evoking scenes from the historic past, I will denounce the stupidities of the present."

Ernestina put her hand on his shoulder. "But sweetheart, where do you think you are living? They won't let you. And if they do let you, so much the worse for you, because with the first article they will arrest you . . ."

"My only weapon is the pen."

"You know what you are doing, but remember: you're not living in a democracy. Excuse me. I don't want to interfere. All right . . . I have to do some shopping in the city. Could you take me with you, on the way?"

"Aha."

"And will you take me too?" Manucho asked of his mother.

"Of course."

"And Baby Bear?"

"Of course," his mother repeated; and with a glance she silenced Gilberto.

At the newspaper office, Gilberto had his first confrontation with reality. "You are persona non grata with the army," Lara spit at him, "and don't compromise me if you don't want the Colonel to shut down the newspaper." Gilberto left, furious.

"Lara is a coward!" he confided to Ernestina who, together with Manucho, was waiting for him in the car. "He brags of being a liberal, a progressive, but he is a coward. He doesn't want to print even one line from me. My poor country!"

During the trip back, Gilberto's rage was transferred to the motor, and the car began racing at high speed.

"For God's sake, Gilberto!" Ernestina pleaded, seeing that, to rid himself of his indignation, he was raising his fists and shaking them. "Don't let go of the steering wheel. We'll run off the road!"

The road, between the hill and the cliff, snaked up and down around sharp curves; the blues of the sky, the greens of the trees, the grays of the rocks fled out of his way, terrified.

"Stop, Papa, please stop!" Manucho screamed, "Baby Bear has to get out."

Gilberto, as if he had heard nothing, continued railing against the dictatorship.

"Stop, Papa. Baby Bear can't stand it any more!"

Nothing. The car had gone insane.

"Gilberto!" Ernestina cried, "didn't you hear? Put on the brakes. Baby Bear has to do his duty. Don't you understand? Stop at once."

"All right. All right. I was looking for a suitable spot," he lied.

The car stopped. Ernestina and Manucho hid behind a thicket. After a little while, as they were returning, Manucho held back, looking behind him.

"Don't worry about Baby Bear," his mother told him. "As soon as he sees you in the car, he will come running. Get in."

"Don't shut the door yet, Mama," Manucho said, in a low voice, and then aloud, "Baby Bear, come quickly or Papa will be angry!"

Gilberto, without saying a word, got out as if he were going to hit someone, and then, with a tremendous slam, shut the door, got into his seat, and took off.

"Papa, Papa! You left Baby Bear in the middle of the road! Stop, please stop!"

He lifted his foot a little from the accelerator, but NO SIR! he wasn't going to yield any more! And he pushed his foot down again.

"Baby Bear got left behind," Manucho cried. "Baby Bear!" And he burst into tears.

"Stop!!" Now it was Ernestina giving an order. "Stop, I tell you. Stop and turn around . . ."

Gilberto paid no attention.

"He's just a child!" Ernestina reproached him, "why do you take out your anger on him?"

And she clutched Manucho against her breast. And the more she tried to console him, the more he wept. And weeping, weeping, the child went to sleep.

The hum of the motor made the two adults maintain their own silence, obstinate and resentful. Finally they arrived. Ernestina struggled to open the door and at the same time lift up the sleeping child.

"Let him be," Gilberto told her, "I'll carry him."

"No! Not my son." Ernestina stressed the possessive, MY son— "I'll carry MY son, myself. I suppose you must be very satisfied. You have behaved . . ."

Gilberto lowered his head, scaled the steps up to the house, opened the door, and held it until Ernestina went in with Manucho in her arms.

The argument—Manucho now in bed—was inevitable.

"You have no feeling for me," Gilberto complained. "The country is in the hands of savages; they throw me out of the university, they deny me any use of the press . . ."

"Don't raise your voice. You're going to wake up the child."

". . . and you, what do you expect of me? That I should start playing with a bear?"

"No, with your son."

"What do you want? That before I sit down in my chair, I am to ask permission of Manucho in case the bear is already spread out there and I might sit on him? You don't give a fig for my ideas. You care more about the fantasies of a little child about an animal."

"Shush. Manucho might hear you. Tell me, what's wrong with a child six years old inventing a little bear?"

"What's wrong, what's wrong? Well nothing . . . Let him become a liar . . ."

"Ah, better so. A liar? . . . Better so . . . Because otherwise you treat your child as if he were a mental retardate. And also, look in the mirror. He invents his own world, and don't you do the same thing? You invent a utopia."

A clever hit. How could this be? What had happened during the year he was in the United States, that Ernestina had become so argumentative? He had never seen her fencing this way. But he returned to the attack. He could not, he could not, he simply could not close his mouth. He had to drown his feelings of failure. Failure as a professor, as a citizen, as a husband, as a father. Out of control, he said whatever entered his head. He said that if he had known that he would come back to a wife and a son both turned into idiots by an imaginary bear, he would never have returned. Moreover, that at this very moment he wanted to pack his bags and leave once again.

Voices. The house was filled with voices.

"Listen carefully, Ernestina,"—the voice was cutting, more threatening than admonishing—"that cursed little bear will drive us apart . . ."

"It's you, it's you, not the little bear . . ." and the voice broke into sobs.

"To the devil with that bear!" the voice exploded.

And in the silence that followed, they heard the imploring voice of Manucho, "Papa—a—a!"

Gilberto and Ernestina looked at each other apprehensively. Could Manucho have heard what they had been saying to each other? Ernestina fell back into her chair. Gilberto rushed up to the child's room. There he was caught by the eyes of Manucho, looking at him without blinking. This was not the vacant look that had surprised him on the day of his arrival at the airport. This was a gaze full of intelligence, a serene regard, cold, profound, that pierced his soul. Something had entered into this child that had made him leap from one age to another. An instant maturity. And Gilberto, filled with remorse, finally understood what he had only suspected during the argument, that what the discussion was really about was discontent in their marriage; that the little bear, more than just a little bear, was a scapegoat that he was using to unburden himself of his unhappiness. Only the violence was strong enough to open a way out for his feelings, completely blocked by moral constraints. Ever since childhood he had been that way. His parents had never shown affection, perhaps from a horror of being common, nor did they ever kiss him when he needed tenderness. Always he had to swallow his tears alone, and harden himself. He grew up repressing all manifestations of sensitivity; he had to store his energy to use in matters requiring will power. But now, with his will power badly bruised and weakened by his recent failures, his feelings responded to the searching look from Manucho.

Manucho and Baby Bear, a small world within the hardly larger world of Ernestina and the household. To see them from above was very moving, after all. Feelings that engendered other feelings: guilt, remorse, hope, tenderness. Yes. He, even he, became tender. Poor child! He felt that if he were to become reconciled with Manucho, all would go well with him, with Ernestina of course, but also with his country. Countries too are children: they have their Baby Bears. And he had been implacable, inflexible in his intellectual manner of condemning his nation's myths. He knelt down beside the bed, caressed the head of his child and whispered, "Listen, my sweetheart. Do you know what we will do tomorrow? You and I are going to find Baby Bear. I bet he is waiting for you in the same place where we left him. He is going to ask you why you left him in the middle of the road, and then you will explain that I was to blame. How does that seem to you? Eh?"

Manucho's face held that inscrutable expression that no adult is capable of understanding when a child becomes serious.

"So. What do you say? Very early tomorrow morning shall we go together and find Baby Bear?"

And Manucho answered, softly, "What little bear are you talking about, Papa?"

The Wisteria

Last night I went to bed very happy with my solitude and my bachelorhood and, oddly enough, today I woke up yearning for a woman. What had I dreamed? For years nothing like that had happened to me and the truth is that I am not at an age when things like that happen. Senescence, they call it. I am not among those who are interested in remembering their dreams, but this time, on waking up, I again closed my eyes and tried to remember what had inspired in me such a desire to love and be loved. In the darkness behind my eyes, I was able to imagine only the trace, the hollow, the form which the forgotten dream had left in my memory. Thus, to rid myself of the obsession, although I still wanted to sleep, I dressed, left the hotel, and started my first walk through the unknown city.

Turning a corner, I discovered a park enclosed by a wrought-iron fence, but with its gate open. I entered. Not a soul was there. It was one of those gardens which belong more to art than to nature. The architect-gardener, in designing it, had selected plants for their plastic properties and used them as material for construction. Not a trace of natural disorder remained. All was artistic order. Between heaven and earth, the human intelligence supplied plant symbolism. The pine and the palm symbolized the solidarity of north and south.

A line of cypresses resembled the wall of a secret cloister. Shrubbery, trimmed back with clippers, was reduced to geometric forms. Even birdhouses had been fabricated and hung from the branches, like little chalets.

But in spite of all this, the green patterns, the geometric forms of the flower beds, and the haughty tilt of the tulips created a certain enchantment. Enchantment that made me smile when, walking along paths pretending to be labyrinthine, I reached a scene where, too ostentatiously, they had brought together the typical elements of a classic painting. For an instant my eyes held the memories of scenes from museums. The painters, who had tried to picture the garden of Paradise, not knowing what it looked like, had bathed the canvas in many shades of green and against that happy background, pictured a few European ladies, very white and lovely, who without undue modesty had removed their garments. They were showing us an Eve, but not an Eden. Well then, in the garden that I visited this morning they had erected a statue of Falconet's *La Baigneuse* above a grotto. From the grotto, a miniature waterfall poured down into a pool. And in the pool was mirrored the nude bather. The scene did not lack its marble bench in the shade of a pergola over which a wisteria was climbing.

The wisteria vine comes from China. In paintings of the Han Dynasty, the landscapes are a happy accident of nature, open, asymmetric, with vegetation growing without the help of gardeners. It struck me then that the transplanted wisteria must find itself ill at ease in the midst of the artificialities of a European garden.

With its enormous clusters, the wisteria reigned supreme over the springtime. I sat down under this marvel of light and fragrance. I held still, waiting for . . . what? Perhaps an adventure that would satisfy my yearning for the woman with whom I had awakened? I could not say how long I remained thus. My attention wandered inward, downward, toward a dark flow of images, images of nothing. It was as if I had regressed to the point of transition from animal to man, before the emergence of language and the power of reasoning capable of distinguishing sensations, fantasies, memories, dreams, desires, and fragmentary thoughts. And suddenly I was roused from my stupor by a kiss on my right cheek. My whole body rejoiced.

Bah! It was a little flower that, falling from the vine, had brushed my cheek and was now reposing at my feet. Although I understood the cause of my error, the effect of the sensation of the kiss persisted, and I ended up feeling pathetic. I was accustomed to my solitude, but at that moment I felt more than alone, I felt abandoned.

More than that, I felt that all the human race had sailed away from me in a sidereal fleet, abandoning me forever. Now I was the last man on earth. This self-pity then changed in tone because in some manner I realized that the fact of being the last man on earth might well mean that the fleet could also have abandoned the last woman on earth.

The little flower that caressed me was only the advance scout of an invasion. Others followed. It could be that a breeze shook its clusters or that the wisteria, precocious in its flowering, had now reached an early maturity, but what is certain is that a rain of flowers fell on my head and over the lawn. The indecisive color of the wisteria, translated into the murmuring sound of the sea, of a rippling sea, rose in me as two merging metaphors: the blue-violet sea of which our blind Homer sang was being sprinkled over us; the rippling violet-blue of the dusk of which the poet Panchito Lopez Merino sang was spreading over the lawn and over me. And then I stopped being literary because I was distracted by something peculiar: immediately to my right, the bench was untouched by any flower. The lawn and I were covered with flowers, but the vacant portion of the bench beside me held none.

Vacant? No. An invisible woman must have been seated at my right, at the right of the cheek where I had felt the kiss! The flowers kept falling. But only on my right were they being displaced in the air. It seemed that a solid form, below, resisted and redirected them. Some of the flowers fell away rapidly; others slipped along slowly. To better appreciate the spectacle of the rain of petals as they outlined the form of a transparent woman, I rose and moved away a few steps. Immediately, three or four flowers fell where I had been seated; on the other hand, at the side, the bench remained dry, untouched. Little by little, in that air untouched by the petals, there appeared the features of a woman's face; features so vague that they seemed rather to be a reflection of a face in the water; water like that which at the moment was trembling between the grotto and the pool. And when the vision was complete, I saw a naked woman. I held out my hands, ready to embrace her. The apparition disappeared. I waited for it to form again, but then I observed that the petals were falling onto the bench where she had been seated.

The iridescent bubble had burst, but now I know that the daydream in the garden repeated the dream I could not remember that morning waking up in the hotel.

The Innocent Child

The widow Hannah Goldstein gave a sigh of relief when, finally! her son, León, went off to the National High School. It had been necessary to shake him in order to make him get up, bring him his clothes so that he could dress, fry his eggs so that he could have breakfast, hurry him up so that he wouldn't be tardy, go with him to the street door so as to bid him goodbye with a kiss, and even there check his notebook to be certain that he had not forgotten his notes on the horrible drama of Lope de Vega that they had deciphered together. He still behaved like a child, although he was already thirteen years old. She sighed with relief, but her smile was tender.

The house and store occupied a corner. The living quarters fronted a poor street. The portion used for business faced a wealthy avenue. Along the poor street—a tunnel of hostile facades to the left, indifferent trees to the right, broken paving-stones below and, above, a threatening sky—León walked toward the high school, nervous, she knew how very nervous. She knew moreover that the image of the street as a tunnel was not just her own notion but the same one that León had just transmitted to her telepathically. León, at that same moment, must have been feeling imprisoned in a tunnel that was taking him from his home to the feared high school. A mother senses what is taking place inside her son, doesn't she? She feels his palpitations just like when she was carrying him in the womb. Thinking carefully ("Ah, now my imagination is awake!"): her womb was the tunnel through which her child entered into life; and in being born he entered into another tunnel, the world, from which there is no exit other than death. ("My goodness! The blame for these happy thoughts is this winter sky, so loaded with black clouds. That cloud in the form of a fist must be wanting to tell me something.")

After dressing, with care but unprovocatively, she went through an inside door from her rooms into the store. She found it cold, with the cold of July. She lit the stove. A dictionary had been left on a chair; she put it back on the desk. She looked about her with satisfaction; in the bookcases and on the tables was the human babble, but classified in perfect order. Her husband, who had grown up in England, had given the store the name of Solomon, thus, with the English spelling, not so much because he himself was named Solomon, but rather because what name was more appropriate for a bookstore than that of the wise author of *Proverbs*—especially for a second-hand bookstore, specializing in history books, as the sign on the store window announced. Solomon, who fifteen years before had established the store opposite the synagogue, died without suspecting that it would soon be menaced by hatred originating in the Old World. ("And I, here, alone with all these books.") Counseled by the Rosenbergs, she had had the "omon" erased, and now the bookstore was named "Sol." Already, they told her, other store windows had been stoned. Bad times. "The too much discussed 'Jewish problem' has been created by anti-Semites. Then I didn't think of myself as Jewish, but now, with these persecutions . . ." Clara Rosenberg had said. Incredible that Clara could have forgotten that she was Jewish. If her friend had married a Rosenberg, as she had married a Goldstein, and all that long before the persecutions started, it must have been for some reason. It was certainly not by coincidence. The feeling of being Jewish could not be just a reaction to aggression from outside. Within her, at least, it was born and reborn. But in one sense the Rosenbergs were right: the agents of rancor were taking over the city in that ominous year of 1936. The air, infected with prejudice, filtered into the classrooms. Had they not assigned the high school children to read that unreadable play only because it was anti-Semitic? Broken store windows, classrooms contaminated with prejudice . . . ("One of these days they will attack the synagogues.")

Her own thought startled her because she heard it explode. Explode outside of her head. Explode in the avenue. It was a small bomb exploding, followed by much shouting. Looking out the store window, she saw that they were throwing bombs at the synagogue opposite her. Big boys, screaming, were throwing tar-bombs. And one of those filthy things had touched the Star of David, and the tar was dripping down.

At that very moment, a man with a gray beard entered the bookstore. He was wearing a black trench coat and a black hat. As if he had entered a theater after the action had started and, in the darkness, could find no empty seat, without saying a word, without turning his gaze from the lighted stage, he stood near her chair. Although he was a stranger, Hannah sensed that he too was regarding the street scene with a quiet horror. Now, while some of the boys were nailing up a sign on the doorway of the temple, others in loud voices were shouting their slogans to the people who were passing by in alarm or stopping to see the fun. It seemed they had no fear that the police might arrive. Brutes, brutes! And there they were, a few yards away. Her poor store window, if she had not already altered the name "Solomon"! Would the abbreviation "Sol" save her? With her gaze fixed before her Hannah murmured, "What barbarity! Have you ever seen anything like this before?"

And she heard a grave voice, with those sibilant foreign s's answering, "I? Yes. Many times."

She turned her face to the man. The blackness of his trench coat and hat, seen from the side, had impressed her as being respectable, but seen from the front they showed stains, wrinkles, and tears. His hair and his beard, grown long from neglect, added to his poor appearance. She could not guess his age because, even though he had an old man's stooped shoulders, his face was bright with his youthful eyes. Her imagination, now watchful, began to stir. Who could this man be? He looked like a costumed mummer in a cheap carnival. And when one starts imagining a person in disguise, what happens? (Here, her imagination took wing.) Immediately she thought of him removing his costume, pulling off his beard, his wig and his cardboard nose, until he is left with a . . . with another costume, which in its turn . . . Her imagination flew even higher. A single body with multiple masks? The image was reversed. Not like her name Hannah, a palindrome, which is the same whether read from the right or from the left, but like the number 6 which, when read upside down, is 9. Turned upside down, the image of a body with many masks was changed into a mask with many bodies. A single face—like the face of God, according to Genesis—had passed from generation to generation and now, precisely in these evil times, was being worn by her son. What problems would that Jewish mask be creating for her son at this very moment at the high school?

"It is a shame that such things happen."

"They have always happened," the strange voice answered.

"Not here, not in this country."

"Not here. In other places."

"Ah. In Hitler's Germany."

"And in other places. Earlier. Much earlier . . ."

A few automobiles braked and picked up the boys, who, from the cars, kept blowing their mocking trumpets in all directions.

"May I sit down? I am very tired," said the man, and sat down. When he stretched out his legs, Hannah noticed his boots, soiled and torn. ("It would have been better for this man to go to a shoestore than a bookstore.")

"Rest for a moment. Are you looking for any book in particular?"

"No. I no longer read books. I have read all that there is to read."

"And how can I help you then?"

"If you give me something warm to drink . . ."

Surprised, she opened her eyes and almost laughed. ("What could he want? A bowl of soup? He's in the wrong store.") She didn't know what to do.

The man passed his gaze over the bookcases and commented, "The 'Sol' of this bookstore was a 'Solomon'."

His voice had no ring of reproach, but it did not please her.

"How do you know that? Are you from the neighborhood?"

"Oh, I know everything. But one of those books open in the store window has the old seal: 'The Solomon Bookstore'."

"Ah." ("I will have to get rid of it.")

She plugged in the samovar which she kept prepared for herself, and, in a little while, served him a cup of tea.

"You must have traveled a lot, right?"

"A lot."

"Throughout Europe?"

"All over the world."

"And you say you have seen scandals like this one in other places?"

"In other places and in other times."

"Times? What an exaggeration! You mean to say years. You're not that old."

"I said times."

"What you know of other times you must have read, not seen."

"I have seen them. In other times, I have seen violence worse than that of today."

From where could he have come, this know-it-all? Many queer types were moving freely around in the city: bohemian artists, philosophers without philosophy, originators of religious cults, mystics, maniacs, liars . . . Would he be one of them? He was speaking with conviction, but is this not perhaps the manner of speaking of these impostors?

"I have traveled so extensively through countries and through epochs that I could be a professor of geography and history."

A modest gentleman, wasn't he? So Hannah decided to give him a little of his own medicine.

"Around here we are all historians. My husband was one. Myself, I read a lot. I write . . . And already my son is showing an affinity for history. Right now he is at the high school."

"It's good that he is not here. He was spared the spectacle of those fascists."

"Yes, he was spared the spectacle here, but not the one over where he is. At this moment, he must be suffering at the school. There is anti-Semitism now in the classes too, you know."

"I am not surprised."

"He has a literature professor who is a madman. Irresponsible. A fanatic. A sadist. Imagine, he had required the children to read *El Niño Inocente* or *El Segundo Cristo* by Lope de Vega. Poetry! And even worse, from the beginning of the seventeenth century. How could a child understand it? I don't know with what sinister intent the professor selected that piece as a text for reading, although, seeing the tar they are throwing at the synagogue, I am beginning to understand. Lope took an incident that occurred during Easter Week in 1490, imagine! Before the discovery of America! According to Lope, a few Jews from the town of Toldeo kidnapped a Christian child, subjected him to the same tortures with which their elders, according to Lope, had tormented Jesus, and then ended up crucifying him. . . A repugnant ritualistic murder . . . What do you think? To give those atrocities to children to read, imagine! And especially to my child who is a Jew . . . So that he should feel ashamed of being Jewish? So that we should all feel ashamed, eh?"

"There is no reason to feel ashamed. That crime never occurred. It was invented. Spain needed saints and in order to create them, it was necessary to feed racial hatred. Tell this to your son."

"Oh, if only it were true! But unfortunately those people work from documents. Lope based his work on chronicles . . ."

"Which also were lies. I know it. I know it because in those years I lived in Spain, I was in the town of La Guardia, I knew the Jews of Toledo very well. And later I met the authors of those chronicles . . . and even Lope de Vega."

("Let him run on. Now he is going to start saying that he met Jesus Christ.") The man was denouncing the lies of others, but he himself was a liar. Moreover, more than a liar he had the look of a madman. Not only was he dressed like a madman, but his gaze was mad, his eyes were childlike, yes, but too intense. He said that he could have been a history professor. Why not? He probably had been a history professor and became mad reading all those stories. And in his madness, he believes himself a witness to all those epochal events. Another Don Quixote. Perhaps he became mad reading, not the histories, but those novels about machines made to journey through time. Or he believes himself a spirit with a wandering soul . . . ("I am imaginative, but that fellow is crazy.")

The man returned the empty cup. With difficulty, he got up and walked to the door. "Moving, always moving . . . Like the world . . . On and on and on . . . The world spins and all the colors of all the flags become a single white flag; and all mankind, homicidal, is a single suicidal man . . ."

And, about to leave, he turned. "Don't forget to tell your son what I have said. It will be good for him. And give him this as a memento." He put his hand into his coat, took out a coin, and gave it to her.

It was a very old coin, worn and old. Hannah felt a strange wave of dizziness. Suddenly her mind was emptied of ideas and filled with foam. She was floating in a sea of time, numb but happy, as if drugged.

At noon, León returned. It wasn't necessary to ask him how it had gone—his clenched face told it all—but she questioned him.

"I will never go back to that school!" he cried, in a rage. "Do you know what the professor did? He made us read aloud from that cursed book. That's what he did. Each one of us had a role. And he gave me the role of the child from La Guardia. You understand that? Only to humiliate me . . . Because they all know that I am a Jew, and they looked at me and laughed . . . He made me speak like a Christian against the Jews . . . Mama, I felt ashamed. First, being Jewish, one feels responsible for all that Jews do and have done, isn't that so? Reciting the verses of Lope de Vega, I felt ashamed for the cruelty of those judges from La Guardia toward an innocent child . . . against me . . ."

"No, no. You mustn't feel that way. All that business about the tortures and the crucifixion is lies and nothing more."

"Hmmm! Who knows? No one now can be certain about those things of the past."

"I am certain."

"How?"

"Because someone told me about it, someone who was there and saw everything, everything that happened and everything that did not happen. He told me about it." And she placed the coin in his hand, the coin which was a Roman dinar with the effigy of Augustus.

"The Wandering Jew told me."

"Ah. So he came through here?"

Lycanthropy

I climbed up onto the train just as it was pulling out. I went through several cars. Filled! What was going on that day? Did everybody want to travel? Finally I found an empty seat. With some effort I placed my valise up onto the baggage rack and, giving a sigh of relief, let myself fall back into my seat. Only then did I notice that in front of me, also seated beside the window, was none other than the banker who lives in the apartment next to mine.

He smiled at me ("What teeth!" Red Riding Hood would have said) and I suppose that I too smiled at him, although if I did, it was unwillingly. To tell the truth, our relationship was restricted to saying hello when we accidentally met at the door of the building or when we were together in the same elevator. I could not be ignorant of the fact that he was involved in business affairs because once, after congratulating me on a science fiction story that I had published in a newspaper, he introduced himself, extending a card—"Romulo Genovesi, Doctor of Economic Science"—and offered me his services in case I should wish to invest my savings. "You," he told me, "live in another world; I live in this one, on which I have a good grasp; now that you know this, if I can be of service to you . . ." On other occasions while the elevator rose or descended eighteen floors, Genovesi spoke to me of economic conditions in the country, of enterprises, banks, interest rates, policies, markets and a thousand things I don't understand. Such was the financial genius who was smiling at me when I dropped into my seat.

I would have preferred to forget my poverty, but the mere presence of that speculator brought it back to me. I had prepared to rest during the remainder of the journey, and suddenly I saw myself forced to be polite. If, in the elevator cage, I respected the practical talents of my neighbor, now, in the railroad car I feared that the talents, precisely because they were adapted to ordinary reality—a reality I reject every time I invent a story—would turn out to be boring. The horizontal movement of the train, longer than the vertical movement of the elevator, was going to kill me with boredom. Even worse, the success that Genovesi was having in his economic operations was not reflected in a face that should have shown satisfaction, contentment, happiness. On the contrary, his appearance was gruesome.

We were the same age, but (if the mirror did not deceive me) he looked older than I. Older? No, that wasn't it. There was something—how can I express it?—something mysterious. I can't explain it. It seemed—how to express it—that his body, wasted, worn out, must have survived various lives. To me he had always looked thin, never robust; nevertheless, his was the thinness of a fat man who had lost weight. More, more than that. It was as if the loss of weight must have occurred many times, and, with becoming first fat and then thin, with repeatedly storing fat under the skin and then removing it, his face had become deformed. His ears were still erect; his nose was prominent, his eyeteeth solid, but all the rest was flabby and drooping: the cheeks, the lower jaw, the folds of flesh, the hair, the bags under the eyes.

His sunken eyes gave out that cold look that one associates with intelligence; without doubt Genovesi was very intelligent. There was no reason to doubt it, considering the fact that he was a Doctor of Economic Science. The difficulty was that his intelligence, his skill with numbers, computation, and problem solving, was always boring to me.

Could he have read my mind? He abandoned his economic theme and switched the conversation to my field of interest, the literature of the fantastic. And, as in the elevator he counseled me about earning money, now, in the train, he regaled me with weird stories that I could use in my writing "so as to become famous . . ."

As if I needed them! I who, with a tiny seed of madness, could grow a forest of sophistic stories or, from an insignificant street scene, construct windy towers, uninhabitable palaces, cathedrals for atheists: I, a veteran, emotional, fantastic, arbitrary, spontaneous, grandiloquent, and a genius, why the devil should I need this vulgar stockbroker to help me write stories? His fatuity made me rebellious, but I suppressed my rebellion (fortunately, when I swell up with pride I hear in my head the buzzing of a sarcastic bee) and let him talk.

His monologue followed the form of a spiral. He took off from a central point, exact, logical, which, until then, I had supposed to be the permanent home of all the technical professions. The first turn of the spiral was only slightly imaginative. He limited himself to suggesting that I write a story about the case—"rigorously truthful"—of Siamese twins, joined at the shoulder, but separated surgically at the Guemes Sanatorium. Each one of them, in order not to feel any pain during the operation, had engaged, telepathically, a different anesthesiologist. One of the Siamese called a Hindu, who put him to sleep; and the other called a Chinese, who put needles into him.

Of course, his kind of truculence did not inspire me with any story. Nor was I too surprised that a Doctor of Economic Science should relate seriously a story that he had heard from the sister-in-law of the cousin of a nurse; after all, treatment by acupuncture, hypnosis, and parapsychology, although unorthodox, had been accepted by various doctors. But yes, I was sufficiently surprised when, in a second turn of the spiral, Genovesi left behind witch doctors and miracle mongers, and took off into the region of pseudoscientific conjecture—namely that our planet had been colonized by extraterrestrial beings, no less—and, in a third turn, he endorsed the existence of witches, shamans, sorcerers, and spiritualists.

By a strange coincidence, while Genovesi was delving deep into the occult, the darkness of dusk was obscuring his face. And I was scarcely able to make it out when, expanding further with his convictions, he went from myth to alchemy and from astronomy to metapsychosis. Nor did he stop there. In succeeding spirals of his monologue, he wandered off into what is hidden in the Great Beyond.

He who, as an economist, would never have signed a blank check, was extending credit to just any miracle monger. Taking advantage of the critics of reason, who limit knowing to mere phenomena, he postulated that there must be irrational faculties and extrasensory capacities of knowing absolute reality; and from this axiom, he deduced that there must be a predisposition to believe that even the unbelievable is possible. It was possible, therefore, that man might live in time that is cyclical, parallel, or returning; possible too were reincarnations, telekinesis, premonitions, levitation, taboo, and voodoo . . .

Genovesi disinterred the same fantastic ideas that I have seen, alive and well, in my own stories, with the difference that, for him, the supernatural was not a whim of fantasy. He lacked the poetic gift to convert irrational feelings into beautiful images. How could I explain to that credulous man that the only magic that counts is that of the imagination imposing its own forms on a chaotic reality, without any more purpose or benefit than to entertain through the art of lying? And even that imagination is not spontaneous, since it has value only when it is joined with intelligence. Reason is a weak, inexperienced, vacillating, and scolded little servant, recently arrived in biological evolution, but without whose services we could not enjoy our leisure, liberty, and happiness. Ah, Genovesi might be very skillful in his jugglings in the banks, but in his commerce of fiction with me, the poor fellow emerged from swampy dreams with a neurotic's delirium, a child's innocence, and a savage's superstitious fears. He accepted everything except reason. And with all of this, without knowing it or caring to, he justified his pillage with the words of Unamuno: "Reason is anti-life," and repressed any urge to accept the words of Ortega: "Man came from the beast, and to the extent that he neglects his reason, he returns again to the beast."

Thanks to the fact that they had not yet turned on the train lights, the night of the world outside, a night without moon or stars, penetrated through the windows and reigned inside as outside. Were it not for the voice, I would not have been certain that the bulk in front of me continued being Genovesi, until the train drew near a city lost in the pampas and the lights alongside the tracks began to pierce the darkness. Each flash illumined Genovesi for an instant. While his discourse continued to unroll the spiral of superstitions, his face appeared and disappeared, and when it reappeared, it was no longer the same. Genovesi was being transformed. The intermittent flashes from the side of the moving train that were changing his features, coincided with the leaps his thoughts were making from one delusion to another. What I was seeing and what I was hearing complemented each other as in a movie; and the movie was a nightmare.

At that moment we entered a tunnel darker than the night and

Genovesi became only a voice that, to me, sounded strangely hoarse. The voice began to tell me that there are men who change themselves into wolves.

"Bah, another little story about lycanthropy," I said, "Petronius told it in the *Satyricon*."

"No, no!" and the voice emerged from the darkness itself. "Forget about Grecian lycanthropy. In the province of Corientes, we call them wolflings. I assure you, they exist. They howl on moonless nights like this one, and they kill. I know from experience. Believe me. They kill . . ."

And then something hair-raising happened.

Hair, mine, not his, stood on end when, leaving the tunnel and entering the station, the light illuminated the face of Genovesi completely.

Terrified, I noticed that while he repeated, "Believe me, I know the wolfling exists," he was being transformed. And when the transformation was complete I saw there, crouched in his corner, a financial genius who had changed himself into a very great fool.

Imposture

Fate, with its right hand, gave a blessing to Valentino and, with its left hand, a curse. The blessing was that an unmarried uncle departed for the next life, leaving him a fortune. The curse was that, as he entered the bank, a terrorist bomb erased his face.

Valentino, before the blessing, had been an exquisite pauper, and he was an exquisite rich man after the curse. When he was poor, he covered up his poverty by disguising himself as a bohemian: he never paid his debts, he neglected his appearance, formed no relations with the bourgeoisie, showed no inclination to work; all this in order to be taken for a romantic type from *Scènes la vie de Bohème* by Murger and from *La bohème* by Puccini. Well then, as a rich man, in order to give his wealth an aura of aristocracy, Valentino, without ceasing to be romantic, disguised himself as gothic. He covered the horrible burns on his face with a mask of black velvet, and to make himself still more interesting, he wrapped his solitude in a mantle of mystery. Feeling himself to be the hero in a gothic novel, he used his money to buy himself an illusory world. He would have preferred to have recourse to the supernatural, as did the authors of the novels of terror which he loved passionately—Horace Walpole in *The Castle of Otranto*, for example—but, clearly, the supernatural could not be bought. So he had to be satisfied with appearances. He distorted reality by surrounding himself with weird objects. He abandoned old friends, reconstructed a mansion in San Isidro, and secluded himself, not as an anchorite but as a sybarite. He furnished the rooms with a scenic designer's whims: curtains, mirrors, tapestries, screens. The pieces of furniture were restless: they were always anxious to be used in some different manner. The entire house acted like a body with a soul. Quarters for the sensual pleasure of every organ, for the spiritual pleasure of every urge: to live, to dream, to hide. On the roof, he installed an observatory so that he would not miss the stars of heaven. Looking out from the balcony, he would contemplate at his feet, as if it were the moat of the *Castle of Otranto*, an expanse of water diverted from the Río de la Plata. Gothic novels also influenced the arrangement of a museum room, at the door of which a medieval suit of armor stood guard, lance in gauntlet. There was a library with the classic books dealing with madness, and a long hall which lent itself to concerts, ballet, and drama. It was assumed that Valentino was the observer, but it was he who, within himself, hoped that the musicians, dancers, and actors entertaining him were in fact the observers of the impudence with which he flourished his black velvet mask, his scarlet cape, his green sombrero and his golden cane.

The musicians, dancers, and actors could never talk with him. From the stage, they saw him stretched out in the only lounging chair in the empty hall. A small inaccessible island. Athough they never managed to see Valentino's eyes, the artists suspected that those eyes, through the mask, were judging them coldly. The masked man, at the conclusion of the concert, ballet, or drama, would applaud and, without more ado, exit with a kingly tread. The butler was entrusted with paying them.

In reality the butler was entrusted with everything. Knock-kneed, humpbacked, and hairy, he seemed to have escaped from the same gothic novels that inspired Valentino in the decoration of his grotesque residence. The two men understood each other without having to say a word. The servant guessed the desires of the master. A perfect relationship. The master, with his mask; the servant with his cardboard face; for that is the way it appeared, so impassive, imperturbable and expressionless was he.

Valentino's life, no matter how reclusive, could not remain secret. Without wishing it and indeed without knowing it, he became famous. And with the years, his fame became legendary. Now it was not enough for the people to describe him as a mysterious eccentric; they endowed him with vices, sins, orgies. They did not always condemn him. At times, on the contrary, they envied him the sumptuous life they attributed to him.

Clemente, one of the actors in Valentino's private theater, could not contain his envy. "How easy it would be," he thought, "to kill him and take his place!" That multimillionaire hid his face behind a mask. ("Doesn't he realize that carnival week is over?") And he kept himself sealed in silence. ("Could he be mute?") So, faceless and voiceless, nobody knew him. He, Clemente, at least knew something about him because, from the stage, he had occasion to observe his movements and measure his tastes and habits. They had the same physique, and, for an actor, what problem would there be in imitating his gestures? The real problem was in killing him and taking his place without the butler knowing it (luckily there was no hound in the house that with its fine nose would be able to discover that he was an intruder).

Clemente studied the comings and goings of the butler, and one Saturday morning, when he saw him go out on errands, he entered the mansion, killed the owner, stripped him, and took possession of the mask. For a moment, he contemplated the handsome face of the dead man. Then he dressed himself in his clothes, attached the mask and, as if the house had infected him with its gothic madness, placed the corpse inside the armor, and sank that heavy weight into the pseudo-medieval moat.

The butler returned with his purchases. Everything in order. Nothing had happened here. The routine of the mansion went on unaltered. The butler performed his duties, and Clemente adapted to his routine. What luxury, what refinement! This was certainly the good life!

So proud was Clemente of his imposture that he did not suspect that the identical idea had occurred to others. The masked man that he had murdered had not been Valentino but an impostor who, in turn, had assassinated another impostor. Each impostor believed that he was unique. Only months later, in a dark corner of the cellar, seeing an armed fist descend upon him, would Clemente understand that his destiny had been the continuation of a series of murders. A series similar to that of the lesser gods, who, according to the gnostics, replaced each other one by one.

No one in the mansion knew what was happening except the butler. He was keeping good account. He noted immediately the disappearance of the armor and at once deduced that a third impostor had just sunk the corpse of the second impostor inside it in the moat. With equal perspicacity the butler had noted that the soil in the garden was turned over where the second impostor had buried the first. And even before that, he had noted the bricks which, thanks to the masonry of the first impostor, had walled up Valentino in the rooftop observatory. He also noted empty spaces in the library

shelves or changes in the reading habits of his master; without
doubt the taste for gothic literature no longer prevailed. And he
noted that the impostor, believing him asleep, from time to time
would sneak off to the city to assure himself of a more normal life, if
only for a few night hours. But the butler never unsealed his lips
since his job as butler suited him very well. He refused to have
hounds in the house precisely to prevent their noisy barking and
olfactory indiscretions from disturbing the peace of his employment; a steady employment, like that of the phantoms who remain
in the same castle while generations of the castle dwellers are renewed. And the truth is that the butler was almost as unreal as a
phantom. At most he was the embodiment of a symbol: he was an
element in the binomial system: "Servant plus master." He formed
part of a social institution. In such a combination of two persons,
each had to trust the other. Neither should interfere with the other.
The master of the moment should take care not to betray himself
with one word too many. For his part, the servant should pretend not
to know the personal identity of the men who successively employed him. Protected by his own mask of servant, what did it matter who was behind the mask of the master! The mask, like the
crown in a monarchic rite—"The King is dead, long live the King!"—
signified the continuance of the invariable in the variable.

Like an allegory without a key, wouldn't you say?

Would to God

Gonzalo Inigo, editor of *The Freethinker*, finished editing his
counterattack on *The Catholic*. He read what he had written and,
like the other Creator, "saw that his creation was good." Above all,
his final sentence was good, framed between two monosyllables: "If
atheism is the possibility of explaining the world without recourse
to the hypothesis of a personal god, we are all atheists, yes."

He, at least, when writing about matters that his director assigned to him—matters as varied as those in an encyclopedia—
never thought about God. He was like Laplace. Once Napoleon asked
the author of *Mechanique Celeste*, "Where does God fit into your
system?", and Laplace answered, "I have never had need of that hypothesis." Gonzalo would have answered the same question in the
same manner, but it never went further than that. In that leftist peri-
odical everyone blasphemed. Not he. For that reason his fellow edi-
tors suspected that Gonzalo had a loose screw in his ideology. He

defended himself: to speak ill of a non-existent God was as ugly as to speak ill of an absent person. His "ism"—that of Marxism—was the visible uniform in which he dressed (or rather, in which they dressed him); but at times he kept his own ideas to himself, invisible, and then his uniform appeared not to fit him, and his colleagues saw him as badly dressed.

Having finished his article, he still had to perform another duty: to check the final printing before the presses began to print out the newspaper.

The day's work had been long, and Gonzalo was looking forward to returning home, where his wife was alone, hoping for him to come back because together they were awaiting their child who, according to the doctor, could be born at any time. They were frightened. They were very young and had not finished tasting the first honeys of matrimony before Mother Nature handed them the bill. What!? Pay so soon for the joy, and pay for it with no less than a child, especially when they were so poor, so very poor? And Soledad, so weak, so sickly—would she survive the childbirth? He had suggested that they should not pay the bill, but she preferred to pay. If she had refused an abortion because she felt it to be murder, he would have convinced her that the fetus was not a living being but still only an inseparable part of the mother's body, though alive and important; but he did not need to argue because she, without ethics or theology, had accepted naturally the burden of all women since Eve.

He hurried his pace in the early-morning darkness. Finally, after turning a corner, he saw their one-room apartment, their beehive, their little convent. He went in. Soledad looked at him through glassy eyes. "The contractions have already started," and she touched her swollen stomach. Although it was more distended than some weeks before, it was evident that while she herself was getting thinner and thinner, the child within her was growing fatter. He must now be everywhere, pushing even at her lungs.

"This couldn't be another false alarm?"

"No. I am sure it is not. The pain in my back, the contractions . . . Everything on schedule, as they told us. The bag will break. We must go. The suitcase is already packed." Gonzalo helped her up; carefully they went down the stairs, and got into a taxi. "Please, hurry . . . to Maternity . . ."

Poverty, poverty, poverty, along interminable corridors smelling of carbolic acid. A picture of Jesus, young and handsome, hanging on a wall. "Bad taste," Gonzalo thought, "what is an unmarried man doing in a maternity ward?" Soledad started to breathe in a strange rhythm. Gonzalo kissed her hand, forehead, cheek, and she, with her mouth searched for his. "I must be ugly, very ugly . . ."

"Sweetheart . . ." his voice broke and he could not console her.

They put her on a small stretcher—her face, disfigured, did not appear to belong to that swollen body—and they took her away. After a little while, a doctor and a nurse approached Gonzalo, too respectfully. The doctor took him by the shoulder and spoke in a low voice while the nurse studied him silently. Scarcely had he heard the first words when a dizziness emptied his head: even the waiting room itself became pale. Those first words mentioned a "complication." Dangerous, doctor? Well, a complication is always dangerous, but although the problem seems more difficult than we anticipated . . . The doctor continued speaking. Gonzalo was no longer listening to him; the words entered his ear but he heard them without understanding. From all the sounds, he retained only "a complication, difficult." The doctor squeezed his shoulder affectionately and then Gonzalo heard him say that within two hours they would tell him the results of . . . And Gonzalo again did not listen.

He stayed alone, in front of a glass door through which he saw the backs of the doctor and nurse receding. He had read a folder on childbirth and could not erase from his imagination the horror of the details: blood pressure, temperature, enema, exploration by finger or apparatus, a pinched membrane, the acute pain of the dilation . . . And if they found the baby dead? They would remove from the womb a reddish mass, viscous, repugnant, whose only resemblance to a human being would be through the bas-relief of a crushed face . . . He feared that at any moment, a weak scream would reach him through the walls, and so as not to go completely out of control right there, he rushed into the street.

He circled the block. And in pacing along its four angles, his feet described a squared O. The section of the city was reduced to a map similar to the graph paper that Gonzalo used in editing the newspaper. Thus, as on his graph paper, the pencil, guided by the squares, is able to form rectangular letters (not all, not the X, for example), his feet, in the city blocks, started to write the letters of his wife's name: Sol . . . Soledad . . . He felt compassionate, fearful, guilty, oppressed . . .

His legs were tiring. If only there was a small park, with a bench! He was about to sit down on the curb when he saw a church. From above, a pseudogothic gargoyle stuck out its tongue at him. Marxist ideology, armed in that sad 1936 with its latest slogans, made him see the church as a symbol: superstition, middle class, political power, military dictatorship. The church: supplier of opium for the masses, a spearhead of unjust power, a conspiracy of the rich, an enemy of reform. But he was so tired!

"My God, how tired I am!"

He bit his lips. What have I said? The "My God" must have just slipped out. He entered the church and sat down in front of the altar. "What would the comrades of the *Freethinker* say if they saw me in a church!" he thought. "But I'm here because somehow I have to sit down, don't I?" He looked at a Christ, at a Virgin. The same as those of the church where he had made his first communion.

His first communion, at eight years of age. That morning, instead of going directly to the church, he had amused himself spying through the keyhole of an empty room, and although he saw that it was empty, he also saw an impossible eye spying at him from inside; and that eye at the other end of the keyhole made him so afraid that he went running out to church.

How well-made the world had appeared to him when he was a child—a world scarcely bigger than the house where he was born and grew up; a house of many rooms, stairs, and patios that at the same time that it protected him, reserved for him a room where he could be free. The world could be infinite but was always a protective mansion under whose roof his parents represented a delegated divine love, not too distant, while he played freely in the flow of events. In the mica of a little stone, he was delighted to see the smile of a little star. A quick look in the mirror was sufficient to make all the city clocks mad. It was all the same to him: finding the mystery in the snail, with his eye, with the finger that tried to make it run, with Father Iturralde's religion, with the little book belonging to the teacher Rosa Anselmino, with the spiraling of surprises, or comparisons, or definitions, or simply, finding the mystery by putting himself into the shell to live with the snail, to turn into a snail. One was at that time whatever one wanted to be. All dreams were fulfilled. How beautiful, that world of his childhood.

Afterwards came the crisis and total ruin, of home and faith. And now! . . . Was it cowardly to no longer dare to go beyond oneself, beyond reason, beyond truth? Inside, he was timid; outside, he was a terror. Two modes of life, as in this church where he was, where inside there was reverence for Christian images, and where outside it was permitted to startle the world with pagan gargoyles, one of which had stuck out its tongue at him when he entered. He remembered the atheistic sentence between an "If" and a "Yes" which he had written hours before, and he felt that to go on thinking that way would finally make logic contradict itself and, humiliated at having entered a dead-end street, blow the top of its head off with one shot.

Was it worth the trouble to think, when you know beforehand that, beyond a certain point, logic can do no less than contradict itself? Was it not better to believe without thinking, like Soledad?

"Ah, perhaps at that very moment Soledad had already . . ."

"Would to God that everything goes well," he murmured, and he nailed his eyes to the figure nailed to the cross.

("I have said 'Would to God'; nothing more. If they take that 'Would to God' for a prayer it's not my fault. I didn't pray. But 'Would to God' that Soledad . . .")

Light suddenly entered through the rose window, and a dark corner of the church was filled with color at the same time as another kind of light entered into Gonzalo, and illumined in him a dark zone long forgotten. Now he understood the words of the doctor that before had been only a confusing noise. "Don't worry," he had said to him, "because everything will turn out all right." The meaning of that "Everything will turn out all right" spread all through him like a blessed dawn. And Gonzalo smiled as if in truth he knew that all would be well.

And with the light step of an optimist, he headed back to the maternity ward.

A Bow Tie and a Mirror

The father, Enrique. The son, Enriquito.

Enriquito, on that snowy night, in dress suit, had to attend a New Year's Eve party. Enrique goes to help him dress.

Enriquito is a student of the angry generation that never wore anything but feathers and T-shirts. Enrique, although he was in his good times a nice boy, had never worn a "tuxedo."

When the suit arrived from the store, they believed that the only difficulty would be in the buttons and cuff links of the dress shirt, on the loops and buckles of the vest. The difficulty turns out to be that the tie, a long worm, has wings and changes into a butterfly. Enriquito doesn't yet know how to tie the bow and Enrique has long since forgotten.

The bow tie that he had constructed thirty years ago was not black, like this ceremonious "black tie" that his son has to wear to the New York City College dance, but red, à la Maurice Chevalier; but the difference in color is no excuse since the knot of a bow tie, be it black or red, winter or summer, in New York or in La Plata, always has the same folds. If it is difficult to tie, it is because the father and son are face to face, Enrique's hands at his son's neck. "It's one thing," Enrique is thinking, "when your fingers are working at your own neck, and quite another when they go to work at somebody else's neck. Another fellow's neck is more suitable for strangling than for adjusting a bow tie." And he laughs.

"What are you laughing at?" Enriquito protests, and takes a step backward because the laugh of his father smells of tobacco.

Father and son.

Very much alike in all ways except for the good humor of the father and the bad humor of the son.

"Enriquito," Enrique is thinking while he takes a step forward to make up for the backward step of his son, "is how I was at his age; I look at him and I see myself when, at his age, I looked at myself in the mirror."

Mirror?

Ah, yes, the mirror . . . An idea occurs to him. Tying the tie for his son, face to face, forces him to move his fingers in an unusual fashion. Perhaps if they both stand in front of a large mirror, his fingers will work normally . . .

In spite of his son's grumbling, the father places him in front of the mirror while he stands behind him. He passes his arms over the boy's shoulders and starts to fix the tie.

Before, when they were face to face, his hands were palms outward, toward his son's neck. Now that he is standing behind the boy and the two are looking at themselves in the mirror, his hands are palms inward, directed toward his own neck. Yet what he sees in the mirror is that his hands have stopped at his son's neck. A comical variation of the theme of the "double": he will be doing his own tie, but around another neck.

And Enrique bursts out laughing.

"What are you laughing at?" Enriquito protests. His father's laugh is spraying his nape, but he can't move away because the mirror on the wall blocks his path and two arms are holding him from behind.

Without ceasing to laugh, Enrique, half-hidden by the body of his son, examines the mirror, which, in duplicating things distorts them. They had length, width and depth; now the mirror is distorting the depth. They had rights and lefts well-positioned; now the mirror is turning them around. His fingers don't know where to go. They are lost in a tangle of sensations. The sensation of sight contradicts that of touch. This sensation of cool and smooth, is it because he is touching the silk of the bow tie or because he is seeing the glass in the mirror? Devilish mirror! The illusion of symmetry shifts deceptively. Enrique's hands occupy two locations at once. They move along Enriquito's throat, here, on this side of the mirror, and along the throat of Enriquito's double, over there, on the other side of the mirror; in reverse movements, they play, here, with the real bow tie, and also, over there, in the depth of the mirror, with its reflection. With things both here and there, the mirror has turned space into madness. Patience. To start fixing a tie in front of that lunar swindler has been an error. He says to himself, "Why am I failing? I did not fail on that evening, fragrant with jasmine . . ."

And that jasmine evening presents itself like a fairy with all her cortege of myriad reminiscences and, in passing, speaks to them of the kingdom lost to the heart, that remains nostalgic, and to the head, that denies its grief. Space turns into time. It is time. His hands continue moving in three dimensions, but are directed now by the memory. Thousands of leaves of the almanac fly in a backward flight of decades and, by enchantment, the world is young. Adolescence enters where the body shows the least wear, in the hands, open wide. They are long and fine. There you can find strength, touch, agility, precision, elegance. In a flash, his fingers recover the skill of the young at play. Chinese shadows. Dwarf puppets—every fingernail a tiny face—in a scene of bones. Hypnotic spidery gestures. Prestidigitation with cards. Arpeggios on the piano keyboard. A sieve of nerves through which the poem is filtered.

Enrique closes his eyes. New Year's Eve, not in the winter of 1957 with snowflakes white as jasmine, but in the summer of 1927 with jasmine white as flakes of snow. He has had seventeen Februarys. He is in La Plata, dressing in front of his mirror. The dreaded moment of the bow tie has arrived, indocile and antipathetic; although, on the other hand, he remembers the color of Irma's lips: Irma! Irma! Irma! He will dance with her, tangos and tangos, in this night's fiesta. A warm rush of life mounts up in his body and he starts to hum "Canaro in Paris." Magic! In his fingers he feels the flower of the bow tie being born. He opens his eyes and is surprised to see in the mirror that the tie he has made is black, not red like the tie of Maurice Chevalier.